OPHELIA & LYAN ARE

DEAD MEAT

AN OPHELIA LEGACY NOVEL

SPENCER STONER

INDIGO
Livonia, Michigan

Published by Indigo
an imprint of BHC Press

Library of Congress Control Number:
2017941028

ISBN-13: 978-1-946848-21-5
ISBN-10: 1-946848-21-2

Visit the author at:
www.authorspencerstoner.com &
www.bhcpress.com

Also available in eBook and Audio

Book design by Blue Harvest Creative
www.blueharvestcreative.com

ALSO BY SPENCER STONER

THE OPHELIA LEGACY

BOOK 2
THE THIRD LIFE OF OPHELIA

MULTI-AUTHOR COLLECTIONS

IN CREEPS THE NIGHT
CONTAINS THE STORY "ON THE WAY HOME"

ACKNOWLEDGMENTS

I wish my Father had lived to see this become a reality. He, like my Mother, supported my writing wholeheartedly. My whole family has done so since I was twelve (which was awhile ago) and don't think that I don't appreciate it. With all my heart.

To my Mom: Thank you for reading the stuff during my teens that in retrospect was crap and telling me it was good. Malia: Thanks for reading my stuff now and telling me what you really think. Kalani: Thank you for inspiring a bunch of the characters that will populate not only this novel but many other stories. Mele': Thanks for helping me develop the temperament to actually finish writing a whole book. To my brother-from-another-mother Jim who not only has inspired characters but some of the more, shall we say, light-hearted moments in many of my stories. And Erikka helped build the groundwork and flesh out the noble Yo Bunpy people among many other contributions.

Finally, my Mom and Malia were the willing guinea pigs who read this when it was in its rough (and it was rough) draft phase and helped make it better. I also appreciate my friends in the Dark Fairy Queen and Her Brilliant Minions writing group who further helped polish the book into what you have in your hands today. Let's see where that takes us, shall we?

CHAPTER

ONE

"SEVER HIS HEAD from his shoulders." The charcoal black skinned woman's voice echoed from the stands until it finally reached the woman standing in the middle of arena.

Ophelia turned to look down at the man kneeling before her. His bald head glistened as streams of sweat dribbled down his brow. Blood trickled from the wounds in his legs that toppled his ability to stand on his own boot wrapped feet.

Orison had been nothing but good and caring to Ophelia. He'd even saved her life on more than one occasion. The look of pain on his face at the woman's betrayal was the only attack he had left.

That was why Ophelia's voice was screaming in the back of her mind to stop. But her hand lifted the sword anyway. A wicked smile that wasn't Ophelia's stretched over her lips even as the voice in her head yelled so loudly that the murmuring crowd was drowned out as they watched.

Orison had been given more of a chance than the rest of the party that had come to these lands with him in search of Ophelia. He was given the privilege of Trial by Combat, a tenet whole heartedly embraced by the Xaviour Tribe. But that wasn't to say it was fair.

The human had been stripped of his heavy armor, instead given flimsy studded leather to wear instead. He was also given an unfamiliar weapon, a short sword. For a man who had specialized in using a two-handed mace, it was awkward for him to carry to say the least.

Ophelia, on the other hand, wore sleeves of plated metal and layers of chain mail to protect her during the fight. The scimitar in her hand, with its curved blade, felt out of place in her hand yet her skill with the weapon couldn't be denied.

Stohbease enjoyed Ophelia's showmanship when the time came for the execution because it was as much hers as the slave's. A glass orb, glowing faint violet, fluttered between the black skinned fingers of the woman who owned Ophelia, before it rested in her palm. It was more accurate to say that the kill was the noble's more than the Ophelia's. She enjoyed watching the slave act out her will and the smile on Stohbease's face showed that joy and unnaturally extended onto the sword woman's face as well. Then her jewel wrapped wrist twitched.

It barely took a flick of Ophelia's wrist to slice through Orison's windpipe. Blood immediately started spilling down the front of the man's body, covering him like a macabre, ruby colored apron. His mouth moved in what looked like a curse but no sound could come anymore.

Ophelia's true voice, though, screamed in her head. "He only came because Harby asked! His only crime is being loyal!"

Stohbease swept her hand in the opposite direction and Ophelia turned the curved blade back toward Orison. The cut took more effort, but the man's head fell to the dusty ground all the same. The black skinned woman let out a satisfied sigh that Ophelia's body (but most definitely not her mind) echoed.

Orison's hazel eyes stared at the woman as his life drained away and words came from his mouth that weren't his own. "Why would you want to leave this, assassin? This is what you were made for. Don't let Harbenigyr take this from you."

Ophelia woke, jumping to a sitting position on the grass covered ground. The trees surrounding the clearing kept her scream from echoing. The woman wiped the sweat from her brow as she tried to will the last images from her dream out of her mind's eye.

The last embers of the campfire to her right still radiated light but it didn't give off any comforting heat anymore. The sun was threatening to rise from the beneath the horizon and evict the frost but hadn't done so yet, so the chill in the late spring air was in full force.

"The same nightmare?" The disembodied voice of the long, straight bastard sword rang in the cool predawn air.

The sword had been in her possession for almost as long as she could remember. It, no he, was a trophy from her first kill and, even then, the sword not only spoke but never truly shut up. It was not until much later that the woman learned that the consciousness in the bastard sword had been an actual person in his, shall we say, previous life? Even then, his name was sure to have been unusual.

"A memory, Havarti, but yeah." Ophelia sighed then lifted herself to her feet. "It's just history getting more ancient every day."

Whether or not the words she said convinced either of them, the sentient sword called Havarti found its way onto the woman's back. Either way, the woman wasn't going to be getting anymore sleep so it was time to get moving. She kicked the bedroll back into its compact cylindrical shape and tied it closed before slinging it over her right shoulder.

With the exception of her sword, the roll of barely cushioned leather was one of the few things left she could call hers. All thanks to an ill-advised card game in the last town she had passed through two days ago. She would have gone without a bed that night as well, if not for one of the male players across the table offering to share his room with her.

He gave her a place to sleep, a little bit of exercise just before and one more thing... a small bag of gold coin that the man had been so generous to let her take, or likely would have been if he'd been conscious when she left. Men were always more generous if you were gone before they woke up the next morning.

That would, at least, pay for a room when she finally met back up with Lyan at the Burly Brawl Tavern. It was about as close to a halfway point between Lyan Yo Bunpy's homeland and the region where Ophelia had been plying her trade as a sword for hire.

She'd received the message from her friend nearly a week ago to meet there. That was pretty much how some of their best times together started. In fact, the action the barbarian brought the mercenary into in the past had been her main source of income so Lyan's letter was timely.

Ophelia would almost surely beat the barbarian to the tavern since she hadn't found an actual job since her... forced service under Stohbease. Whatever could she do to pass the time? The thought, while not completely evicting the memory of the unpleasant dream, did make a stream of memories of more pleasant sleepless nights wash over her and a smile spread across her face.

The sun rose over the treeline only to be covered by distant clouds moments later. Not that the idea of facing less heat during her trek was a bad thing. It was still going to be a long walk but that would give Ophelia plenty of time to gather herself and refocus on whatever kind of trouble Lyan had in mind for the two of them this time.

The handle of Havarti, the bastard sword Ophelia carried, protruded out just above the left shoulder of her red trench coat, the scabbard itself actually resting along the mercenary's back inside the lining of the knee length leather garment. As company went during a long hike, Ophelia could have done worse than a snooty sounding disembodied voice. At least he knew some fun limericks.

The woman had worn the trench coat for so long that it now fit her perfectly, wherever the leather showed signs of wear or damage, it was repaired to fit her body shape. But she wasn't the trench coat's first owner. He had fallen in battle years ago. So it was now Ophelia's to keep as a trophy or a keepsake. Add to that the battered and scratched plates of armor that ran down and around her right sleeve, it was apparent that she was no stranger to combat.

She was a tall woman, just reaching six feet tall, but the clothing she wore under the coat would have only completely covered a woman of only four feet in height. Her shirt, such as it was, could be described as little more than a halter top; made of green silk and black leather like material on the sides that seemed to be able to stretch or squeeze unnaturally. In this case it squeezed her chest to make the woman's cleavage, already ample in its own right, protrude higher in the low cut material to make her breasts look bigger. If you didn't wear heavy armor in her trade, you had to at least make sure you looked good.

Skintight pants, made from the same black leatherish material as Ophelia's top, were nonexistent at her round hips down to her mid thigh. A fashion that the mercenary had borrowed from a half-elf archer she knew. The only splash of color was where Ophelia's belt buckle fastened together. From there and down her inner thighs was the same green silk that made the middle of her top. The woman didn't like to chafe.

Ophelia's chocolate colored hair, including the two long braids that ran down either side of her face, fluttered in front of pale blue eyes and obstructed the woman's vision, albeit for only moments at a time. Those distant clouds didn't stay that way for long and the weather turned foul over the last hour or so but the mercenary didn't seem to be bothered by the wind. In fact, her tanned skin didn't seem to even notice the drop in temperature by turning red or even raising goosebumps.

When the building finally came into view, it brought a smile to the woman's face. The Burly Brawl Tavern, almost literally in the middle of nowhere, was a simple two story job that was made of wood with worn shingles on the roof and had rooms for rent but none of that mattered at the moment. A good old smelly tavern was one of Ophelia's favorite places in the world for a very simple reason: they had booze.

Finally, the door was within reach. With a heavy push, the slab of oak swung in and Ophelia was met with the sound of... silence. In all of her visits this place was never silent no matter what time of day she arrived. Her thick eyebrows pressed together as she stepped inside, much slower and more cautiously than she had planned on only moments earlier.

People filled the entire lower floor of the building. Their mouths were moving but no sound was coming out. One by one, each person's attention shifted to Ophelia at the entrance and they all started yelling something the mercenary couldn't hear. Then a sudden flash of silver filled her vision.

"Son of a—"

BLINK

The sword slashing for Ophelia's neck embedded itself into the door she had been standing beside. All it managed to cut, though, was the faint violet silhouette Ophelia had left behind. It would be inaccurate to have called it a flash of light, more like the impression of something you stared at lingering on the back of your eyelids once you closed your eyes, just there to be seen by all.

Ophelia found herself standing on the opposite side of the door next to the heavily armored man that held the sword embedded in it. She had just "blinked". It was a magical defense mechanism that came from an intricate set of runes tattooed onto her back. In the event of an attack or some other surprise, Ophelia would teleport a few feet out of harm's way.

That was the theory anyway. In practice, blinking had a couple of problems.

The armored man turned to face Ophelia where she now stood, pulling his sword free of the door with barely a grunt of effort and again swung for her neck. If it had been up to Ophelia, she would have blinked behind him to gain the element of surprise. Unfortunately, she couldn't control where she "landed". That was the first problem.

Ophelia instinctively raised her armored right arm to block the incoming attack. It hit with such force that she stumbled back, spinning into a table and knocking it over before she was able to right herself. If she had been able to control her blinking, Ophelia would have avoided that strike. That was the second problem: It didn't always work.

The armored man pushed the attack, not giving Ophelia enough time to unsheathe her own sword. All she could do was throw her armored limb in the blade's path to block the strike. Sparks flew each time the metals connected, filling the woman's ears with what sounded like steel cookware being slapped together.

The man reared up with all the power he could muster, bringing the blade down with all the strength he and gravity could combine together. Ophelia raised her arm, hoping the armor could stand the blow when she suddenly found herself standing behind her attacker.

His blade split her after image in half, burying his blade into the slatted floor. Ophelia felt her lips tug into a smirk at her change in fortune.

While her right arm was wrapped in metal, she had made a point of keeping her fingers armor and glove free. On the back of her hand, though, was a nice thick piece of metal that protruded just past her knuckles. Her arm was already reared back when she had raised it to block. Now it was going to change its intention.

Tapping his shoulder with her left hand, the armored man turned to face Ophelia just in time to take a heavy, steel augmented punch to his temple, knocking him out cold. The woman chuckled to herself as she nodded in satisfaction.

Her grin stretched even wider when another idea came to mind. "You got any rope?" She asked the stunned looking barkeep.

CHAPTER

TWO

CALEB GROANED AS he returned to the land of the conscious. He immediately regretted it. His head felt as if it was being used as a sledgehammer against a stone wall. His vision was blurred, although it didn't stay that way for long.

As it cleared he saw that woman, Ophelia, sitting immediately across from him. She straddled the wooden chair she sat on, the slotted back rose up between her legs and the woman rested her elbows on the top edge of the back rest.

She wasn't wearing her long coat anymore. It was draped over the foot of the bed behind her, the bastard sword still resting inside its custom made scabbard.

Her arms were as toned as the rest of her. Walking and fighting, it seemed, was a hell of a workout. Sitting like this, eye to eye, Caleb could see that they were just about the same height, too.

"Well hello again!" Ophelia sounded unnaturally chipper as she spoke to him, much like someone talking to a small child. "I have to admit. This is a pretty amazing thing."

Ophelia held up a small, puce trinket that looked like the head of a shaft of wheat. She waved it back and forth in front of Caleb's hazel eyes to make sure he got a good look.

"Such a little thing casting a mute spell on an entire building full of people just so they couldn't warn me about your little ambush." Her thumb and forefinger tensed and the trinket shattered into tiny, barely visible pieces. "It raises a few questions, doesn't it?"

As she smirked at him, Caleb heard a knock to his left. He gingerly turned his head to look in that direction and saw the door. Ophelia's smirk didn't leave her face as she gave the person permission to enter.

The door opened into the room, obscuring the man's view of the new arrival. He heard several heavy footsteps before his vision was filled with bright blue.

After blinking a few times, he saw a woman, even taller than Ophelia and himself and heavily muscled. Even more so than him, as well. It was odd clothing, to be sure, but she wore even less than Ophelia.

Pastel blue fur wrapped around her chest, barely containing breasts bigger than Ophelia's. Two straps of leather looped over her shoulders, holding the garment in place as well as adding somewhat more to the laughable amount of protection the armor likely provided. Her bottoms were the exact same way, pastel blue fur, but she also had a massive white ball of cotton mounted on the back. And he would have sworn the fur was... sparkling?

Her furry boots started at her thick thighs and ended in what looked like rabbit feet. Giving her a second look, Caleb could see that rabbits were a heavy theme in her wardrobe. She had a dull metal buckle shaped like a stylized bunny on a strap of leather across her chest that clasped between the two shoulder straps, although the buck teeth he expected to see seemed sharper.

Long straps of leather wrapped around the base of her stout neck, leading down to a pastel helmet resting against the woman's fur covered upper back, complete with long ears, the insides of which were pink unlike the rest of the fur covered bits. One, though, was folded in half.

Her forearms were covered in the same blue fur, with leather straps to hold heavy metal armor shaped like rabbit heads in place on top of the hair, with the saber like teeth reaching down well past where her fingertips would reach. He'd hate to be punched by such a thing.

That was when it occurred to him. He cursed under his breath as the woman closed the door behind her, turning so that he could see her left side.

She carried a shield, complete with a saber toothed rabbit etched into the front. It was made of wood and lined in the pastel blue fur with a heavy metal grommet mounted right in the middle of it. Dangling just under the round piece of wood were two severed heads. And he recognized both faces as they swung back and forth in and out of view.

It was as he feared. This woman, this barbarian was...

"Hey there, Lyan." Ophelia smiled wide as she greeted her obviously expected friend. "Glad you could make it. With presents, too!"

Lyan Yo Bunpy of the Yo Bunpy tribe of Bunny Barbarians from the Land of the Long Toothed Rabbit. She was supposed to be dead by the hands of the very men she now carried the heads of dangling under her shield.

Her face turned to look at Caleb. The two thick braids she kept her ebony hair tied in barely moved with the motion. Her dark brown eyes narrowed and the mocha skin around her mouth sank into heavy lines as she frowned at the man.

"This is him?" She asked, not acknowledging Ophelia's greeting. "This is the coward who attacked you without raising any declaration of battle?"

Ophelia nodded, a clicking noise coming from the corner of her mouth. "That's him in all his glory." She chuckled.

As Lyan's eyes scanned down the man, her face went from stern to a mask of confusion. "Why is he naked?"

Caleb looked down at himself for the first time. Loop after loop of rope was wrapped around his ribcage and arms. Oddly, his chest was completely exposed, the bottom half of the glyph tattooed onto the middle of his torso, that looked like a life sized crimson hand reaching out from his abdomen, peeked out from under the rope.

He could feel his wrists tied together behind the back of the chair he was sitting on and his shins, from ankle to calf, tied tightly to the legs of the wooden chair. He expected to be out of his armor but this?

He was well muscled, having the same workout regimen as Ophelia. Although Lyan's musculature put even his to shame. Even though Caleb knew not having his clothes was supposed to have the effect of humiliation, he was inwardly thankful that it was warm in the room.

"We didn't want him to escape did we?" Ophelia smirked up at the taller woman. "Besides, he's hot. Why not get a look at the goods?"

She laughed even as the barbarian woman looked somewhere between confused and disturbed. It only lasted for a few moments before she stepped up to the man.

"Who sent you to kill us?" She growled before throwing a back handed punch to the opposite side of his head that Ophelia struck to knock him out.

Caleb's blonde hair fell in front of his eyes, blinding him. She didn't hit him in a way that the gauntlet's "teeth" would have pierced his face. He was thankful for that.

That is, until he felt the barbarian's hand wrap around his locks and lift his head. He was suddenly eye to eye with the disembodied heads of his compatriots.

"As you can see. You all failed." The look on the Yo Bunpy woman's face made Caleb's breath catch in his throat.

She dropped the heads, one of them actually landing on his left foot. If he could have moved, Caleb would have shaken it off of him.

Instead, he could feel what he thought was Adrian's nose pressed between two of his toes.

"Lyan, you're not going to get any answers that way." Ophelia grinned at her friend as she lifted herself from her chair.

Ophelia practically pirouetted as she whipped one of her legs over the back of her chair to finally stand at one side of it. Her hips swaying as she walked, she made her way over to Caleb until she was sitting on his lap. Resting her arms on his broad shoulders, she straddled him much like the chair she was on only moments ago.

"Guys love being tough and maybe even sacrificing their own lives to prove they can't be broken. Like them." Ophelia shifted her weight to one side as she motioned to the decapitated heads at Caleb's feet. "We already know you're a strong, macho man. Don't we?"

Caleb's mouth hung open with no sound coming out as Ophelia smiled sweetly at him, her hands wrapping around his shoulders, massaging them. She leaned in close, her soft chest pressing against his as her lips brushed over his ear.

"But we don't have to be enemies." Her warm breath washed over the sensitive skin of his ear. "I, for one, always welcome a new friend. But we can't really relax together if we always have to look over our shoulders, can we?"

Caleb gulped. His breath came in short gasps as he tried to turn his head away from the woman sitting on him. This was not how he had expected things to turn out.

"I can't. He'll kill me." He muttered, keeping his eyes closed tight and trying to think of something, anything else.

"I can take him out of the equation for you." Ophelia whispered, slowly rocking back and forth on top of the man. "Come on, the poking sensation in my thigh says you like the idea."

Grunting to himself, Caleb violently shook his head. Inadvertent or not, he head butted Ophelia and suddenly saw stars as pain overrode... other sensations.

When his vision cleared, it was to the sight of an annoyed looking woman. The silence in the room felt as if it would crush them all before Ophelia finally spoke.

"Okay, plan B."

Caleb suddenly fell backwards in his chair, the back of his head scraping against the wall until he came to a jarring stop against the floor. The breath was knocked out of his chest and he tried to gasp for breath but his chest wouldn't move.

Looking down at the man, Ophelia sat on his rib cage, putting her full weight on Caleb so he couldn't breathe. "Listen, I like a chiseled set of abs as much as the next girl but I am not above killing you and finding a set that doesn't have a creepy hand tattoo on them. Who sent you?"

Blood pounded in Caleb's temples as he shook his head, which rested vertically against the wall while his torso lay horizontal on top of the chair laying on the floor. He tried to will air into his lungs but the same wiggling that had distracted him earlier now kept him from getting any breath at all.

"Who sent you?!" Ophelia's hands slipped from his shoulders to wrap around the base of his throat.

Feeling his life starting to drift away, Caleb nodded. He felt Ophelia lift herself to let him get just enough air to talk.

"Perett. Perett sent me." He rasped.

"Who in the gray hells is Perett?" Lyan asked, coming into Caleb's field of vision.

His mouth moved but no sound came out. Ophelia lifted herself again and he continued.

"He runs all the brigands around Valen Court." Caleb cleared his throat to keep himself from coughing and losing more air. "He wanted you all out of the way before he expanded his business to Dianmeyer."

"Dianmeyer?" Ophelia looked up at Lyan, unable to hide the worry all over her face. "Harbenigyr and Josie?"

"Anyone who knows of Harbenigyr's Order would also know that we would come to their assistance in the event of an attack." The barbarian said to the mercenary.

The Order of Kuan Yin was a group of clerics that originated from a system of islands to the west of the continent. While they did carry weapons for self-defense, they were hardly an army.

Their mission, the main way they spread the word of their goddess was to set up a sanctuary in towns and aid residents medically, even aiding in childbirth. No preaching, just service.

That was how Ophelia met Harby. She awoke to him applying healing balm to her skin. She never asked for help. The cleric just came to her aid.

Ever since then, Ophelia had always thought of Harbenigyr as a younger brother, even helping him finally find the courage to get together with the woman he would eventually marry. Even with that, the cleric had saved her far more than she had ever helped him.

Harbenigyr had taken ownership of a small castle called Dianmeyer and, over the ensuing years, a village had grown around it. Now it was under threat.

Caleb coughed uncontrollably as his lungs were suddenly allowed air unrestrained. Ophelia stepped over to the bed and snatched up her long red coat.

"Let's go, Lyan. Someone's trying to kill us again." She pulled her coat on as she stepped out of the room.

CHAPTER

THREE

IN THEIR TRAVELS, Lyan very rarely needed a horse to keep up with the rest of her traveling companions. Her training, as well as custom made blessed boots, as a Yo Bunpy warrior made her able to run over long distances almost tirelessly.

This time, though, could be filed under "special circumstances". The duo had a lot of ground to cover in as short of time as possible. That meant a full gallop for as long as the horses could hold out. Not even Lyan Yo Bunpy could keep that pace for long.

They were lucky that the tavern also had a stable. The horses they rented were panting, steam rising from their mouths as the day cooled into late afternoon. Fortunately for them, they had reached the one place the two women could cut a full day off of their journey to Dianmeyer: Etigran Pass.

Ophelia slipped off her horse and started for the gateway that signaled the official beginning of the path over the mountain range. There was a sign warning about avalanches but Lyan didn't bother to look over the details as she led her horse up beside her companion.

An old man with red hair that was in no way natural and pulled back into a ponytail stepped up to the women with a polite grin on his face. "What can we do for you ladies tonight?" He stood proudly, adjusting the long black fur lined robe he was wearing.

Lyan looked up at the still blue and gray sky. The sun was still visible, just barely kissing the top edge of the peaks. She looked down at the spindly man who was a head shorter than Ophelia which made him that much shorter than the barbarian. Judging by the stare she was getting, his eyes just came up to Lyan's chest.

"Aren't you a little ahead of yourself, old one?" The Bunny Barbarian nodded down at him, the bobbing movement of the tall ears on her helmet pulling his attention away from lower down.

"Oh, er, not by much." He looked back up at the sun himself, pulling his robe's fur lining tighter around him as if he had a chill, before turning back to face the women. "It goes down fast around here. Looking to hole up for the night?"

Both shook their heads. "No, sir. We need to push on once we get our steeds watered and fed." Lyan said.

The old man grunted, shaking his head in reply. "You're not going to have much time to get over the pass before total blackout."

"We'll chance it." Ophelia chimed in before Lyan could reply. "We've got friends who need us on the other side."

"Okay but don't say I didn't warn you." His ponytail whipped from one side to the other as the old man turned toward the small pond that rested beside the guard post that also likely served as his house. "Once the sun goes down, I would get off your horses and walk them the rest of the way. It gets narrow on the pass and you'd be no good to your friends lying dead in a gully up there."

"Thanks for the tip." Both women said at the same time.

"And don't be surprised if you come across what's left of anyone else who didn't take my advice lying around up there. I may be old but I know these mountains." With that the man guided the horses to the watering pond and retreated back into the house.

It didn't take long for the horses to refresh themselves but it still took longer than the barbarian woman would have liked. Lyan tapped her foot impatiently, kicking up a small cloud of dust that enveloped her legs up to the knees, as Ophelia led both horses back to her.

"Did that guy creep you out as much as me?" Ophelia asked as she mounted her horse.

"You know I don't know fear." Lyan adjusted the long Yo Bunpy Tribe spear that rested under the horse's saddlebags before slipping onto her saddle proudly.

"That's not what I mean." Ophelia glanced back at the old man's house as they started up the mountain path. "That house doesn't seem to fit him. It was so down to earth and simple. Not like it belonged to someone who dyed his head some color that doesn't occur in nature."

Lyan grunted in agreement. "Indeed. Creepy."

"Ladies, it is impolite to gossip about a man behind his back." A disembodied voice rang quietly in the air.

Ophelia turned to look at the source, the sword handle peeking over her left shoulder. "Who asked you, Havarti? I mean, really, you're acting like you were the one with redder than red hair."

What could only be described as a harumph came back in reply, "Back when I had a body, the pressure to maintain as much of your youth for as long as possible was quite the powerful motivator."

Lyan arched an eyebrow. "So you are saying that you used to dye your hair red?"

"Red? Oh, dear me, no no." The sword said. "I went with a simple but elegant mahogany hue."

"Mahogany?" Ophelia shook her head. "I swear you are just handing me material to mock you with now."

"Harumph."

The women rode up the trail as fast as they could on the uneven terrain. In the gloaming, the fading light of the day forced them to hug the mountain side while leading their horses to traverse some points, it got so narrow. It was a miracle, at least in Lyan's opinion, that she could find footholds for herself, let alone their steeds.

The light of day was fading fast, especially with them surrounded by mountain peaks on all sides. Even Lyan's brightly colored furry armor seemed a mere shade of gray while Ophelia resembled more of a shadow than a person.

Their pace was slower than they would have liked but steady. The change in terrain was gradual at first, but the road eventually started to slope downward. Then it started to widen until the women felt it was again safe to ride side by side. Even then they could see little more than each other in silhouette.

They hadn't galloped more than a few paces when they heard a faint cry on the wind. "Please help." The voice sounded hoarse and strained.

Lyan straightened up to her full height in the saddle. "Who is there? Identify yourself!"

After a few seconds, the voice came back. "Please, do you have some water?"

Lyan slipped from her saddle and onto her feet, squinting into the darkness, trying to find the source of the voice. "Identify yourself and you may have water. Otherwise..." With a faint whisper of wood sliding against leather, the Bunny Barbarian freed her spear.

Ophelia looked anxious to keep moving but when she saw Lyan dismount, she knew it was pointless to try and get her moving again. "Hold on a second. I have a torch here somewhere." Ophelia grumbled to herself about 'warrior's codes' and the inanity of such things until she found the object of her search.

With a quick strike of flint, sparks leaped up and ignited the torch, bathing the immediate area in orange light. Just at the edge of the fire light was a man who was lying against the mountain face, his left leg resting at a very awkward angle.

"I fell off the trail up there." He pointed straight up, well beyond where the light from the torch could reach. "And I haven't had a drink of water in two days."

Although the man seemed to be around the same age as Ophelia appeared and a little younger than Lyan, judging by his dark hair and eyes with no hint of wrinkles, his cheeks sank into his face seeming to try and make him look older but also serving to confirm his story. The rest of him was bordering on rail thin as well. Apparently he hadn't eaten in some time, either.

His white shirt was caked in dirt and the left leg of his black trousers was ripped all the way up to his hip, exposing his obviously broken leg. Though no bones protruded, red flesh above his knee hinted at some kind of infection just under the surface of the skin.

Lyan and Ophelia looked at each other. The slightly shorter woman motioned further down the trail with her eyes while the barbarian motioned back to her saddle bags. Ophelia's eyes narrowed. Lyan growled under her breath. The sword woman frowned. Lyan sniffed.

"Fine, fine. We'll give him one bladder of water and you can set his leg but then he's on his own, okay? There's bound to be another sentinel at the base of the mountain we can send for him."

The Bunny Barbarian nodded as Ophelia again grumbled all the way back to the saddlebags. The bladder of water sloshed back and forth as she cradled it in one arm, the other hand still holding the torch.

She stomped over to the young man, shoving the base of the torch into a crack about shoulder level in the rock face. That made a small shower of sparks rain down over the young man, who didn't seem to notice.

He looked up at her with a faint smile on his face. "Thank you." He said weakly.

"Don't thank us yet." Ophelia said as she knelt down beside him, popping the cork loose from the bladder. "Lyan still has to straighten your leg out."

The young man took a long drag of water, a few drops finally slipping down his chin to leave a couple of clean paths on his dusty skin. "That won't be necessary." To demonstrate, his leg straightened up to a normal angle and, with surprising agility, he hopped to his feet.

"I wasn't thanking you for the water." He snickered at them, practically dancing to some unheard tune. "Or the offered first aid. I was thanking you giving us a chance to catch up to you. We were having a dickens of a time keeping up."

The water bladder fell to the ground, forgotten as it spilled its contents into the dirt. In a quick, practiced motion, Lyan and Ophelia were back to back with their weapons drawn and ready for a fight.

There wasn't anyone but the young man who grinned back at them in a way that seemed mirthful, although his eyes showed nothing but malice. On his thigh, just above his knee, the red flesh wasn't inflamed but rather a tattoo of a similar style to Caleb's back at the tavern. Instead of a hand, though, this one was of a talon from some kind of a bird of prey that could have easily cradled a human head if it were real.

"What the hell are you talking about? Where are your men coming from? Your back pocket?" Ophelia asked, bouncing in place and ready to fight.

In answer to the woman's question, a piercing screech filled the night sky. The sound of flapping wings came from above, circling the women. The "we" he was referring to weren't men at all.

A massive beast dropped to the dusty ground, just at the edge of the torch light. The wings, covered in layers of chocolate colored feathers, folded onto the body of a giant cat with golden fur. The fur gave way to pale feathers at the creature's forelegs, talons of a bird of prey bigger than the thin man's tattoo scratched at the dirt.

Its falcon head loosed another screeching call and two more beasts joined the first on the ground. They were griffins, massive beasts that fed on any kind of meat they could get their talons on whether it be fish, fowl or human. Why would animals like that be following the bidding of this man? How was he even able to command them?

Ophelia didn't have much time to consider those questions before the three griffons leaped at her and Lyan. They were animals used to hunting in groups and the coordination showed it well. When one snapped its beak at Ophelia, another lunged at her exposed back when she turned to dodge.

But Ophelia and Lyan were well practiced at fighting together as well and the Bunny Barbarian's spear slashed at the second griffin. The shaft crushed one of its forelegs and snapped it down the middle to make the talon hang limply. It cowered back but the third beast lashed at Lyan to cover the escape of the wounded one.

The beak of the griffin facing Ophelia ground against Havarti's blade so hard that yellowed bone shaved away. It released the sword and quickly pulled away when it realized the metal wouldn't buckle under the force.

The wounded animal took up to the air, into the darkness, while the other two circled around the women. Their weapons were up at the ready but then the injured griffin pounced on Lyan's horse, the beak of its eagle head plunging into the defenseless creature's jugular vein while its remaining talon ripped at the torso.

The barbarian reared back with her spear, readying to rescue her steed when one of the circling griffins saw the opening and launched. Ophelia tackled the beast before it could reach the other woman but after they tumbled through the dirt, she found herself pinned under the beast that was easily twice her body weight.

Its beak wrapped around her throat. Just as it started to pinch shut Ophelia was suddenly looking at the night sky with no animal obstructing her view. She was behind the griffin, still on her back in the dirt. Ophelia had blinked.

The beast that would have been Ophelia's killer hadn't noticed that she was no longer under it yet. But neither had Lyan. The Bunny Barbaran had only seen her friend get pinned to the ground by the winged creature and was charging to the mercenary's aid.

The other griffin took advantage of Lyan's single minded effort to save Ophelia by leaping for the fur covered woman's exposed back. Ophelia stuck out a leg and, with a quick spin of her body, knocked the feet of the barbarian out from under her.

Lyan fell to the dirt face first but the griffin flew over her and landed on the other beast that had pounced the mercenary. The two animals tumbled in a heap as Ophelia hopped back onto her feet and hurried over to the Bunny Barbarian.

"You okay, Lyan?" She offered her unarmed right hand to the other woman.

Lyan stood back up without Ophelia's aid. "A simple shout of warning would have sufficed."

"Sorry." Ophelia turned her attention over at the man they thought they had been helping. "Who the hell are you anyway? What do you want with us?"

The two griffins untangled themselves. They started snapping and hissing at each other until the young man let loose a sharp whistle.

"Azula! Zuko! Focus! The rest of the pride will be here soon." As soon as the beasts under his command calmed, the young man looked over at the women. "I am merely a humble servant looking to make things right in this chaotic world. With some help, of course."

Even as the flying beasts returned their attention to Lyan and Ophelia, both women couldn't help but notice heavy scratching noises came from the nearby edge of the road. True, they were well below the peaks of the mountains now, but there was still plenty of height to kill someone if they fell over. The fact that something was climbing up the sheer face of the cliff...

An immense hand, as big as a platter a waitress in a tavern would use, reached up and pulled an equally massive, and hairy, figure behind it. It was an ogre, a female one by the look of it, complete with massive under bite, thick muscles and a not so bright but surly look on her face.

As she came to stand on the mountain pathway, she was tall enough that the top of her head was out of reach of the torchlight, almost twice as tall as Ophelia and Lyan. She also took up far more than her fair share of room on the road.

Then two more males climbed up on either side of the ogress. They were even taller and wider with their entire heads obscured in shadow.

"Don't panic. We still have the advantage of mobility." Lyan muttered to Ophelia as they again pressed back to back with the barbarian facing the incoming giants while the mercenary kept Havarti pointed at the griffins.

The ogres stomped toward the two women. As they reached Lyan's prone horse, the wounded griffin picking meat from the carcass, one of the ogres wrapped its ham fist around the dead steed's throat and pulled.

The griffin reared back as the body that served as its latest meal and perch was ripped out from under it. With a single beat of its wings, it hovered in the air for a moment before setting its three good legs back onto the dirt. It wanted to snap at the new arrivals but the thin man made a noise that somehow warned the animal off that plan of action.

The dead horse slid across the ground, spooking Ophelia's horse. It turned and ran back the way it came up the mountain. It almost immediately fell off the side, unable to see the thinning road. The sound of it neighing in terror as it fell into the abyss below echoed between the peaks.

Lyan and Ophelia glanced over their shoulders at each other. They seemed to have the same thought at the same time. Both women turned their backs to the griffins to face the ogres.

The winged beasts took the bait and launched themselves at the barbarian and mercenary. Ophelia felt herself blink out of their way while Lyan spun out of their path, being sure to give the closest monster a smack on the back of its head with her shield.

The griffins flew into the ogres, who barely took a step back. But that step took them all uncomfortably close to that cliff they had just scaled and they struggled with the combination of balance and winged creatures tangled between their legs.

The two women sprinted down the slope. The path was quickly widening so they could run all out without worrying about following their horses off the the side of the road.

The torchlight, and the monsters gathered inside it, shrank away as the distance between them and the women quickly increased. Ophelia smirked at Lyan's comment about having the advantage of mobility. It turned out to be true thanks to the bulky but very not agile ogres.

The trail curved around the mountain and both women kept their pace up, running as fast as their feet could carry them. Still, when a group of armored silhouettes blocked their path, they were able to stop themselves before having a collision.

They were in a military style formation, with torches lit and carried by several figures in the rows behind the front. That would make it so at least those leading the group would have better night vision. It also made it more difficult for anyone looking at them from ahead to see the loyalty the troops, giving them a momentary advantage while it was unsure whether they were friend or foe.

Not that Ophelia or Lyan had much doubt. They had no friends on this mountain. Ophelia counted no less that twenty rows of helmets, lined up in five columns.

"Don't panic. They are surely overconfident in their numbers." The barbarian whispered as she moved the sharp tip of her spear back and forth between the many selections of targets.

There was something odd about this group of soldiers. At least the mercenary thought so. It took her a moment to decipher what was so troubling about them.

They weren't moving. At all. No matter how disciplined a battalion was, there was always one that would have to adjust a belt, shrug a shoulder weary from carrying a heavy pack or even just taking a deep breath to either recharge from a long march or stave away sleep from standing guard.

These soldiers did none of these things. At least not until Ophelia took a step toward them that brought them just within reach of Havarti's blade.

In perfect unison, they all reared back and drew various weapons. Swords, clubs, each bigger than the one previous glinted in the light of the torches. That was when the mercenary noticed something else.

Between the layers of metal armor there was no skin. There was only bone. They were literally skeletons and this was an undead army. No wonder none of them had to even take a breath.

"Don't panic." Ophelia scoffed as she glanced over at the barbarian. "They're already dead."

The sound of three massive ogres charging down the path behind them, accompanied by the sound of more screeching griffins than the mercenary and Bunny Barbarian faced a moment ago filled the air. Lyan shrugged at the other woman and they charged into the lines of bone and metal.

Skeletons weren't exactly known to have supernatural strength. Hopefully having nothing but sinew holding them together would make them more brittle and they could get through before the air power and behemoths could reach. Ophelia slashed for the neck of the nearest skeleton holding a torch and a longsword.

The undead creature's head flew from its shoulders and she started for the next. The first didn't fall, though, and chopped for the woman's neck much like she had to it.

Ophelia ducked under the strike. When she looked back up at the skeleton warrior, she saw the undead being place the flame from the torch in its hand at the base of its neck, as if it was going to light it like another torch.

It worked. The monster tossed the now extinguished length of wood to the ground and its skull was now replaced by what looked like a demon's head sculpted in fire! It reared back and shrieked its displeasure at Ophelia.

"Okay... panicking is looking like a better idea now." She said before bringing Havarti down on the creature again.

The ogres joined the fray, wading into the swarm of skeletons toward the barbarian and mercenary. As the undead broke and fell out of the massive creature's path, they did like the skeleton Ophelia faced and used their torches to replace lost limbs of bone with those of flame.

Lyan continuously stabbed at the ogres as they closed the distance but the razor sharp blade of the rabbit head stylized spearhead, while it sliced into their flesh, didn't seem to cause them any pain. The Bunny Barbarian and Ophelia found their backs pressed against each other as the creatures surrounding them left less and less room to stand.

Lyan was going to say something to the other woman but Ophelia suddenly disappeared as a talon whipped through the violet outline that remained. The griffins had joined the fight.

Ophelia blinked again and again in the swarm of monsters. She felt herself starting to get dizzy as the mercenary shattered one fleshless limb from another before finding herself landing beside yet another whole monster and needing to regain her bearings. Ogres and griffins were bigger and slower but plenty of their attacks connected as the tide of bone started to overwhelm the women.

Ophelia felt her own ribs cracking as she saw Lyan's pastel helmet fly off her head when an ogre's fist connected against the barbarian's face. But still, both women kept fighting.

The beasts piled on top of them, Ophelia's blinking finally stopped completely and all she could hear over the dull thuds of landing blows and screams of fury was Lyan repeating, "Don't panic! Don't panic! Don't panic!"

INTERMISSION

Ophelia sat hunched on the stool in the tent that was serving as her home while she recuperated. It was as spacious as anyone could wish for, big enough to fit a family of ten with room to spare, and the walls were made of leather from various giant rabbits that grew in the region.

The mercenary's coat and shirt laid on the ground beside her bed in the back, neatly folded by... someone who had been in their earlier. Havarti rested on top of the red leather square, idly humming one of the few soothing melodies that Bunny Barbarians sang.

Unless she was mistaken, it was the story about the love that had formed between one of the Yo Bunpy's storied ancestors and a woman from the clan they had just conquered. Romance or pillaging, Ophelia wasn't sure if the Bunny Barbarians knew the difference, really.

The Yo Bunpy cleric sitting on another stool behind her sprinkled powder that smelled like mint laced excrement from some animal over the wound on her back that severed one of the many runes tattooed on her skin. He had done the same to the wound on her abdomen, which was actually the other end of the same stab wound. Now Ophelia was concentrating to keep the stinging sensation from making her turn and smack the man she knew was only trying to help.

The flap to the entrance of the tent opened and Lyan stepped inside. Her pastel helmet was covered in white snow that quickly started to melt thanks to the roaring fire in the center of the shelter. She pulled the overlapping flaps closed and finally turned to face the inside of the tent.

Tugging at the folded ear on her helmet, the piece of armor slid off. "How is she doing, Bawb?"

"Bawbory, if you please, Prophesy Child." The cleric responded.

He then slapped the wound on Ophelia's back. It had been explained to her that it was to promote blood flow and allow the medicines to better circulate through the wounds but she had noticed they only did so on her back. It was as if they were trying to make her blink but it had not worked in the weeks they had been doing so. Again, Ophelia had to keep herself from damaging the healer in response to the action.

Only the clerics of the Yo Bunpy tribe called Lyan "Prophecy Child" or the "Child of Prophecy". She had been born on the night of some astronomical alignment that some ancient cleric said would herald the birth of the one promised to destroy the "Great Evil". It was meant as an honor.

Lyan hid her disdain for the title and dumped her helmet onto the floor beside the entryway. "Very well, Bawbory. How is she?"

"Wide awake, alert, and here in the room. Thanks." Ophelia answered for him. "He's just finishing up his torture session and getting ready to go have a smoke."

"It's hardly torture, milady." Bawbory retorted as he sealed the small canister of powder. "It is a herbal mixture prescribed by your colleague Harbenigyr himself."

That was the only way Ophelia would let any of the clerics touch her was if they used the Order of Kuan Yin's medicines. As much as she enjoyed staying with the Yo Bunpy, she wasn't much of a fan of their healing rituals that involved more bloodletting and chanting than actual treatment. It had never been an issue since she never really needed healing from them. Until now.

"Where is Harbenigyr, anyway?" Lyan looked around the tent as she asked.

"He watched over Ophelia until dawn." The Yo Bunpy cleric answered, lifting himself to his feet. "Now it is his turn to rest."

With that, Bowbory excused himself and stepped out into the snow. Ophelia shivered at the sudden chill his exit caused but the fire replaced the lost heat almost immediately.

"You look like you are feeling better." The Bunny Barbarian stepped over to the other woman.

Ophelia shrugged. "Still haven't been able to blink since—" She pointed at the wound in her stomach then whistled, her finger moving to point to the wound in her back with the sound.

One of the fringe benefits of blinking was that it sped up Ophelia's healing. It wasn't a miracle cure but after blinking a number of times, if the ability would start again, she wouldn't even have a scar from where she was impaled anymore.

"No one is expecting you to get over it all in one day." Lyan grabbed the stool the cleric had been using and sat across from the mercenary. "You bested that mad woman Stohbease and left her tribe in chaos. Take some time to revel in the glory! I've even commissioned our bard to write a sonnet detailing your victory."

"I'm not in much of a reveling mood." Ophelia said as she stood up.

The barbarian nodded, still sitting. "So I've heard. Edge has been beside himself, waiting for a chance to share a bed with you again."

"He practically needed a ladder to reach the mattress last time." Ophelia chuckled but immediately regretted it as pain shot through her midsection.

She reached up to cradle the bandage on her stomach, stuck to her skin with the goo that served as the second part of the medicine, mixing with the powder to do... something that Harbenigyr explained but Ophelia couldn't understand. But it was taking too long. She had already been in the Yo Bunpy camp for over a month and nothing had changed! All anyone did was coddle her, tell her how none of this was her fault...

Havarti felt something change in Ophelia. "My dear, don't do anything rash." He warned.

"Lyan, I want you to hit me." Ophelia said turning to face the other woman. "Right now."

The barbarian blinked up at the woman. "What? Are you crazy?"

"Hit me, Lyan." Ophelia's hands clenched into tight fists. "It's a simple enough request."

Lyan rose to her feet. "No, Ophelia. I will not fight you. Not now."

"Why not? We've sparred together for years. We even fought in the Squared Circle." Ophelia caught her tone veering dangerously close to begging.

The Squared Circle was a small field in the public meeting area of the Yo Bunpy camp, cordoned off by a series of leather ropes made from remnants of saber toothed rabbit skins. It was where the warriors challenged for leadership or to settle any dispute within the tribe.

"We did so to show my tribe that women could be warriors, too." The Bunny Barbarian unfastened the fur lined gauntlets, with the saber teeth that protruded beyond her knuckles, and pulled them off her arms. "Up to that point they refused to recognize that I was female since the Child of Prophesy had to be a warrior."

"And now you won't fight me because I'm all used up and not worth the effort now?" Ophelia felt a sting behind her eyes that had nothing to do with the medicine she'd been given.

"That is not true!" Lyan felt a rush of anger but kept it in check. "I will not fight you now because you still need to recover. I will not fight you simply because you want to punish yourself over Orison!"

Ophelia kicked the stool she'd been sitting on out of her path and into the fire. There was a slight limp to her step as she recovered her balance. It was obvious the wound was bothering her.

Lyan tossed her gauntlets away. "I can understand your frustration, Ophelia. I really can."

The other woman glared at the barbarian.

"Remember when I left the tribe?" Lyan asked. "Do you remember why?"

The mercenary's thick eyebrows pressed together. "It was after we captured Dianmeyer, wasn't it? Your father had you lead the Yo Bunpy warriors into battle. His best friend died, right?"

The Bunny Barbarian nodded. "He wasn't just my father's friend. He was the only man I have loved."

Ophelia didn't know what to say.

"Not that he knew." Lyan continued. "Being the Child of Prophesy, I wasn't recognized as a woman so I could not confess my feelings to him. He died saving my life, in my arms, and I still couldn't tell him."

Lyan held out her arms as if her muscles were reliving the events of that day. As a warrior, though, the Bunny Barbarian did not cry. But her face still reflected the hurt and turmoil the memories brought back to the surface.

Lyan cleared her throat. "After that I demanded my father recognize me as his daughter so that, as a woman, I could speak at his pyre and confess what I had been hiding. He refused. That was when I left."

"I... I didn't know." Ophelia wanted to do something to comfort the other woman but knew that any gesture would be shrugged away at the moment. "I thought you left because you thought your father wasn't pleased with how you led the Yo Bunpy."

The barbarian let out a heavy, long held breath. "It was as much for his death as my cowardice at accepting beliefs I knew were insipid and not fighting for what I knew was true. But you came after me. You reunited me with my people. My family."

Ophelia shook her head. "All I did was prove that you could have boobs and wield a sword at the same time."

"By challenging my father to force him to recognize female warriors. To recognize me as such." Lyan nodded again.

Ophelia stepped over to the bed at the back of the tent and sat down of the foot of it. "Did you ever get over how, you know," the mercenary motioned to the other woman's still raised hands, "how he died?"

"I do not blame myself anymore." Lyan sat down on the bed beside Ophelia. "But I still miss him. I still have not found anyone that could match his place in my heart."

The mercenary arched an eyebrow. "Really? No one? After all this time?"

"I am not like you." The Bunny Barbarian sighed. "I cannot lie with any man that catches my eye. They must be able to stand up to me in battle and, as the Child of Prophesy, it is somewhat of a challenge to find one able to shoulder such a requisite."

"Just because you have standards..." Again, Ophelia chuckled and, again, the wince betrayed that she regretted it.

"I will not tell you not to blame yourself for Orison's fate." Lyan pressed a hand of comfort onto Ophelia's shoulder that the barbarian would have shrugged off if the gesture had been the other way around. "But I will insist you recognize that while it was your hand that ended his life, your hand was not in your command at the time."

"I'll try." The mercenary nodded.

The silence lingered in the tent for a long while but neither woman moved or dared any action that would end it. Until Ophelia came to some unspoken decision and turned to Lyan.

"Just because I can't fight now doesn't mean we can't come up with a plan of action for when I'm better, right?" She said.

"That's true." The other woman agreed.

"Blinking or not, I'll need to get back in the swing of things." Ophelia started, her words leaving her mouth at a speed that betrayed her anticipation. "Where could a couple of hot hired swords like us go to make some coin?"

Lyan looked as if she was about to kick an already injured animal. "The only real unrest in the region is south, where the Xaviour Tribe is fighting amongst themselves to resolve the vacuum of power you left when you killed Stohbease. And I will not allow you to return there."

Ophelia frowned. Although she had no desire to go back there anytime soon, anyway. Her teeth clicked together as she racked her brain for any ideas.

"You think I could maybe get another loan from Rayflintr?" She asked.

"For what?" Lyan wondered why the other woman would want money at all, let alone more, from the Yo Bunpy Tribe's Chief Cleric.

Ophelia chewed on her lower lip for a moment. "I was thinking that since I can't really go any further north than here, I could head out west. Maybe see if I can find out some information about the Great Evil for you."

Out west was primarily protected by the Light Bringers, a force that declared itself a multinational police force of knights. They were an effective means of keeping law and order in that region, hence why there were no reports of major troubles out that way.

There was still the occasional brigand or thief, although Lyan thought it likely that Ophelia could handle most any of them even in her current condition. She nodded and stood up.

"Very well. As soon as the clerics declare to able to travel, I will have Rayflintr... loan... you some money and you can scout the west for word of the Great Evil." Lyan declared, then started for the entrance to the tent.

"Thanks." Ophelia said after her.

"But we will meet at the Burly Brawl Tavern six weeks later so you can share your findings with me. Perhaps even set off to fulfill my calling from there." The barbarian smirked back. "Agreed?"

Ophelia and Lyan fought well together. One could call that level of skill a calling. The other thing they do just as well, if not better? Drink. Now that was a calling they could both get behind.

"The Burly Brawl Tavern." Ophelia smirked back. "I always liked the honey bark ale there."

CHAPTER

FOUR

ONCE OPHELIA AND Lyan were beaten to the point they couldn't raise a hand to defend themselves, one of the ogres slung the Bunny Barbarian over his shoulder while several skeletons hoisted the mercenary onto the back of a griffin.

The skeletons that had burning limbs extinguished the fires causing many, but far from all, to tumble to the ground to never rise again and the black out the old man at the beginning of the pass warned Ophelia and Lyan about enveloped them all. The darkness didn't seem to bother their captors as they walked at a pace that gave the impression that they could see everything in their path.

The bouncing Ophelia was subjected to first jarred her out of her dream and back into consciousness. It steadily worsened the pain in her ribs with every step. It also made her unable to tell how much time had passed before she noticed that they had marched into a cave. The group turned this way and that and soon neither Ophelia nor Lyan could tell the direction they had come from or the way back.

Finally, both women were thrown to the floor. The voice of the almost forgotten thin man that lured them into this trap again floated across the women's ears. The words, though, were not directed at them.

"Take everything off." He ordered the beasts. "There can't be any chance of them sneaking any kind of tool or weapon inside."

Ophelia felt something tugging on her boots, then the cold rough bone fingers of a skeleton unfastening the belt of her pants. She tried to bat away the arm of the creature but the ogress' massive hand suddenly pinned her face into the dirt, threatening to crush her head like a grape.

Between the ogress' fingers, Ophelia could see that Lyan was being treated with equal care. Her pastel armor was unceremoniously tossed into a pile in the corner of, for lack of a better term, room.

Then, again, Ophelia was lifted into the air. Her baby blue eyes struggled to focus until they saw a round hole in the wall just big enough for her to fit inside coming closer and closer. The woman wasn't claustrophobic but just the sight of the limited space made her stomach turn.

And it didn't stop when they dropped her inside. She started sliding down the thin hole, feeling the rough gravel dig into her skin as the woman's momentum made her go steadily faster. Ophelia didn't even realize she was screaming until the hole stopped and she was deposited into another wide room. Rolling to a stop, pain racked her body and the only good she was able to find in the situation was that the floor was cool against the burning scrapes on her skin.

Ophelia groaned and her body vehemently protested as she lifted herself up to her knees. She looked around, hoping her eyes just hadn't adjusted to the dark and there wasn't really nothing around her. Then she heard a faint, echoing bellow.

The noise quickly got louder and Lyan barreled from the same hole Ophelia came from and into her and knocked the mercenary back down off her hands and knees. Ophelia groaned and her left arm cradled her right side that was searing with pain. The barbarian, who came to rest on her side with her head and shoulders down by the other woman's knees, didn't move at all.

"Lyan?" The ground behind Ophelia glowed faintly violet with the light radiating from the runes on her back as she rolled onto her side and nudged the larger woman's shoulder with a bare foot.

Still, the warrior woman didn't move. Ophelia felt her stomach tense up and, pushing through stabbing pain in her side, lifted herself back up to her knees. Crawling over to the Bunny Barbarian, Ophelia sat on her knees and shook the woman's shoulder again.

"Yo Bunpy, tell me you're not dead." She said, her voice stern like a military officer speaking to a lower ranked soldier.

Even with her ears ringing from the beating both women had taken, Ophelia could still hear her own heart beat anxiously as Lyan stayed still. "Lyan?" She felt her breath catch in her throat and Ophelia's mind suddenly filled with so many shades of regret.

Her throat acted like it had forgotten how to make sounds as Ophelia again struggled to find the words to apologize when the big woman suddenly groaned and fell rather than rolled onto her broad back.

"Not dead." Lyan's voice sounded muffled somehow. "Humiliated but unfortunately not dead."

The mercenary didn't have the energy to laugh with relief that her friend was alive but she did feel the tension in her body suddenly release, having to stop herself from falling on top of the Bunny Barbarian and give her the closest thing she could to a hug in her current state. "Since when has not being dead been a bad thing?"

"When they stripped me of my honor and dumped me in this place to suffer whatever indignities they have planned next." Lyan's voice sounded like she was muttering, barely opening her mouth to speak.

Ophelia frowned, held what little air she could in her chest, and forced herself to her feet. A not at all tough sounding squeak escaped from her and the mercenary cradled her broken ribs tighter as she steadied herself.

"Stripped you of your honor?" She spoke around quick gasps for breath. "Was that in the left or right cup of your top?"

Not that the standing woman could see it but Lyan's gaze locked onto the glowing symbols tattooed on the other woman's back. "It is the traditional battle armor of a warrior of the Yo Bunpy tribe." The Bunny Barbarian could feel little droplets of spittle splash her cheeks as she spoke.

Ophelia grunted in response as she clumsily turned in place to try and get some sense of bearings in the room. "Sounds like you still got some pride in there to me." She finally said, looking back in the direction the barbarian woman lay, or at least where she was pretty sure she was laying.

It was far too dark for either woman to see anything with real detail, even after their eyes adjusted, so Ophelia turned her attention to helping Lyan get vertical. They had succeeded in getting her into a sitting position when the sound of locks unlatching and the squeak of rusty door hinges moving caught both their attention.

The room suddenly filled with blinding light. Lyan raised a hand to shield her eyes but Ophelia's left arm stayed cradled around her ribs and she just couldn't get the right to move high enough to do the job. So she squinted, hoping her baby blues would adjust as quickly as Lyan was suddenly able, albeit shakily, to hop onto her feet.

Two figures stepped inside the room, both wearing highly polished black armor from head to toe. They both also had cloth bundles under each arm. After half a dozen steps they stopped well out of reach of either woman.

Ophelia's eyes finally got comfortable enough that she was able to take in her surroundings. The room was bigger than the woman thought initially and she and Lyan weren't even in the middle of it. In the middle, off to the women's left, a stream of water as thick as one of Lyan's massive arms spilled from the ceiling into a basin carved into the floor itself. It must have had some kind of drainage because the water flowed continuously but the basin showed no sign of overflowing even though the water was up to the brim.

Chains lined every wall of the room. Some lengths even hung from the ceiling. Judging from their stillness and the amount of rust coating them, however, they hadn't been used in some time.

The only ways in and out of the room were the hole behind her and Lyan and the doorway that was blocked by the two guards. They dropped the cloth bundles to the stone floor at their feet before one of them spoke.

"Clean yourselves up in the fountain." The guard's voice was tinny through the metal helmet that completely enveloped his head. "But do not drink the water if you want to live. Then get dressed and you will be taken to meet the Judicator."

"What's the Judicator?" Ophelia asked, although looking defiant when you were naked, dirty and injured wasn't a easy task.

Neither guard answered as they turned and started back for the door but the chatty one did say, "The door will remain open so that you will have light to see but do not think it a path to escape. It leads only to the Judicator."

Ophelia started after them but quickly realized that she wouldn't be able to catch up as she was now. Judging from the grunt and cough of pain behind her, Lyan must have had the same thought but come to the same conclusion as well. Both she and Lyan looked at each other and that was when the mercenary was able to get her first good look at the Bunny Barbarian since they had been taken prisoner.

"Oh, ouch." Ophelia hissed, a look of concern crossing over her face.

The entire right side of Lyan's face was purple and swollen to the point that her eye was completely shut. The reason that her voice was muffled was that her jaw was more than likely broken so her teeth were clenched tightly together.

"Can you get to the fountain?" Ophelia asked.

Lyan nodded and started limping toward the water. "Are my injuries that severe?" Her hand rose to gingerly poke at the swollen bruising.

"You look like a blueberry about to pop." Ophelia tried to give her a joking smirk as she pulled her left hand away from her torso and into the running liquid.

"I don't think a little water is going to fix it." Lyan said matter of factly.

Ophelia splashed her handful of water onto the taller woman's face and started to gently rub the purple skin. "No but we can at least clean it a bit and see if it's really as bad as..."

"What?" Lyan asked just before her eyebrows pressed together. "I see two of you now."

"The swelling is going down." Ophelia quickly cupped another handful of water and splashed the barbarian again.

The swelling almost completely disappeared with the second splash and Lyan's eye was completely open again. Her cheek was still discolored but even that was starting to fade.

"It's a healing spring." Ophelia felt the need to state the obvious.

Lyan nodded and reached into the fountain herself with both hands, splashing her face again before starting to work her way down. Ophelia followed suit, only able to use her left hand effectively. Still the effects were immediate. The scrapes caused by the slide down the hole were gone in seconds. As she filled her hand again, she suddenly wondered just how powerful this spring was.

Lyan's left arm was almost completely scarred from shoulder to wrist by the former owner of the blue fur, a twelve foot tall lightning spitting saber toothed rabbit, that now made up her armor. In fact, much of the skin on her upper arm was permanently scorched black from the encounter. Ophelia leaned as she filled her hand again to look around the stream of water to see if that was still the case.

The Bunny Barbarian's old wounds remained. So the fountain wasn't able to heal years old wounds and scar tissue. When Ophelia splashed the water on her right side, she discovered another limitation.

A yelp of surprise and pain escaped from her lips, her vision flashing white. When her senses came back to her, Ophelia couldn't help but wonder why she wasn't flat on the floor. That was a simple answer: Lyan caught her.

The heavily muscled woman's right arm was behind Ophelia's shoulders while the barbarian's left was around her waist. Not only had Lyan kept the mercenary from falling to the ground but she also avoided her most obvious injury.

"Well," Ophelia started to talk even though breathing was still an effort. "We know that the fountain only heals wounds that are skin deep now." She chuckled without any real sense of amusement as she glanced to her left and blinked in surprise a second time. "Lyan, when did you get so pasty?"

"What are you talking about? I'm darker skinned than you." Lyan helped Ophelia straighten back up onto her feet.

Ophelia looked Lyan up and down before reaching out to the fountain again, this time being far more careful applying the healing water to her side. "Not your boobs or your legs. I may just have to use the water here to fix my singed retinas after looking at those!"

Ophelia pushed her head into the stream of water, making it spray all around the basin for a moment. Lyan looked down at herself then over at the other woman.

"I am a warrior. I must be ready for battle at all times." Lyan said, still through clenched teeth. "I always wear my armor."

"That explains the tan lines." Ophelia replied, able now to raise her right hand enough to help her left wring excess water from her auburn hair.

"You are also a warrior." Lyan took her turn dunking her head into the stream of water, not bothering to undo her massive braids.

The Bunny Barbarian tried sucking some of the water between her clenched teeth. Inside of her mouth suddenly felt as if it was starting to burn, especially where she figured the bone of her jaw was fractured.

Lyan spat the liquid out. She couldn't taste blood like before but her mouth ached just as much as before. The barbarian made sure to loose a mouthful of spittle in embarrassingly thin little dribbles (thank her god, the Great Chromatic Rabbit, that Lyan's head was still in the streaming water) from between her teeth before chancing to swallow. What healed the skin apparently would damage anything inside the body.

Finally pulling her head free from the spring, she turned to face Ophelia and continued their previous conversation. "Then why is your skin so evenly colored?"

Still cradling her side, although the bruising that had been there was now gone, Ophelia had already started toward the bundles the guards had left behind. She felt better than before the spring but there was still a hint of a limp in Ophelia's stride.

"I don't like tan lines." The mercenary smirked as she fumbled with the knot tying one of the bundles shut.

Lyan limped over to the other bundle. "That would mean that you would have to be—"

"Naked." Ophelia continued the barbarian's sentence for her.

"A lot." Lyan finished.

Ophelia chuckled and immediately winced. "Dammit! Did they have to break my ribs to bring us here?!" With a grunt of frustration, the woman tossed the still tied bundle away.

"Perhaps it was payback for when you shoved that skeleton's spine up the ogre's..."

The glare on the Ophelia's face told Lyan not to finish that sentence and she didn't. "Could you open this for me? I'm not having any luck one handed." She asked the barbarian just as Lyan finished untying the knot around her own cloth bundle.

The barbarian woman nodded and did so for her. "I wonder what they dress their prisoners in to meet with this Judicator."

Both women unfolded the cloth to see what was inside. Red leather greeted Ophelia while pastel blue practically radiated in front of Lyan. It was their own clothing.

"That I did not expect." Said the Bunny Barbarian.

Ophelia was silent for a moment, pulling her long coat up from the neatly folded pile of clothing. Unsurprisingly her sword, Havarti, and Lyan's spear and shield were not included but each article of clothing was clean and patched up. After the battle to get them to this place, neither one's wardrobe was exactly top drawer but, for some reason, they were even cleaner than when Ophelia and Lyan started away from the Burly Brawl Tavern.

"I think I understand." Ophelia said as she started pushing a leg into her black pants. "It's the same reason they have a healing spring that only treats flesh wounds. They don't care how beat up someone is when they get here as long as they don't look bad when they get in front of whoever this Judicator is."

She was able to use both hands to buckle her belt but reaching any higher with her right caused strenuous objections from her ribs. Ophelia was able to work around that while slipping on her top but working her arm into the armored sleeve of her coat...

"Allow me to help you." An already fully dressed Lyan, complete with helmet although lacking the metal portions of her gauntlets, stepped up behind the mercenary.

Ophelia nodded her thanks and soon both women were dressed as almost exactly as they were when they arrived in the caves. "If they want us presentable, not looking like we've been mistreated, we may just have a chance to get out of this." Ophelia's voice came out as a whisper when she noticed a guard step up beside the door.

"I don't see how." Lyan whispered back, her eyes narrowing and revealing thin wrinkles that Ophelia hadn't noticed before, at the waiting guard before turning back to face the other woman.

"If this Judicator is a law person of some kind, he may just listen to reason and let us go. We haven't done anything to anyone around here." Ophelia explained. "We may just be able to charm him to get the same results if we use our assets right."

Lyan shook her head. "What assets? Our weapons are nowhere to be found."

Ophelia sighed. "No. Our assets." Raising her left hand, the mercenary tapped her chest then Lyan's making the soft flesh of their breasts jiggle with the motion.

"It is time." The chatty guard or another one, their voices could have just sounded the same through their helmets, said.

Six armored guards stepped into the room around the first, surrounding Lyan and Ophelia on all sides as they stood together. The pole axes they carried seemed mostly ceremonial but they were sharpened to the point of lethality if a prisoner tried to attack or run from them.

The sheer number made getting through the actual doorway awkward, since it was only big enough for everyone to go through one at a time, but the hallway itself gave them plenty of room to maintain a four person wide formation, with Lyan and Ophelia in the middle, as they made their way along.

There were precious stones and gold inlaid into nearly everything from decorative suits of armor and even the edging of the stone walls themselves. But nothing gave either woman a hint of where they were or with who they were dealing. The hall intersected into others as they walked and they took a turn here and there. It was starting to get to the point that Ophelia wasn't sure she'd even be able to find her way back to their cell without help.

Then she suddenly straightened up to her full six foot height, her pale blue eyes opened wide. Lyan noticed but, unfortunately, so did the guard to Ophelia's side.

"What is it?" The tinny voice came, the entire group came to a stop and turned to face her.

The thick blades of their axes lowered closer to the women as they awaited an answer from Ophelia. A pained look crept over the mercenary's face as she cleared her throat, eliciting a pang from her ribs to make Ophelia's pain become more genuine.

"I-it it's my ribs. I think they're broken." She started, making an effort to sound pathetic. "I took a step wrong back there and I hurt myself again. Sorry." Ophelia smiled weakly at her questioner.

No one moved for a few seconds until the guard turned and gave the order to resume marching. Once they were walking steadily again, Lyan looked over at the other woman questioningly.

Ophelia mouthed, "Havarti" to the barbarian, motioning back to the hallway in the T intersection they just passed. When she and Lyan first met the Bunny Barbarian must have thought Ophelia was crazy, having arguments with herself when she thought no one was looking. It wasn't until sometime later that the mercenary introduced her to Havarti an enchanted, living bastard sword that could speak for itself but Ophelia also explained that they shared a type of telepathic link so they could communicate silently, on the sword's end at least, and even know where the other was if they were separated. As long as they were within a certain distance, of course.

Chances were that wherever Havarti was, Lyan's weapons were likely to be with him. It wasn't much at this point. But it was more than they had a few moments ago.

They finally came up to a massive set of double doors, easily twice the height of anyone in the procession, made of ebony wood that was polished to the point that it looked like they could have been a light source on their own.

The doors opened as they neared, without the creaking their cell door exclaimed to denote its unkempt state. There was one man on the inside of each door, short and thin wearing simple black robes. Their skin was dark gray, like used charcoal dust, and their ears were long and pointed. Ornate skullcaps hid their hair but their race was obvious and Lyan cursed quietly.

Inside was a round room. Guards like the ones escorting Lyan and Ophelia lined the walls all around and eight tall, thin windows with more small panes than the women could count, lined the walls of the room, showing little more than cave rock face beyond.

Standing in the middle of the room, obviously the most important there, was a woman with obsidian hued skin and long, pointed ears pierced with every type of jewel Ophelia or Lyan could think of naming. The woman was dressed in a black satin dress that stretched from her throat to beyond her feet and draped over the floor. Her waist length hair was silver with intricate gold chains braided into it. Radiating up and back away from her shoulders was what her people called a filigree. Ophelia always thought it was a pretentious way of saying "fancy cape collar". It was over half again as tall as she and was sculpted in the shape of a spiderweb complete with a ruby embedded black widow woven into it. It somehow displayed her rank within the Lytyl Tribe, although neither surface dweller knew how to read it.

Lyan growled under her breath, her knuckles cracking in an effort to restrain herself. Ophelia came to a dead stop just past the door jamb, a look on her face that stretched from wrenching dread to blood searing hatred.

A single curse word slipped easily and loudly enough for all to hear from the sword woman's lips at the sight that greeted her followed by, "The svartalfar."

CHAPTER

FIVE

THE SVARTALFAR WERE a subspecies of elf that went literally underground so long ago it may as well have been forever. A few of the tribes, in more mountainous regions, had their skin turned albino white from the lack of sunlight. They lived hard lives but were well adapted to the harsh environments of the naturally carved out caves.

But the Lytyl Tribe, along the Xaviour and other svartalfar tribes, lived in ground that was so rich in elements that made them able to live in a way that was a dark reflection of life above ground. A side effect of such rich earth was that it turned their skin dark with excess carbon from the soil.

"Not a very promising first impression." The svartalfar woman smirked as she rested her hands on her narrow hips.

The heavy doors to the round room closed behind Lyan and Ophelia with an echoing thud. Half of the group that had escorted the prisoners here took positions in front of the door, leaving one on Lyan's left, one on Ophelia's right and one behind both to guard the two women. All there was between the barbarian and Ophelia and the svartalfar in the satin dress was about ten feet and a rug with intricate runes and designs emblazoned on it.

Ophelia would have liked to think it was her better judgment but, in all honesty, it was probably the sharp pain in her side that kept her from rushing over and beating the life out the woman with the spider themed fashion sense. Guards or no guards.

So, instead, she said. "Being kidnapped, beaten and brought here wasn't much of a 'how do you do', either. So I guess we're both off to rocky starts."

The Bunny Barbarian kept standing at attention, sticking her chest out proudly as she watched the other two women speak. The two saber toothed rabbit teeth that ran down between Lyan's eyes from the brim of her pastel blue helmet to just past her chin hid most of her brow furrowing at Ophelia's reply.

"Beaten?" The woman feigned shock well as she lifted a black hand to her chest. "But you don't have a scratch on you."

"That's because of the spring in our cell. It healed the wounds on our skin but not any of our more serious..." When the mercenary realized her mouth moved but no sound came out, she stopped mid-sentence.

Ophelia's pale blue eyes narrowed at the svartalfar woman. The corner of the black skinned woman's mouth twitched up in a momentary smile, but she otherwise gave no other sign of knowing what was happening. But Lyan noticed as well and tried to say something but had results similar to Ophelia.

"I see you do not dispute that you come here uninjured, after all." The woman said, ignoring that either of the other women even tried to speak. "Then we come to the reason for your audience here."

Lyan's hands clenched into fists and she started to take a step toward the svartalfar. Ophelia's good arm moved just enough to bump the barbarian's wrist, getting the larger woman to see the Ophelia subtly shaking her head as she turned to face the svartalfar woman.

"I'm all ears." Ophelia jibed, half expecting it to be silenced but it came out normally.

The white of the svartalfar woman's teeth stood out against the obsidian of her skin when she grinned. "It is a simple thing, really. You have been brought here to confirm intelligence reports that the Order of Kuan Yin and the Light Bringers are combining forces for an invasion of svartalfar lands."

That took both Lyan and Ophelia by surprise. The only thing that betrayed their reaction was their backs straightening a bit, which no one seemed to notice anyway.

"To what end?" Ophelia asked but her voice was cut off again.

"No objections?" The svartalfar woman was making a production of this, dramatically pacing back and forth in front of the two prisoners as she spoke. "Then you admit this is true and that our conquering our homeland is indeed in the upworlders' plans."

A long low groan, heavy enough to shake the entire room came from above. The svartalfar woman's face turned toward the ceiling, a look of reverence suddenly plastered on it.

"Indeed, I humbly apologize, Lord Judicator." She said. "I did not mean to put words in the mouths of the witnesses."

Lyan and Ophelia looked at each other. They had both thought the fancily dressed svartalfar woman to be this Judicator. Apparently she wasn't, so the question of who was in charge made the prisoners look up themselves.

All the wooden beams in the cone shaped ceiling of the round room lead straight to its center. There, embedded in an oak circle at the peak, was a massive eyeball easily as wide as Lyan was tall. Its amber colored iris darted this way and that, watching the proceedings for a long moment before blinking.

What closed around the eye were not eyelids in the traditional sense. They had the color of flesh, black and gray svartalfar as well as hints of pink upworlder skin, but looked sewn together piecemeal and shaped into a pair of lips. When the eye opened again, Ophelia noticed that there were indeed teeth on either side between the lips around the eyeball itself.

Ophelia couldn't keep from shuddering. Oddly enough, it may have been less disturbing if the teeth had been sharp beastly fangs.

But they weren't. They looked like normal teeth in a mortal person's mouth except for their massive size.

Another low groan escaped from the mouth and Lyan and Ophelia thought it looked as if liquid was going to drip from the iris down onto them. Both women suppressed the urge to step back, away from where they thought the drop would land. But it would likely, and gleefully, be taken as a sign of cowardice rather than their desire to stay clean and dry.

"As you command, Lord Judicator." The svartalfar woman nodded dutifully. "The time for truth has indeed arrived."

Ophelia, and surely Lyan as well, doubted the other woman's desire for the truth. The mercenary had never heard of such a being as a Judicator before in any of her many unfortunate dealings with the subterranean elves but they apparently owed some kind of allegiance to this creature and needed to get its blessing to go to war.

How could this woman hope to get Ophelia and Lyan to help, even with the ability to selectively silence them? Silence didn't equal a confession, at least to this Judicator, and it had already somehow reprimanded the woman for trying to make it that way. Neither the Bunny Barbarian nor Ophelia would say anything that would legitimize her story of Harbenigyr's Order planning to go to war.

"Let us make this interrogation official, shall we?" Some kind of frame under the skirt in the svartalfar woman's kept the material from getting underfoot as she strode over to the thin window opposite the two prisoners. "The Lytyl Tribe's Chief Inquisitor calls upon the known enemy to the svartalfar, Ophelia, to testify."

Ophelia couldn't help but feel insulted. Yes, she had an... unpleasant history with these subterranean people but not all of them. As far a she knew, it was only two different tribes now including the Lytyl. Her hands balled up into fists as she awaited her first question.

"Step forward." The Inquisitor sternly ordered before her fake smile returned to her face. "Please."

Ophelia heard Lyan growl under her breath and worked hard to stifle the urge to do so as well as she started forward. The hard soles of her high heeled boots clacked against the stone floor before she stepped onto the rug. She stopped on the center of the cloth, just as several of the armored guards around the edge of the room started to look uneasy at how close she was getting to the Inquisitor.

"Do you, Ophelia, swear upon pain that you will answer my questions with only truth when you are asked and bring good justice to these proceedings?"

"I guess that would depend on your definition of 'good justice'." Ophelia kept both hands down at her sides, not wanting to appear weak in front of the svartalfar, but her right arm still pulled in tight to her side in an unconscious effort to protect her sore ribs. "I haven't met a Lytyl yet that wanted truth that didn't suit her own ends and, so far, you're fitting that mold to a T."

The Inquisitor visually bristled at that. The human forced herself to keep from smiling in satisfaction. But the svartalfar quickly gathered herself, slapping that condescending smile back onto her face.

"A simple yes or no." She tried to sound civil, no doubt for the Judicator's benefit. "Please."

Ophelia looked from the Inquisitor, back over her shoulder at Lyan and up toward the massive eyeball resting in the ceiling. "Fine. Yes, I do."

With that, streaks of indigo lightning suddenly erupted from the carpet and wrapped around the woman's arms, legs, waist and throat. They crackled and tried to pull Ophelia down off her feet but she forced herself to stay upright even as her knees and, more intensely, her broken ribs screamed with the effort at remaining standing.

"What are you doing to her?" Lyan bellowed, knocking the guard nearest her flat on his back before stomping toward Ophelia and the Inquisitor.

Six guards and six razor sharps axes got in her path before the Bunny Barbarian could reach the edge of carpeting in the middle of the floor. A groan escaped from the Judicator and the Inquisitor nodded toward the ceiling as she skirted around the enchanted material to address Lyan.

"These runes," She indicated the patterns and shapes sewn into the carpet. "Punish those who speak lies or withhold information from the Judicator. He designed them himself."

Lyan looked down at the carpet and the unnatural lightning did indeed emerge from each of the runes. If the pole axes hadn't blocked her way, she would have wrapped her hands around the Inquisitor's throat.

"Then why is it hurting her now?" The Bunny Barbarian still had to speak through clenched teeth and sprayed spittle with each word. "She hasn't said anything. You haven't even asked her any questions!"

The Inquisitor acted as if she was having trouble understanding Lyan. "Oh, it's merely a baseline to motivate the witness to not lie and make it worse for themselves." The obsidian skinned woman skirted back around the carpet and leaned in close to Ophelia, their faces only inches from each other. "Understand what is at stake, human?"

Ophelia already felt beads of sweat from the effort of standing mixed with the pain radiating through her entire torso start dripping down her face. "Just ask your damn questions!" She spat through gritted teeth much like the barbarian moments before.

"My my, it seems both of you missed elocution classes growing up." The Inquisitor snickered, just before another groan of impatience from the Judicator. "Of course, Lord. I shall begin now."

The svartalfar woman straightened up, smoothing the wrinkles that had formed in the front of her dress. She looked all business now, her hands back on her hips as she scowled at the woman in the red trench coat.

"You are familiar with the leader of the Order of Kuan Yin. An elf who calls himself Harbenigyr?"

"Yes." Ophelia nodded and while the lightning didn't disappear, it ceased its strong pull on her, and she breathed a silent sigh of relief.

The Inquisitor nodded in return, looking thoughtful. "Both you and he share the same bigotry against the svartalfar, yes? You hate us." That smirk returned.

"No, we both don't hate the svartalfar." Ophelia didn't like the taste of that sentence as it left her mouth but it was truthful. "He's too kindhearted to hate anyone." She knew the words came out, but she didn't hear the sounds of that last sentence as she spoke.

"I see. You lived among the svartalfar for some time, yes?" The Inquisitor's fingers tapped against her hip.

The Xaviour tribe of svartalfar had tricked Harbenigyr, Lyan and the rest of her friends into thinking that Ophelia had been killed and took her as a slave for "some time". When her friends learned of the deception, thanks to Orison, they entered the Xaviour's caves and gave Ophelia the opportunity to kill their Matriarch, Stohbease, and regain her freedom.

"I was enslaved by the svartalfar for a short while. Yes." The only one of her words that anyone heard was "yes".

"So Harbenigyr, who has never experienced the luxury of svartalfar hospitality, is the one who holds the bigotry in his heart." The svartalfar woman said.

It was a statement, not a question, so Ophelia wasn't required to answer. That didn't stop her, or Lyan for that matter, from trying to deny the Inquisitor's conclusion. It fell on deaf ears or, more accurately, came from silenced vocal chords.

"Tell me, Ophelia," The Inquisitor tapped her fingers along her hip after Ophelia and Lyan stopped trying to speak. "Does Harbenigyr have a preferred steed?"

Ophelia scowled back at the obsidian skinned woman. "Where are you going with this?"

The Inquisitor folded her arms over her chest. "Answer the question, please."

"You want to know his favorite color, too? How about what kind of dessert Harbenigyr likes after a long day?" The mercenary sneered before suddenly buckling down to her knees.

Burning pain scorched through Ophelia's body and she wasn't able to see anything but white while her ears rang with agony. There was nothing else but the pain and the pulling. The pulling. Straight down as if it was dragging her to hell itself.

Eventually, her sight did return and all Ophelia could see was carpeting. She couldn't move, couldn't lift herself up. Pain still arced through her body, concentrating on her broken ribs, which now felt as if one stabbed through her skin. She was pretty sure she could feel the warm trickle of blood running down her side.

Then she heard the Inquisitor's voice again. "You did promise to answer all questions in a timely manner, my dear. Stalling for time by mocking the Judicator will not avail you here."

Ophelia's breathing came in shallow gulps, none of them enough to alleviate the sensation that she was feeling of being smothered. Ophelia was just able to turn her head, the heat of the friction of the rug's threads against her forehead stinging, to at least see the svartal-far woman.

"I would. If they..." She struggled to speak, each breath shooting what felt like a burning dagger into her side. "Had a.... point."

"Oh, but they do, Ophelia." The Inquisitor smirked down at her, pulling one of the stray braids that had fallen in front of Ophelia's face out of her field of vision. "Now, tell me, does Harbenigyr ride a griffin?"

Ophelia nodded. "Yes. Triton. A wingless... griffin Harby... rescued from.. being slaughtered... by some farmers."

Again, every word but "yes" came from muted lips. But this time, from this low angle, Ophelia could see a familiar looking puce colored head of wheat twirling back and forth between the svartalfar's black fingers.

The Inquisitor straightened back up to her feet and looked up to address the Judicator directly. "Let the record show that the mercenary, Ophelia, corroborates that the leader of the Order of Kuan Yin was the likely rider of the griffin that led an ambush against a peaceful svartalfar caravan in the north caves a fortnight ago."

"No... No I... didn't." As Ophelia gasped, she felt the unnatural lightning that had been holding her suddenly come loose. "I only.. said that.. Harben...igyr had... a griffin."

As Ophelia spoke, able to be heard, she lifted herself to her knees where a growing puddle of blood rested. Crimson covered one of the blocky indigo runes from where the lightning had manifested. She had a feeling that it also had something to do with why they weren't active anymore.

Ophelia heard grunting behind her and struggled to look back and see what was happening. Lyan was lying face down on the cold stone floor, along with five or six of the guards that were out cold. Two, though, stood on either side of her with the blades of their pole axes resting against the back of her neck. Another sat on her back, restraining her arms so she couldn't use them to attack anymore.

Ophelia didn't have the strength to restrain the smile that came to her face at the thought of Lyan taking on all those guards just to help her. But the visual of the end result made the smile fade quickly.

The Inquisitor rested her hand on the crown of Ophelia's head and turned her to face the svartalfar woman again. "It is enough. Along with other evidence, I have been able to show that the Order of Kuan Yin is a clear and present danger to the Lytyl Tribe and must be destroyed."

Ophelia's voice was again silenced as she tried to protest. Then she realized she was starting to feel light headed.

The puce head of wheat again twirled between the Inquisitor's fingers. Ophelia thought the svartalfar had missed her calling. With her finger dexterity and being able to hide the little magic trinket, the Inquisitor would have been a hell of a pick pocket. A master thief.

Although, she was committing a far greater crime by helping whoever gave her the trinket to instigate a war against an Order that was little more than a group of doctors and healers. Harbenigyr had delivered his own child when his wife went into labor for the gods' sake!

Again, Ophelia tried to protest but she started to list to the side, unable to straighten herself. Her right hand reflexively reached out to try and catch herself but immediately regretted it as a new flash of pain came over her.

"Poor dear." The Inquisitor smirked down as the human fell into unconsciousness. "I guess you were injured after all."

The svartalfar woman motioned for the guards to pull Lyan back up to her feet. New bruises were forming all over the muscular woman's body but, beyond her broken jaw, didn't seem to have any major injuries. She rushed over to the unconscious Ophelia and scooped her up in her thick arms.

The Inquisitor spoke to Lyan as much as the guards. "Take them back to the cell and then fetch a healer to treat Ophelia's wound. Assuming she survives both she and the barbarian will face charges of aiding and abetting a war criminal and the Judicator will schedule when they are to be executed."

Without a word Lyan and Ophelia found themselves back in the cell with the spring. The Bunny Barbarian gently lowered the other woman down beside the spring and started splashing water over the bloody gash in her side.

"She needs far more attention than that." A voice that was little more than a whisper drifted across Lyan's ears.

"Who's there?" The barbarian felt spittle dribble down her clenched chin as she jumped to her feet between Ophelia and where the voice came from, her fists ready to pummel.

A shadow peeled away from the corner of the cell and stepped toward the pastel blue fur covered woman. She didn't make any threatening gestures. In fact, once she revealed her presence to Lyan she didn't move at all.

"Are you the healer?" Lyan's brown eyes narrowed at the darkness draped figure.

"No. But I am the one that will help you escape." The living shadow hissed. "Both of you."

CHAPTER

SIX

"No." Ophelia said.

"But—" The Bunny Barbarian started.

"No!" The other woman interrupted. "I don't trust Nyphistra!"

The mercenary turned away from Lyan to check on the dryness of her top that now hung over a length of chain draped from the ceiling near the spring. Red stained the edges of the green silk sections, even after over an hour of trying to wash the garment in the cell's lone source of water. Now that their appearance in front of the eye mouth thing they called the Judicator was done, the svartalfar didn't seem to care how they looked.

At least they sent a healer to treat Ophelia's wound. A long length of bandage was wrapped around her torso, covering her breasts and down to just above her navel. From behind, it covered the top half of the runes tattooed into her back but they still glowed faint violet through the fabric.

The bandages were wrapped tight enough that the woman couldn't quite get a full breath but at least she had full use of both of her arms without debilitating pain washing over her. The Lytyl

Tribe always did insist on their prisoners being healthy before they were executed.

Lyan, who was able to move her jaw now with only a mild ache after the healer's visit, continued to speak even as Ophelia's back was turned to her. "We do not have many options here. Nyphistra gave me a map with a path up to the surface and we worked out how to avoid the guard patrols. The magician helped you before. Why do you distrust her now?"

The Bunny Barbarian wasn't overly pleased that her fate was tied to a plan from a duplicitous magician but, as she said, their options were few. In fact, Nyphistra's plan was their only option outside of being executed as war criminals. So Lyan was going to do all she could to get the other woman on board.

Ophelia didn't feel her top was dry enough to wear yet and turned back to the barbarian. "Her version of help before left us unable to fight back and Folken as a slave in a loin cloth. And that was the high point of her plan!"

The Bunny Barbarian frowned, remembering the part of Nyphistra's escape plan she liked least. She would not be able to retrieve her spear, gauntlets or shield before getting to the surface.

"You did get out. She kept her word then, did she not?" Lyan said, her massive arms crossed over her equally massive chest.

"And it just happened to up Nyphistra's standing in the Lytyl tribe hierarchy as a result." Ophelia felt a chill run through her, whether through the clammy air or her feelings toward the wizard or the svartalfar in general, she wasn't sure. "Just imagine how much higher she'd go capturing a couple of escaping war criminals."

Ophelia snatched her long coat off another length of chain and slipped it over her shoulders. She effortlessly slipped both arms into the sleeves with barely a squeak from the metal wrapped right one or herself. The coat didn't feel right without Havarti or at least his scabbard pressing against her back and she reflexively wiggled from side to side to try and get more comfortable.

"She does claim to be trying to change the svartalfar for the better." Lyan repeated what Nyphistra told her, although the barbarian wasn't sure she believed it herself. "If it's true, we have a chance to get out and warn Dianmeyer. If she is false, our fate remains unchanged."

Ophelia grunted. "There are fates worse than death, Lyan. I lived one until you and Harby came and got me out and I won't let the Lytyl do that to me again." She turned to the Bunny Barbarian. "I hope you get out, Lyan. I really do. As for me, I'm going to kill every last svartalfar bastard that comes for me with my bare hands until one of them finally gets lucky."

"I will return for you again, Ophelia." The Bunny Barbarian stood tall and proud as she spoke, her tone one of taking an oath. "Once I've warned Dianmeyer we will come for you like we did before."

The other woman shook her head. "Don't bother. Even if I had Havarti, I'll be dead long before you could get back here. Just make sure Harby's Order gets word of what's happening."

The conversation ended there. Both women eventually lay down on the stone floor but only Ophelia seemed to actually sleep. Lyan waited, her fingers tapping back and forth across her hard abdomen as she went over historic battle plans in her head.

The faint pop of a timed explosive snapped the Bunny Barbarian out of her reverie. Nyphistra had planted the little magic trinket in the lock before the healer arrived and the wizard fled. This was the best and only time for Lyan to escape back up to the surface.

The Bunny Barbarian quickly rose to her feet and stalked over to the door, peering out for any sign of alerted guards. She glanced back at Ophelia and saw that her long coat was still wrapped around her like a blanket and she hadn't moved a muscle.

Lyan couldn't force Ophelia to come, or realistically even carry her the whole way to the surface, though the thought did come to mind. With a sigh, the barbarian slipped out into the hall and gently closed the door behind her.

The map of the path out was drawn into the scorched flesh of Lyan's scarred arm. The markings were only slightly darker than the actual skin so the Bunny Barbarian could see it only because she knew what she was looking for, unlike anyone who would or could have searched her.

Now it was coming to use. Lyan was tempted to try and find her weapons but Nyphistra didn't mark that room on her map, insisting that the timing to avoid the guards patrolling the path to the surface had to be precise, and the only hint the Bunny Barbarian had was Ophelia's head tilt toward a hall where she sensed Havarti.

So escape was her best choice. Then to come back with troop of warriors, preferably Yo Bunpy, to retrieve her property and avenge Ophelia's murder. It might have to wait until after whatever battle the svartalfar Inquisitor planned for the surface but Lyan would surely make the Lytyl Tribe pay for all they had done.

The idle mutterings of pairs of guards floated towards and then away from the barbarian, in just the pattern the magician said they would come and go, as long as she was in the proper hallway at each time. The conversations started coming more often, and easier to hear as the barbarian went along.

She must have been ahead of schedule, because a pair of voices came from around a corner that Lyan didn't expect. Looking around, her only option for a hiding place was behind one of the decorative suits of armor that rested just inside a shallow recess.

It is normally assumed that because of their brightly colored armors Bunny Barbarians stood out against any background they were in so hiding and sneaking was impossible for them. While it was true that the Yo Bunpy tribe prefers open battle to subterfuge, they are trained to sneak and can sneak well when the situation calls for it. Even their armor, as long as they avoided direct sunlight, seemed to take on the color of what was immediately around them on the rare occasions they chose to hide.

"The Generals are rallying up the troops a lot faster than usual." The tinny voice of a guard said, as the faint metal clanking of his footsteps got closer. "I guess the idea of the upworlders combining forces really got them worried this time."

"Maybe," Another tinny voice said. "I think it's a power play by the Inquisitor to make the Vizier look bad and take her position beside the Matriarch."

The two black armored soldiers came into view, just over the shoulder of the decorative armor, as Lyan pressed herself tightly against the wall. Her helmet rested on the floor between her feet, the tall ears protruding too far for her to hide effectively if she kept it on her head.

The second guard's helmet squeaked as he suddenly started looking around. "But don't tell anyone I said that," he whispered.

They disappeared around the corner and Lyan slipped out from behind the decorative armor. Putting her helmet back on, the barbarian peeked around the corner after the guards. Unfortunately, they were heading in the very direction she had to go.

Her knuckles cracked as Lyan's fists tightened. Another myth about barbarians was that they only stomped around everywhere they went. That was particularly untrue of the Bunny Barbarians of the Yo Bunpy tribe. Using the thickly padded forepaws of the massive saber toothed rabbits they killed made their boots perfect for walking silently in any terrain. They only stomped when they wanted to intimidate their opponents.

This was not one of those times. Lyan moved more quietly than a soft breeze, quickly closing the distance between herself and the two guards heading down the hallway she had to take.

Her arms stretched out from her sides, making Lyan look as if she was pantomiming a bird gliding, until the guards were within reach. She wrapped an arm around each guard's head, squeezing so tightly that Lyan could feel the metal of their helmets crumple between her biceps and forearms. Just as they started to yell in surprise, the barbarian wrenched her arms back to break their necks.

With a sickening crack, one tumbled straight to the stone floor while the other wheeled around and struck the wall with enough force to crack the wood beam that ran up to support the ceiling. Lyan cringed at the echoing thud the armor made, her eyes darting back the way she came in search of any guards coming to investigate.

The quiet was oppressive in those long moments as Lyan waited. She started down the hallway again, slowly walking backwards and keeping an eye out for more guards. She finally reached the wooden archway with a statue of Matriarch Lytyl, the ancient svartalfar that the tribe was named for, standing in the middle of it. It was just as Nyphistra described. She looked back down at her scarred arm for the instructions.

"Touch the back of Lytyl's hands, then touch her palms. Press your palms into her shoulders, just where they connect to her chest. Then wrap your hands around her hips and twist the statue to its right and a passage will appear."

As the wall lifted up and away from the floor in the archway, it was surprisingly quiet for how big the passageway became. Lyan couldn't help but wonder if svartalfar did everything so intricately and over-complicated. They seemed to have schemes upon schemes and ritual upon ritual for even the most mundane tasks. It seemed a wonder that they could get up in the mornings in a timely manner, let alone organize to start a war.

As Lyan stepped inside, the archway closed just as quickly and silently as it had opened. This was a little used and even less known stairway that was supposed to be reserved for the Lytyl Tribe's nobility as a secret path up to the surface in case of a rebellion or other attack on the underground city in order to preserve the aristocracy.

After a quick walk down a cramped tunnel, the area suddenly widened into a massive cavern. Though she was still underground, the barbarian couldn't see the cave walls as they were so far away.

The staircase on the landing at the end of the tunnel was wide enough that a half dozen Yo Bunpy could march shoulder to shoulder comfortably, as it lazily spiraled up and to the right on narrow spires of rock with arches that spanned the stairs every fifty feet or so to hold torches on either side.

The torches were magically activated by motion and jumped to life as Lyan made her way up the stairs. Apparently the nobles didn't want to sully their hands with soot even if they were fleeing for their lives.

This was it. The home stretch. It would be a long walk up the stairwell to what Nyphistra described as a "hub": A wide, leveled off area where three secret stairways met and combined to lead to one tunnel up to the surface world. Then another half an hour's walk and Lyan would be in the sunlight.

As she neared the hub, something started to not feel right. Lyan's brown eyes narrowed as she tried to find the source of her unease. After a few more steps, it came to her. The last few torches she had passed were already lit, unlike all the ones that came to life at the beginning. That meant...

When the Bunny Barbarian reached the end of the stairway, the hub was filled with as many svartalfar as it could hold. Many were armored guards like the two she had killed but there were also archers immediately in front of the tunnel to the surface. There were also robed svartalfar women whose hands crackled with energy as they idly made archaic gestures with their fingers, working to keep them loose.

There had to be at least forty svartalfar and, in the middle of them was the Inquisitor with a self-satisfied look on her face. She turned as a sharp eyed archer spotted Lyan and pointed her out to the group.

"So it was Nyphistra after all." The Inquisitor's white teeth exposed by the woman's smile stood out to Lyan even at their long distance apart. "I will have to thank her for this glorious bounty she's provided me."

Lyan weighed her options. Fifteen armored svartalfar with pole axes, five magicians and twenty archers and the Bunny Barbarian without a shield or a weapon. If she was lucky, the magicians would cast spells that used lightning to attack her. Since her armor was made by a creature that literally breathed lightning, it couldn't hurt her. But there was also fire, ice, acid and a plethora of other types of magicks they could fling at her besides the lone one that was harmless to her.

Charging head on was a death sentence, assuming she even reached the armored guards before she was riddled with arrows, Lyan wouldn't get within arm's reach before being chopped or skewered by at least a dozen axes.

"Whoever lets her body fall into the abyss gets to follow and retrieve it." The Inquisitor announced.

As much as it pained Lyan to admit it, she only had one real option: tactical retreat. Cursing loudly to herself, the Bunny Barbarian turned and started down the stairs just as she heard the first barrage of arrows dive past her head.

Going down was much faster than going up with the aid of gravity and running as fast as her padded feet could carry her. The barbarian felt random dull thuds of arrows impacting but not piercing the strips of furry armor against her back as she ran. It was a miracle none found the flesh of her broad back.

The guards started yelling as they charged after her. Fortunately for Lyan, they were still a group and moved slower than her, even when charging.

As she reached the opening of the tunnel, she again smiled at her good fortune. The archers would be useless in such a confined space, the magicians, too. The tight tunnel would also nullify the guards' number advantage and maybe give her time to figure out how to open the passage back into the system of hallways, forcing them to split up in search for her. The barbarian had a better chance against small groups or pairs than against the whole force at once.

Lyan hurried all the way back to the beginning of the tunnel. She hadn't noticed how flat the wall looked on this side. She knew the archway was in the wall. It, in fact, made up most of the wall when it was open. But she couldn't see any mechanism to open it on this side. Were the svartalfar so paranoid that they even had a secret ritual to open a secret passage from the side that was supposed to be secret in and of itself?

Apparently they were. The loud squeaking and clanking of armor told the barbarian that the guards had reached the entrance at the other end of the tunnel. Their numeric advantage was still nullified, perhaps if she could get one of the guard's pole axes from them she could use it to fight back. They weren't all that different from her spear, after all.

A purple cloud suddenly appeared beside Lyan and, just an instant later, was replaced with Ophelia, who looked around in confusion as she took in her new surroundings. The mercenary turned and grinned wide when she saw Lyan standing beside her looking dumbfounded.

"Ophelia? How—what are you doing here?" Lyan said, her eyebrows painfully close together.

"I got lonely." The woman shrugged back.

As the first guard appeared and charged them, Ophelia lifted Havarti and slashed down on the long handle of the ax, splitting it in half and making the svartalfar in the armor stumble forward before having his head removed by the bastard sword chopping through the thin space between the helmet and torso pieces.

"You have your sword!" Lyan said as she eyed the ruined pole ax at her feet. "I don't suppose..."

Ophelia shrugged one shoulder, then the other and Lyan's shield slipped from her back and into her free hand. She tossed it to the barbarian as she jabbed Havarti through the eye hole of the next guard charging down the tunnel.

"What about my spear?" Lyan didn't want to appear ungrateful as she sandwiched the next guard's head between her wooden shield and the immovable stone wall.

"Oh, yeah. Your spear." Ophelia slashed at the next guard before jumping back against the flat wall to avoid the guard's own attack with his ax. "There's a story about your spear."

"And what's that?" Lyan asked as she drove the edge of her shield into the throat of the same guard that made the mistake of focusing his attention on Ophelia.

It was starting to get crowded in that thin tunnel. The next guard had to step over the dead bodies of his comrades.

"Well, you see—" Ophelia started just as a steel rabbit head with razor sharp saber teeth stabbed through the wall only inches from her head.

CHAPTER

SEVEN

Ophelia didn't open her eyes when she heard the pop and the door slowly open. Lyan shuffled around and stopped at the cell door. She seemed reluctant to leave but finally did so.

After a slow count to one hundred Ophelia lifted herself to her feet. She slipped on her long coat and started for the door. Then she turned back to the chain where her top rested and plucked it from the rusted metal.

Ophelia slipped out the door and pushed it back into place, just as Lyan did, and started down the hall. She followed halls as she made her way to where she felt Havarti, but must have been too far away to yet even mentally hear his snooty accent. And while she walked at a good clip, she still stopped at each intersection to peek around for any stray guards.

Even for this time of night the keep seemed understaffed. The svartalfar didn't even trust each other in their own deepest held territory and the fact that there weren't any to keep track of each other seemed wrong somehow. If events were shaping up the way she was figuring, and if Lyan was indeed in the middle of it, a lot of people with pointed ears were going to die. Starting with a certain svartalfar wizard who looked like a living shadow.

Despite hitting a couple of dead ends, Ophelia reached the door that led to Havarti much faster than she thought she would. She turned the brass handle and found it locked, not much of a surprise there. But when she stepped back to put her shoulder into it to smash the door, the slab of wood swung open.

The mercenary didn't move toward or away from the door. She simply waited for what was bound to be the inevitable svartalfar wizard or some type of soldier to step out and attack. None came. She didn't even hear any movement behind the door or inside the room. Finally, Ophelia peeked her head inside and groaned.

Nyphistra was standing inside with Havarti, still in his scabbard but in her hands. If the Inquisitor's skin was obsidian, the wizard was a shade darker than that. You couldn't even make out any of her facial features she was so dark. Even the "whites" of her eyes were black, leaving purple irises to surround black pupils. That only made her pink tongue stand out even more when she spoke. The movement of the muscle was almost hypnotic.

"You will not be harmed here." The wizard's voice came as a hissing whisper.

Never any louder than that, but no matter how raucous it was around her, even in the heat of battle, Nyphistra could be heard clearly. Every syllable. And something about that irked Ophelia.

The wizard's clothing had been tailored in much the same way she wore her skin... black. She didn't wear baggy clothes like the lower ranked svartalfar wizards. Nyphistra dressed in the finest satin dress and a billowing silk cloak the Lytyl Tribe could afford. The only hint of color to her was a silver leg brace that peeked out from a slit in her gown that went up to the svartalfar's left hip, the foot looking like the talon of a metal bird of prey.

As Ophelia finished sizing the other woman up, she stepped into the room and closed the door behind her, slipping the latch back into its locked position. It was the armory, at least an auxiliary one considering that she could walk from one side to the other in about ten steps.

Along the far wall, from one side of the room to the other, were pole axes like the ones that every guard carried. In the middle of the space was a line of two sided racks of weapons of various types that stretched the entire length of the room, as well. The rack closest to the mercenary held daggers, along with Lyan's spear, shield and gauntlets, which were obviously tossed there in a hurry. The rack closest to Nyphistra held magic wands of various lengths.

Ophelia stopped about three steps away from the svartalfar woman. "There's no one on this side of the fortress. You sent Lyan into an ambush, didn't you?" It may have been phrased as a question but the tone made it a statement.

Nyphistra slowly nodded. "Not by design. I'm afraid our tribe Inquisitor is on to me and seeks to usurp my position."

"On to you? You make it sound like you are the victim in this when Lyan is marching to her death." Ophelia balled up a fist as she stepped up to the living shadow, trying to decide whether or not to throw the punch.

"There is still time to save her." The wizard hissed. "If you take the barbarian's weapons to her and then make your way back to me, you may still be able to obtain your freedom."

As if offering an olive branch, Nyphistra held the bastard sword up to the taller woman, who snatched it and slipped it onto her back in a quick, practiced motion. Ophelia was still trying to decide whether or not to strike, this time with Havarti instead of her hand.

"Havarti guided me here. Why didn't he warn me that you were here waiting?" Ophelia glanced back between the sword and the svartalfar.

Nyphistra held up a familiar looking puce wheat head. "Apparently this effects more than just a living person's voice. I took it from Inquisitor Aylosha while she was busy gloating to some of the nobles."

Ophelia's eyes narrowed at the little object. "That's the second one of those I've seen." She reached out and took it from Nyphistra, who didn't make a move to resist.

"It was a, for lack of a better term, gift from the man with which Aylosha is colluding." The living shadow moved for the first time, away from the rack of wands, as she continued. "A human named Perett has promised to help her destroy me in exchange for letting him use the tunnels to the north to ambush the Light Bringers and overthrow the Valen Court."

Valen Court was the city that served as the home base of the Light Bringers, an organization that enforced law and order throughout the region with their authority being recognized across every country. It also held the eponymous Valen Court that served as the court system for war criminals. If those were to fall...

"Perett." Ophelia chewed on her lip thoughtfully for a moment. "One of his men said that he was planning to attack the Order of Kuan Yin and Dianmeyer. That's what eventually got us down here."

The wizard nodded again. "Perett's early forays into our tunnels weren't sanctioned. He can somehow control griffins and brought them down with him. They attacked several patrols before Aylosha discovered him and learned his actual plan to attack the Light Bringers on their flank."

Ophelia's pale blue eyes flicked toward the door as she scooped up the Bunny Barbarian's equipment. "What does that have to do with Harbenigyr?"

Nyphistra sighed, a sound that made the mercenary's ears itch. "Nothing for Perett, save that he is the only one the svartalfar have encountered who uses a griffin as a steed. Destroying the Order of Kuan Yin simultaneously would not only help Perett but provide our tribe with a foothold to invade the surface without the worry of Light Bringers interference, which was the reason I've given to the Matriarch to deter unnecessary violence up to this point."

"Your Inquisitor is willing to wipe out an entire keep, an entire town full of people just to move up in rank in your tribe?" Ophelia slipped the shield's carrying straps over her shoulders so the round piece of wood rested on her back, keeping an eye on Nyphistra every second.

"Yes. Aylosha will start a war if it discredits me and allows her to take my place at the Matriarch's side." The wizard answered.

"Well too bad for you." Ophelia stuffed the metal rabbit heads of Lyan's gauntlets into the pockets of her coat and flipped the latch to unlock the door. "If I get Lyan back and in one piece, maybe we'll figure out a way to help you. Where is she?"

"Along the eastern wall is a shrine to Matriarch Lytyl—" Nyphistra started but was interrupted by the door suddenly smashed off its hinges and into the armory.

Ophelia jumped just out of the path of the splintered wood, her bastard sword already in hand. An armored guard stepped inside, and then another, each with their pole axes leveled toward the mercenary.

"Friends of your—" The sword woman started to ask as the first guard jabbed the sharp, heavy blade at her abdomen.

She stepped to the side, out of the weapon's path. He was awkwardly close for her to use Havarti's blade on him but with a quick twist of his handle, the bottom half pulled away to reveal the dagger it concealed, Ophelia buried it in the guard's throat.

She looked back up toward where Nyphistra had been but she wasn't there. The mercenary turned her attention to the second guard and saw the wizard behind him. Nyphistra was almost a foot shorter but she reached up with both hands on either side of his metal enshrouded head. The same kind of indigo lightning that the Judicator used on Ophelia now leaped back and forth from fingertip to fingertip through the helmet. After only seconds, the metal started to glow red hot and a sickening gurgle came from inside the helmet as the guard collapsed to the ground.

"Aylosha took most of the men who were supposed to guard this side of the fortress into the hidden stairway with her in anticipation of my escape plan for you and Lyan." Nyphistra stepped over the man she killed and into the hallway, mostly to avoid the puddle of crimson liquid that started to form under the dead guard's head. "Your sword has the instructions on how to open the passageway."

Ophelia didn't thank the svartalfar. She figured not pushing the woman to the floor showed enough gratitude for the moment and Ophelia started down the hall to the east. She heard the clanking armor of more guards coming up almost immediately but Ophelia turned the corner before they spotted her.

"You fools." Nyphistra's voice came to Ophelia's ears as clear as if she was standing right beside her. "The human already took what she came here for. Go to the western gate and keep her from escaping!"

Ophelia rushed down the hallways. Unlike before, she didn't check to see if guards were in the halls ahead. Holding Havarti in her left hand, Ophelia's right was wrapped around Lyan's spear with the length resting under her arm. If any guards did end up in her path, they would likely be skewered by a steel saber toothed rabbit head before they realized what happened.

As she approached an intersection, Ophelia let out a yelp of surprise when the spear was suddenly wrenched to the side and sent her spinning down the wrong corridor. Stopping herself inches from toppling a decorative suit of armor, Ophelia looked down the corridor opposite her to see what took the spear.

Her pale eyes opened wide at the sight of the massive svartalfar, easily over seven feet tall. He held Lyan's spear in one hand and a pole ax in the other. The dark elf didn't wear any armor but was built as if he was made of granite, a very large block of granite. He wore a black uniform trimmed with gold, meaning he was an officer in their military. That was something quite rare for a man in the svartalfar's matriarchal society.

He didn't have an overbite or an under bite but his jaw looked as if it was three sizes too big for the rest of his head. That was impressive considering how big his head was... along with the rest of him.

"Prisoner, in consequence of your attempt to escape, your life is now forfeit." The svartalfar's voice was a deep baritone that practically caused the walls to reverberate with his words.

And then the ax chopped down at Ophelia's head. She jumped back to avoid the strike, swinging Havarti to sever the head of the blade from the staff but not before the razor sharp metal buried itself into the stone floor and caused a crack to radiate all the way to the wall behind Ophelia.

That the man was strong was an understatement. But when he turned his head and started to bellow down the hall for back up that told her that he was smart, too. Not the combination Ophelia needed in an opponent at the moment.

Confusion was all over his face when his yelling didn't get past his lips. The svartalfar officer tried again but with the same result. Silence.

Ophelia smirked, taking his moment of confusion as a chance to strike. Unfortunately, not only was the man strong and smart but quicker than he looked, too.

The big man tossed the staff that had formerly been his ax at Ophelia's legs, making her trip. Spinning around as she fell onto her back, Lyan's shield made her slide across the stone floor and stop immediately in front of the muscular soldier foot first. The Yo Bunpy spear streaked down for Ophelia and she did the first thing she could think of: Kicked both of the officer's shins simultaneously.

It worked. The force of the kicks pushed her just far enough out of the way that the spear buried itself into the stone floor between her legs. The extra force came from the svartalfar dropping to his knees, one of his hands landing beside the spearhead to brace himself up and he let out a pained groan in forced silence.

So many jokes suddenly flooded Ophelia's head but she didn't get a chance to even spout one before the fist that had been wrapped around the spear thrust for her face. She rolled back, thankfully out of his reach but in the split second it took her to whip the red leather of her coat back behind her, Ophelia had another strike to dodge.

This time she didn't even have an illusion of grace as she lunged to the side, down the hallway that lead to her destination, landing in a heap and jarring her still aching ribs. Ophelia scrambled up to her feet, pointing the tip of Havarti's blade at the svartalfar officer's chest to keep him from thinking that charging her was a good idea.

As she steadied herself, four more guards charged down the hallway opposite Ophelia. Even with the officer's voice silenced, the power of his strikes must have caused plenty of noise for them to come and investigate. Ophelia cursed her luck.

"Mind you, my dear, we must leave this rabble behind and find Lyan!" The familiar, snooty voice of Havarti echoed in Ophelia's mind.

"And why have you been so closed lipped until now?" She muttered as the armored guards took positions around the massive officer, who now once more pointed the Yo Bunpy spear straight at Ophelia.

"That dreadful device must have stayed tuned on me until you switched its focus onto that beast." Havarti answered.

The svartalfar were smart enough to stay out of reach of her sword, but they knew they had the advantage at the moment. And every second Ophelia spent here was another Lyan was on her own, unarmed and without back up against whatever the Inquisitor had waiting.

She just needed a few seconds lead. She was outnumbered against five men. What could she do? Five men. Men.

Ophelia frowned, fighting the urge to roll her eyes as she straightened up out of her fighting stance. Before the svartalfar could even wonder what she was up to, Ophelia's free right hand reached up and pulled the bandages covering her breasts down.

Each man froze for just a moment but it was enough. Before they shook their heads to regain their senses, Ophelia was already out of sight down the hall.

Hopping over two dead soldiers that appeared to be Lyan's handiwork, Ophelia was at the arch and statue moments later. The screams of rage from the five svartalfar echoed down the hall when they came upon their fallen comrades, reminding Ophelia that she only had seconds.

"Back of her hands, her palms, shoulders." Havarti hurriedly instructed.

The officer beat the others to Ophelia, whose focus was solely on the statue. Her hands were just moving to Lytyl's hips as Lyan's spear stabbed for just under the woman's arms to skewer her chest cavity.

In a flash of purple haze, the mercenary suddenly found herself in a dark tunnel standing beside the pastel blue armored barbarian. Ophelia couldn't stop herself from grinning at the dumbfounded Lyan, relieved that she was still alive.

"Ophelia? How— what are you doing here?" Lyan hurriedly asked, obviously confused.

"I got lonely." She shrugged back.

An armored guard like the lower ranking ones chasing Ophelia emerged from the tunnel and charged them, the mercenary lifted Havarti and chopped the long handle of his ax in half, making the svartalfar in the armor stumble forward before having his head removed by the bastard sword.

"You have your sword!" Lyan said.

Ophelia realized that Lyan could have armed herself with the ax she just chopped to pieces. But Lyan interrupted the other woman's incubating apology with "I don't suppose..."

Ophelia was suddenly aware of the weight resting on her back and shrugged one shoulder, then the other to free the Bunny Barbarian's shield into her right hand. Ophelia tossed it to Lyan as she jabbed Havarti through the eye hole of the next guard charging down the tunnel.

"What about my spear?" Lyan asked as she sandwiched the next guard's head between her shield and the stone wall.

"Oh, yeah. Your spear." Ophelia jumped back against the wall to avoid another guard's attack with his ax. "There's a story about your spear."

"And what's that?" Lyan drove the thin edge of her shield into the throat of the guard that just attacked Ophelia.

It was getting crowded in the tunnel. The next guard had to step over the dead bodies of his comrades to get at the women.

"Well, you see—" Ophelia started just as a steel rabbit head with razor sharp saber teeth stabbed through the wall only inches from her head. "Grab it and pull!"

Following her own instructions, Ophelia wrapped both hands around the wood shaft, just under the sharp, stylized spearhead. Lyan followed suit and both women tugged with as much muscle as they could.

The spear's tip pierced the armor of the guard rearing up with his ax to attack, piercing his heart and he collapsed to the ground on top of the other guards that came before him.

The wall behind the women was suddenly hit with something massive. It was so heavy, in fact, that it dislodged the mechanism that held the passageway closed and the wall started to lift away from the floor. Before the next armored svartalfar could get through the tunnel, the women already rolled through the narrow opening and were back in the torch lit hall.

On the floor, the immense officer was dazed, lying atop all four of the guards that followed to support him. Ophelia slipped Havarti back into his scabbard and wrapped her hands around the giant svartalfar's collar.

"A little help here, Lyan?" She grunted and she pulled the officer to his feet... mostly.

The Bunny Barbarian wrapped her arms around the man's thick chest and hoisted him the rest of the way up. "Why are we doing this?" She asked.

"We have to keep that door from opening any wider and letting the Inquisitor's goons come after us." Ophelia positioned the officer so that he was between the cracked statue of Lytyl and the two human women that held him. "And charge!"

Using the heavy svartalfar as a battering ram, his back slammed into the statue and the likeness of the Matriarch's head buried itself into the wall up to her shoulders. They left the man resting in the arms his clan's namesake and turned to the other unconscious guards, stuffing them into the narrow opening with well placed kicks that dented the metal that cocooned them and wedged the men in tight.

"Not exactly architecture for the ages but it does get the job done." Havarti said as both women started down the hall, back the way they had come.

"I am sorry, Ophelia." Lyan whispered as she poked her head around a corner to check for guards. "You were right. The magician did set us up to be captured."

The other woman took her turn to check the next intersection. "No, Lyan, you were right. I went to get our weapons and she was there waiting for me."

Ophelia explained what happened in the armory, even showing the barbarian the puce wheat head that the Inquisitor had used. "It's exactly like the one that Caleb had back in the tavern."

Lyan grunted. "I told you we should have killed him."

"It was either him or us paying for the damage to the bar." Ophelia whispered as they reached the hall just adjacent of the armory.

The mercenary peeked around the corner and saw Nyphistra pointing in a direction opposite the way Lyan and Ophelia came from and the obedient guard ran off in that direction. After a few seconds, the wizard's head cocked to the side as if hearing or smelling something new.

"It is safe to emerge now." She hissed.

Ophelia kept herself from cringing as her ears itched again. She and Lyan stepped around the corner toward the living shadow.

Nyphistra turned to face them, although it wasn't easy to tell that she did. "We should adjourn to my office. Not even Aylosha would dare to confront me there. We can speak freely and you can… gather yourselves." The wizard's words were pointed at Ophelia with her bandages still out of place and her coat covering only a portion of the woman's chest.

Ophelia looked down at herself then back at the svartalfar, a wide smirk stretching her lips. "You're right, Lyan will want to put her gauntlets on properly."

To illustrate her point, Ophelia pulled the metal bunny heads from the inside pocket of her long coat and handed them to the barbarian. Lyan started fastening the straps around her arms with little trouble as they walked.

Nyphistra sighed. "We will have to discuss our next move. The only way out for you now is via portal but the Gate Keeper is not one of mine."

"Well, we wouldn't want things to start being easy now, would we?" Ophelia said.

"Actually, I would appreciate not being bathed in blood anymore this evening, thank you." Havarti chimed in vocally so everyone, not just Ophelia, could hear.

"Indeed. I would prefer to avoid more bloodshed as well." Nyphistra said as they reached an ebony door encrusted with a fortune in jewels.

There was no knob or handle in it and the places the wizard touched and the gestures she made were too fast and complicated for Ophelia and Lyan to keep track. The door opened silently and Nyphistra ushered them inside.

"With the exception of Aylosha, of course." The living shadow said after she closed the door to her office. "I must strike her down before she shares her suspicions with the Matriarch."

"And what are we supposed to do?" Lyan asked, her thick arms folding across her chest.

"That is simple." The wizard said. "You will become svartalfar."

CHAPTER

EIGHT

"LET ME MAKE sure I understand..." Lyan said as she struggled to squeeze herself into the black breastplate worn by the very guards that were hunting them.

Nyphistra's office, about the twice the size of the armory, was also twice as full of random objects. A long table lined the middle of the room, acting as a focal point that all the other clutter seemed to orbit around. On its surface were vials of fluid of various colors and odors that muddled together in a way was not completely unpleasant, as well as metal... things that neither human could identify.

The rest of the room mirrored the table, although every pile seemed to have some form of organization in that one had objects that appeared to the made of silver while another had ones of gold and yet another pile was of what looked like emeralds. There were also little machines, ranging in size from that of a small rat to as tall as Lyan's waist, spinning or bouncing performing functions that couldn't begin to be guessed.

"Your tribe's Inquisitor has allied herself with a human crime lord named Perett so that she can replace you," Lyan pointed at the wizard. "and the only reason the Order of Kuan Yin and Dianmeyer are involved at all is because Harbenigyr rides a griffin? A wingless one at that."

"A fact that was conveniently omitted when Aylosha questioned Ophelia." Nyphistra hissed.

Ophelia held up the puce trinket again to show how the Inquisitor managed it. "And Perett will attack the Light Bringers who are facing the wrong direction, wipe out Valen Court and cut off the major resistance in the region." Then Ophelia tucked the wheat head away and turned her attention to the crimson silk bundle resting on the stool immediately in front of her.

Lyan's newly acquired guard armor squeaked as she worked to tie her now loose black hair up in a way that it would fit inside the matching steel helmet. "And Perett gained the ability to flank the Light Bringers thanks to the svartalfar tunnels the Inquisitor is allowing him to use?"

Nyphistra nodded. "Leaving the Lytyl armies free to turn Dianmeyer into a stronghold on the surface to attack whomever they please next."

The wizard busied herself by picking up a couple of weirdly shaped pieces of metal and weaving them together. Ophelia scowled as a blue bunny ear again poked out from between one of the many folds that led to the knot that held the silk bundle closed.

"Why didn't this Alowishus woman say another type of creature, anything else but a griffin, attacked the svartalfar before?" Lyan grunted with the effort of getting the helmet down around her hair as she pushed down the piece of armor. "Why this scheme that has to kill countless numbers of innocent people?" The barbarian's voice suddenly shared the same tinny quality of the guards she now resembled.

"Because Aylosha (she emphasized the correct pronunciation to the barbarian) knew griffins were at fault and the Judicator would have sensed the lie." She put the weaved metal aside on the table and picked up a glass cylinder full of thick black liquid. "She has to silence any information that doesn't fit her scenario because if the Judicator is lied to by anyone they would be destroyed. If the svartalfar that it is bonded to the Judicator spoke an untruth, the punishment would be even more severe."

"And that's why Perett gave her that wheat thing." Ophelia said as she held up the bundle triumphantly. "To keep information from coming to light without having to resort to actual lying."

"But you want your people to have a foothold up on the surface, don't you?" Lyan's head squeaked as she turned toward the wizard. "So why help us?"

"My people and I want peaceful coexistence with the surface." Nyphistra answered as she searched through a couple of small drawers. "While the Matriarch and I differ on this, she is no war monger."

The crimson silk was wrapped with gold colored cordage that was also fashioned into shoulder straps. Ophelia tossed it to Lyan and the bundle fumbled from hand to armored hand before the barbarian wrapped her arms around it tightly.

"I cannot see a thing in this helmet." The muscular woman grumbled.

Ophelia smiled back at her. "You look great, though."

"I understand why I am disguised as a guard. I could not pass for a spindly little svartalfar woman." Even Lyan's tinny voice sounded tougher than any of the guards they had encountered. "But why isn't Ophelia wearing armor? She would fit into it easily and not be recognized."

Nyphistra stepped over to the mercenary, holding the cylinder of black goo. "All guards are male and the Gate Keeper will not allow two males to traverse a portal without a higher ranking woman accompanying them."

"Then why don't you come with us?" Lyan asked, receiving a glare from not only Ophelia but, guessing by the wizard's head position, Nyphistra as well.

"I cannot leave while Aylosha still lives. I must kill her before she has an audience with the Matriarch." The living shadow whispered.

"What's to keep her from just marching to the Matriarch's room and talking to her?" Ophelia asked, becoming aware that Nyphistra was steadily getting closer to her.

"A platoon of guards, half a coven of wizards that are loyal to me and a series of traps designed to keep anyone below the rank of Vizier away from our Matriarch without hers or my permission." Nyphistra's hissing seemed to have a hint of pride in it as she spoke.

"And you are the Lytyl Tribe Vizier." Ophelia said, resisting the urge to step away from the svartalfar woman as she got uncomfortably close.

"Indeed. It will take her at least a day to gain audience to the Matriarch without my permission and she must die in that time." Nyphistra's black and violet eyes locked on Ophelia. "Remove your coat and shirt, please."

Hesitating for a moment, Ophelia finally shrugged off her coat before pulling her shirt down around her waist, the bandages thankfully back in place to preserve a modicum of modesty. "Why has so much of the last two days involved me taking off my clothes in one way or another that hasn't been voluntary?"

She heard Lyan chuckle through her helmet and another glare shot the barbarian's way. Nyphistra held up the glass cylinder in one hand while dipping the fingertips of her other hand into the black liquid. The liquid itself was decidedly black but, against the darkness of the living shadow's skin, it looked a couple of shades lighter.

"The Gate Keeper will sense any glamours disguising your appearance." Nyphistra said as her goo covered hand pressed against Ophelia's cheek. "So to pass you as a svartalfar we must use a more subtle method."

The wizard spread the black liquid all over Ophelia's face, turning her skin as dark as the Inquisitor's. The human couldn't help but shiver as Nyphistra's fingers ran over her ears.

"You know, I can put that stuff on myself." Ophelia protested.

The living shadow dipped her fingers into the liquid and continued undeterred. "Even with a mirror you cannot see all of yourself and we cannot risk you missing any portion of your skin. Especially with the dress you will wear."

Having completely blacked out Ophelia's face, Nyphistra rubbed down her throat and neck and moved down to the human's shoulders and right arm. The liquid felt slippery as the wizard's fingers intertwined with hers to make them obsidian colored as well and, again, she felt a shiver. Nyphistra repeated the process on the mercenary's left arm, then moved on to Ophelia's chest.

"This is wrong in so many different ways." Ophelia groaned. "This part I know I can do myself."

Nyphistra tapped the bandages covering the human's torso and they unraveled and fell to the floor as if they had a mind of their own. "Nonsense, I will be putting this on your back at the same time and you cannot see your back."

Lyan was trying, poorly, to stifle her snickering and Ophelia cursed to herself, bemoaning her luck that it was not only cold in this room but also that Nyphistra seemed to be enjoying herself. As the wizard moved to Ophelia's back, the human felt the svartalfar's hands brush over the area where her glowing tattoos were etched into her skin over and over.

Nyphistra grunted, which with her voice sounded like a dagger being loosed from its sheath. "The make-up is a simple concoction of soot and several other non-magical ingredients so it will only cover the runes for a couple of hours before they burn themselves free. You will have to make your way to the Gate Keeper with haste."

The wizard finally stopped caressing and applying make-up to Ophelia's body just above the belt line of her pants at the curve of her hips. As she stepped away from the woman, Nyphistra placed the cylinder on the table and steam rose from her other hand, burning what liquid was left over off the wizard's fingers. Then she disappeared behind a tall, flat piece of bronze that had runes etched all over its surface.

Seconds later, Nyphistra emerged with a sapphire blue silk dress over one arm and a wig of silver hair that was so long it brushed against the floor in her other hand. She handed the garment to Ophelia who tossed her top onto her long coat and then dutifully slipped the dress on.

Now Ophelia had to admit that the amount of make up the wizard slathered on her was necessary with the dress being cut so low that it went down below her breasts and halfway to her navel. The back was cut even lower than that. Even the shoulder straps that held it up were little more than two strands of blue thread. Ophelia believed that there had to be some kind of enchantment to keep them from simply snapping with the first movement of her shoulder.

Ophelia's boots barely peeked out from under the hemline of the skirt. The polished black leather actually complemented the dark blue of the dress pretty well. At least she got to keep her pants on, Ophelia thought as Nyphistra positioned the silver wig on her head. Going from the living shadow's hand to Ophelia's head, the wig didn't brush the floor anymore but it did still reach below the human's waist.

The wizard pulled a few pins made of silver from... somewhere and secured the wig to the human's head before running her dark fingers through it to neaten it up and make it look somewhat styled. Silver strands drifted down in front of Ophelia's sky blue eyes and for the first time in well, ever, Ophelia had a hairstyle with bangs.

"This hair looks so real." She commented.

"It is." Nyphistra said as she turned and opened one drawer, then another in the dresser beside her before she found what she needed. "So are these."

Ophelia's eyes opened wide when she saw a pair of severed svartalfar ears, complete with a heavy ruby earrings in each lobe, dangling between the wizard's thumb and forefinger in each hand. She reached for either side of the Ophelia's head with speed that surprised the human, otherwise she would have tried to dodge.

"You will only need the top portion, of course." Nyphistra whispered idly as she pressed the disembodied ears against Ophelia's own. "I always felt the rubies enhanced the beauty of the dress."

Ophelia felt a quick, stabbing pain in each of her earlobes before feeling the weight of what were surely the rubies hanging there. Nyphistra finally pulled her hands away and tossed the unused black flesh back into the drawer she found it in.

"I enchanted the former owner's ears to bond with yours for as long as you are wearing the dress." The wizard held up a hand to stop

Ophelia's protests. "The earrings have a much stronger enchantment and the Gate Keeper will only sense those. It would look suspicious if a svartalfar of moderate rank approached with nothing of magical power at all."

"Former owner? Moderate rank? Where did you get all this?" The questions escaped from Ophelia's lips before her brain had a chance to tell her she'd regret hearing the answers.

"The dress and ears are from a student of mine who I was forced to eliminate after she stumbled upon a secret correspondence to an upworlder who has been assisting me in my quest. The hair is from the scalp of the Vizier before me. She died honorably in the duel where I won the role of Vizier from her, I assure you. She was the one who aided me in designing the Judicator."

Ophelia wanted to rip all of it off and just yell "Ew, ew, ew!" before the last part finally processed in her mind. "Wait a minute. *You* made the Judicator?"

Nyphistra nodded. "That is why you have not heard of such a thing in svartalfar society before. I have introduced the concept of an unbiased trial to my people. It is no longer as simple as a noble's word of accusation being enough to punish another svartalfar of lower rank. I must now make adjustments to prevent manipulation by magicks not of svartalfar origin to keep our next Inquisitor in line."

Having experienced the Judicator's version of justice first hand Ophelia wanted, again, to beat Nyphistra to a pulp. The human had to remind herself, however, that she had only experienced the painful side of the Judicator's power thanks to Inquisitor Aylosha. Ophelia was starting to regret that she wasn't going to be the one to put an end to the Inquisitor's worthless life.

"Ah, yes. One more thing." The wizard shifted back to the dresser that held the ears. "We must make you look complete for the illusion to work."

Ophelia wondered what horror Nyphistra was going to pull out next and it turned out to be a make-up kit. First, with a small brush the living shadow painted a dark blue lacquer over Ophelia's lips. Then with a different brush, she spread different colors along the human's cheeks and eyelids.

The svartalfar stepped back over to the table and picked up the mesh of wires she put together earlier. "We will have to hide your eyebrows because they do not match your new hair."

Ophelia was about to make a crack about how that was a lot to hide when Nyphistra pressed the wire mesh onto her head, revealing it to be a woven silver and gold skullcap. It wrapped around the top of her head, all the thin wires meeting at a point just between Ophelia's sky blue eyes.

Little metal tines poked through the wig (Ophelia insisted on calling it that to herself rather than the scalped top of another woman's head) and into her own skin. The cap itself didn't cover Ophelia's eyebrows but it held the silver bangs in place so they couldn't be seen no matter how her head turned.

Nyphistra took a step away from the other woman. She was surely looking Ophelia over but there was no hint of her head or even her eyes moving to do so.

Just when the disguised woman thought she'd been as creeped out by the svartalfar as she possibly could, that stillness and... staring proved her wrong. Sighing, Ophelia turned to Lyan, held her arms up from her sides and gave a quick spin. Her chest was barely covered. Her back was even less so, although if worse came to worse the long wig could cover Ophelia's runes as long as they didn't glow too brightly.

"How do I look?" The mercenary asked without much enthusiasm.

"Less like you than I thought possible." Lyan's tinny voice answered.

"Remember, you are one of my apprentices and her guard escort. I am sending you to Maid Gulch to procure a special wine that is an ingredient for a spell I am working on." Nyphistra handed a folded parchment with a wax seal stamp to hold it shut. "That is as close to Dianmeyer as I can get you without rousing suspicion since I have previous dealings with the owner of the tavern there."

"Do not look the Gate Keeper in the eyes." Nyphistra warned. "You are a lower rank and at best it will be taken as a challenge, at worst the Gate Keeper will sense our deception and you will be stranded here and executed. Are we clear?"

"Crystal." Both women answered at the same time.

Ophelia pulled Havarti and his scabbard free from her red leather coat as she gathered up the garments and rolled them up under her arm. She stepped behind the Bunny Barbarian and stuffed the garments into the bundle that the larger woman carried like a backpack, tucking the fold back in tightly afterward. Ophelia started looking for a place to carry her weapon.

"I'm afraid svartalfar wizards do not carry swords. They are too cumbersome to wield while casting most spells." Nyphistra answered the unasked question. "Lyan will have to carry it for you. Pole axes are reserved for duties here, so it will pass unnoticed."

The armored barbarian turned to face Ophelia. Her metal encased hand squeaked as she held out her hand for Havarti. The mercenary only hesitated for a moment before giving him over to Lyan, who mounted the sheathed sword on her hip.

"I will be ever so happy when this unpleasantness is over and I am no longer referred to as 'it'." Havarti chimed in. "Also, I'm liable to rust in this damp subterranean air if we linger much longer."

Ophelia smirked, lightly slapping the wax stamped parchment against the palm of her other hand as she stepped away from the door. "So what are you waiting for, guard? Open the door for your mistress so we can get the hell out of here." She grinned up at Lyan, though the mirth didn't quite reach her eyes.

The taller woman nodded and stepped up to the office's entrance. She pushed on the ebony wood but even against her muscle it didn't budge. She tried again but with the same result. The wizard seemed to find it amusing even without any outward sign beyond watching a few more futile attempts without moving. Finally, Nyphistra stepped around the disguised barbarian, tapped the wood and made it swing open with little more than a brief gust of a breeze.

"Remember, you are to stay behind your Lady at all times, Guard." The living shadow looked up and hissed at Lyan as she passed. "Even in the face of danger, you only jump in the path of a direct physical attack. She is expected to be able to defeat any foe with her magicks while you are little more than her man-servant."

Lyan visually stiffened at the description "man-servant" but continued into the hall. Nyphistra nodded at Ophelia as she passed or was it a shallow bow? Either made the human uneasy and she hurried passed Lyan to start down the hall.

Nyphistra turned and started rubbing her chin thoughtfully as the door closed to barricade her alone back in the office. She stepped up to the bronze slab with runes etched into it and pulled another from behind it and then another and another.

Events were in motion. There was no stopping now. The players were in position. It was time to battle for the heart of the svartalfar...

CHAPTER

NINE

THE GUARD INSPECTED the intricate design stamped into the hardened wax for a long moment before he and his companion pulled open the double doors for the woman they supposed was an apprentice to the tribe Vizier herself. They each gave her a solemn bow as she passed.

Ophelia grinned but made sure they couldn't see it. Once the doors closed, the two disguised women found themselves in a long tunnel, dug directly into the rock all around them rather than architecture like the fortress at their backs. Torches lined each wall, leading off into the distance.

"If I were a duke I could have a woman like that." The voice of one of the guards just made its way through the thickness of the door. "I would love to see if all nobles like her have spider tattoos down…"

Ophelia chuckled and looked up at her own guard. "I could get used to this." She said.

"Don't." Lyan replied.

The barbarian's armor squeaked as she shook her head, not understanding what was so amusing, and they started deeper into the tunnel. Unlike the rest of the fortress, which was purposely designed to be maze like to confound spies and assassins, this tunnel had only one direction: straight ahead. It was a short walk before they reached a portcullis that didn't have any visible means of opening.

The women could see through the bolted together lengths of black steel but beyond two torches there was nothing to see but darkness. That was when Ophelia heard something, faint at first. It sounded like scratching?

"Do you hear that?" She whispered to Lyan.

Lyan's helmet turned from side to side, although her hand found its way to Havarti's hilt. The scratching continued but, as it got closer, it sounded more like dirt being stabbed into again and again. Ophelia's pale blue eyes squinted into the dark, trying to see the source but with no luck.

After a few seconds the barbarian whispered. "Now I hear something. Like scratching?"

The other woman let out a soft grunt. Ophelia's hearing shouldn't be so much better than Lyan's, even through the helmet. The Bunny Barbarian didn't seem to notice what the guards said through the last door they passed, either.

The ruby earrings. Nyphistra mentioned that they were enchanted. They must make the wearer's hearing more sensitive. Ophelia was so lost in thought about her new jewelry that when she turned back to face the gate she didn't notice the glowing pair of blue eyes staring back at her until their owner spoke.

"What brings you to my parlor, young one?"

Ophelia jumped in surprise but, thankfully, no undignified sound came out of her. The disguised human looked back at Lyan then through the gate again.

"I must use the portal to travel to Maid Gulch and procure spell components for the Vizier." Ophelia pulled out her arrogant sounding noble woman voice.

The blue eyes blinked twice before disappearing completely. Out of the darkness stepped an obsidian skinned woman who was... upside down.

No, not merely upside down, she was walking on the ceiling. As the torchlight finally ran all over the woman on the other side of the portcullis, they could see that while, from the hips up, she looked like a svartalfar the lower portion of her body, where her two legs should have been was the body of a gigantic spider. What the svartalfar called, oh so cleverly, a "svartwidow".

The svartalfar half of the woman had silver hair like Ophelia's wig, but clumsily cut into short tufts that stuck out in many awkward directions. Her red eyes blinked back at Ophelia and gave no indication that she had even noticed the figure in black armor standing behind her. Wait, red? The eyes Ophelia saw before were blue.

The svartwidow apparently created her own wardrobe using spider silks, running from wrist to wrist and wrapping around her human-like chest so tightly it was as if she was mummified in materials that many in the upworld would pay a fortune to acquire.

Where her hips started with smooth, dark svartalfar skin changed to the bumpy, rough flesh of a spider's thorax. Eight chitin coated legs, each easily as long as the humans were tall, radiated all around her body from there and into the top of the tunnel. Behind that, her pulsating, spider-like abdomen returned to the smooth, ebony skin but with red stripes that marked out a complex design neither Ophelia nor Lyan could make out at this angle.

At the back of the spider abdomen was a sharp spike as long as Ophelia's forearm. The creature's web spinneret, judging from the liquified white silk gleaming along the tip.

"Oh, I see. Nyphistra has sent you." The svartwidow skittered backwards along the top of the tunnel, making different gestures with each hand. "Come in, come in!"

With a heavy wrench in protest, the linked metal rose to open the way down the tunnel. Taking a quick, deep breath, Ophelia walked after the Gate Keeper with Lyan close behind.

"I do hope you forgive me. I usually don't get much in the way of visitors but the last few days have been so hectic! Wizards and rogues needing to travel into the upworld. I keep telling them that I will not bring them back but they do not listen. Most of them will be killed by a simple halfling, I would bet." The svartwidow just kept speaking, not caring if Ophelia was listening or not. "Had to use most of my beautiful hair to send disgusting ogres to that Loch Aeris above. Offensive creatures. The human with the scarlet hair that herded them didn't even protest when I had to kill one to make the rest stay in line. Its blood tasted like that of swine."

The half spider creature spat and kept talking as she led Ophelia and Lyan down the tunnel. So this was the Gate Keeper that Nyphistra told them about. It was odd that an offshoot race of svartalfar that were thought to be cursed would be tasked with as momentous a responsibility as travel to and from the upworld.

Misbehaving svartalfar youth were often treated to cautionary tales of the naughty children who were transformed into mindless half beast svartwidows for their transgressions, living visual aids of the horrors that would befall them if they ventured into tunnels where the dark elves were not supposed to go. Because that was where the formerly svartalfar, the damned, lived.

But the Gate Keeper could speak full sentences and, apparently work magic that could create portals so she had to be far from mindless. Even then, the stigma of being a svartwidow would be one that should have kept her shunned but here she was leading them to the portal.

From behind, the red lines on the svartwidow's abdomen continued up along her svartalfar half, able to be seen through the sheer silk of her makeshift top. The design looked as if it could have been an hourglass, emptying from her svartalfar half and filling the bulbous spider abdomen, especially by the spinneret where the red looked as if it was full and throbbing with blood.

Finally, the tunnel widened into what must be intended to be a receiving area where the three reached another set of doors. They were thick steel with gold leaf pounded into the edges and a massive piece of ebony lumber spanning both doors, a distance of twelve feet easily. The Gate Keeper scampered off to the side and looked at Ophelia expectantly before turning her red eyes toward the doors.

She expected Ophelia to open the door? Was this some kind of test? The mercenary couldn't possibly hope to lift the wood that barred the door shut. She wouldn't be expected to, being a svartalfar wizard. The Gate Keeper must have expected her to lift the lumber with her magic. The only problem was that the human couldn't use any.

Ophelia looked back at Lyan, silently hoping the other woman had some idea. The barbarian's helmet squeaked as it angled down to face her. Ophelia glanced over at the svartwidow as she motioned at the door. Lyan shrugged and softly slapped her hands together as if getting rid of dust. Ophelia shook her head. Lyan nodded. Ophelia grunted. Lyan nodded again, this time throwing a salute as well.

The armored barbarian didn't see Ophelia shaking her head in protest, although she tried to keep the Gate Keeper from noticing, as Lyan stepped around her and toward the doors. The half spider shuffled up beside the woman disguised as a svartalfar wizard with a confused look on her face.

"Why do you not open the entryway yourself?" Her red eyes narrowed as she stared down at Ophelia.

The svartwidow was easily twice as tall as the human thanks to her spindly arachnid legs, but she had crouched so that her head hovered only inches above Ophelia's. The creature's question sounded like innocent curiosity but her demeanor had an air of malice to it.

Ophelia's mind raced, trying to find something to say even as she watched Lyan stomp up to the middle of the doorway. The massive piece of wood came up from chest height on the Bunny Barbarian up to just above her head and she slipped both hands under the obstruction.

The creature didn't even have to move her legs to sway over to the other side of Ophelia. "It is odd, having your guard attempt to open the way for you."

Ophelia's mouth went dry when she heard Lyan grunt and strain with effort. The wood, unfortunately, didn't rise at all.

"He... wasn't my first choice for guard." Ophelia hoped whatever came out of her mouth next made sense. "But he begged for a chance to prove himself. Since it would not be in battle, I told him it would be here."

Ophelia put on her best arrogant face, complete with sanctimonious smile. The Gate Keeper smirked back and turned to face the doors where Lyan had crouched to get her shoulders under the lumber barricade.

"It doesn't look as if he's going to make it to me." The svartwidow snickered. "The question becomes whether I should allow you to travel through the portal after I eat him for failing you?"

Ophelia's eyes nearly bugged out of her head at that, then snapped back at Lyan. Her hand started up to where Havarti usually rested on her shoulder but she forced herself to stop.

Havarti's voice rang in Ophelia's mind as Lyan stumbled and his scabbard scraped against the metal doors with an ear rending screech. "So this has become a life or death venture. Gate Keeper or not, we may have to kill this beast, preferably before she slays Lyan. Then, dare I say it, find Nyphistra and figure out what we can do next."

The svartwidow looked ready to pounce, rearing up when Lyan stumbled but the barbarian was able to get her feet under her again. Ophelia couldn't help but wince at the obvious effort Lyan was going through to open the doors. Somehow, the barbarian must have known that her life depended on her success. With a loud roar that sounded more like a manticore or a dragon, Lyan forced herself to straighten up under the beam and hoist it up from its metal cradles before dumping it at her feet.

It landed with a solid thud, cracking the stone ground, a yard so from the doors which started to creak open. Lyan was obviously gasping for breath as she stepped off to the side. She pushed one of the doors along with her, maybe, just maybe using it to keep herself upright as she recovered. The Gate Keeper let out a soft grunt and leaned in closer to Ophelia.

"I guess that means he's to be your regular choice for guard now?" She gave Ophelia a wink before starting for the doors.

Ophelia breathed a sigh of relief as she walked after the creature. As she passed the doorway, Ophelia stopped beside Lyan and gave her a worried look. She didn't want to give the Gate Keeper a reason to be suspicious by actually asking if her "guard" was okay.

Lyan's helmet creaked up and down as she pushed herself way from the metal door. She still looked a little shaky but she fell into step behind Ophelia as the svartalfar disguised woman started after the Gate Keeper again.

The room behind the door was smaller than either woman expected. After only about four steps in darkness, torches all around the room popped to life, revealing a stone archway in its center at the top of a short, five step staircase.

The svartwidow had already taken position atop the apex of the arch, motioning for Lyan and Ophelia to come up to the stairway themselves. "You must come upon the ley line to activate the portal." She said.

Lyan had no idea what a "ley line" was. Ophelia, at best, had a basic idea. A ley line was an artery that carried life energies all around the planet, like how veins and arteries carried blood throughout a person's body to keep them alive. Wizards and clerics were suckers for that kind of stuff. Any particulars beyond that were well out of the mercenary's realm of expertise.

A line was carved into the uppermost step, in front of the archway, that was thicker than any of the others (that were more than likely natural cracks anyway). It actually extended down both sides of the stairway and out to the walls on either side of the room. Literal or figurative, that was likely the "ley line" the spider lady wanted them to step onto.

Ophelia and Lyan did so, the Bunny Barbarian being careful to stay one step behind her "Lady". The top step was only about twice as wide as the rest. It would barely have enough room for both women to stand side by side so Lyan stopped on the step just below.

"No no no." The half spider skittered behind the barbarian, pushing her up beside Ophelia, who shifted to make room. "Enjoy this moment, guard. This will be the only moment you will not be behind or under your lady."

The Gate Keeper giggled to herself as she stepped back onto the archway. Each of her eight legs started tapping against the stone in a rhythm that sounded like an up tempo song. Lights started to flicker in the space inside the arch and the svartwidow reached up to her head... and then frowned.

"I do apologize, my dear." The Gate Keeper shuffled down beside Ophelia, one of her hands suddenly sliding through the human's wig. "I've been so busy making portals of late that I have run out of the most important component."

It wasn't until then that Ophelia noticed how sharp the creature's fingernails were. They came to a sharp point about an inch beyond her fingertips and one was making its way to her neck.

Ophelia, on a reflex, almost knocked her hand away but Gate Keeper's blade like fingernail suddenly changed course and sliced a long clump of hair away from above the disguised woman's shoulder. The svartwidow smiled sweetly and made her way back to the arch.

"I hope you don't mind." She said, lifting the silver tresses to her nose and giving them a quick smell. "This scent is so familiar to me..."

Both Lyan and Ophelia stiffened. The barbarian was ready to pull Havarti from his scabbard and Ophelia's hands balled up into fists. The mercenary suddenly realized that she could feel the make-up cracking and crumbling away from the glowing runes on her back.

Thankfully, the Gate Keeper was in front of them and couldn't see that. The svartwidow gave the hair another idle sniff before tossing it into the swirling lights under her. Instantly, it solidified into a picturesque field of wheat with a building resting in the middle of it, against the foot of a steep hill. It had a sign with the words "The

Drunken Dragon" scrawled over the door, complete with a painting of a red dragon holding a comically large glass of wine.

"It reminds me of our former Vizier." The Gate Keeper commented as she swept her body down from the top of the archway just enough to stop Lyan and Ophelia from rushing through the portal.

As the creature's face turned from one woman to the other, the set of blue eyes Ophelia saw before opened in her forehead, just above the silver brows of her red eyes. Both sets focused on Ophelia and the Gate Keeper raised her hands and pressed her palms together as if she was going to pray.

"*Lytyl assalaa kempiali truus sevaltah.*" The svartwidow said.

Ophelia stared back up at the Gate Keeper for a moment. The beast had spoken in the traditional language of the ancient svartalfar, a language that few upworlders knew. This had to be one last test. Ophelia was no linguist, and she by no means was fluent, but she had heard something like this before in her... time with the Xaviour Tribe.

Pantomiming the Gate Keeper's hand positioning, Ophelia replied with, "*Tetetala kominih ke wala, waalah Lytyl.*"

What was it about a svartalfar's face, on a spider's body or not, that made a genuine smile so unsettling? Ophelia didn't dwell on it too much as she gave the Gate Keeper a polite smile in return. The creature backed up and out of their way to the portal.

Lyan was surprised that they didn't feel any sensation as they passed through. One moment they were in a cave with a svartwidow and the next they were standing in the afternoon sun right next to the Drunken Dragon Inn.

The portal closed seconds after both women made their way through and they were standing alone in a field of wheat. Ophelia took a moment to feel the warmth of the sun on her skin even as Lyan pulled the black metal helmet off her head and tossed it away.

Thanks to the bright sunlight, Ophelia noticed hints of silver weaved through the otherwise charcoal black hair of the barbarian. The mercenary's pale eyes reflexively flicked toward her own braids. There wasn't a hint of gray to be found. Lyan was showing signs of getting older, why wasn't she?

Then Ophelia remembered the parchment in her hands, pulling the mercenary out of her revery. Looking down at it, the disguised woman snapped the seal open and unfolded the paper. It was a map of the area around them.

"Let me see the bundle, Lyan." Ophelia said.

Lyan tried to shrug the crimson silk off her shoulders but it wouldn't budge. "I don't suppose..." She muttered, even as she kept vainly shrugging one broad shoulder and then the other.

Ophelia stepped behind the barbarian and pulled the piece of gold cordage that wedged itself between Lyan's breastplate and pauldron and then it slipped off easily. Ophelia unrolled the silk, creating a flat area like a picnic blanket that she crouched onto, laying out the map between Lyan's pastel, long eared helmet and her gauntlets.

"We're here." Ophelia pointed to the dot marked Maid Gulch on the piece of parchment. "The Gate Keeper mentioned sending a bunch of ogres to Loch Aeris over here."

Her fingertip pressed into the blue blob to the west of Maid Gulch. Lyan nodded in agreement, even as she beat at the black armor cocooning her to press it into a shape that would come off easier.

As each elbow guard, codpiece, breastplate and every other piece of armor came off, Lyan let out a louder, more pleased sigh of relief. Finally, she was in only the two main pieces of her armor, covering her chest and hips, and fluffing out her white tail before she focused her whole attention on the map and the woman she stood over.

"Dianmeyer is to the south." Again Ophelia's finger moved. "I think we should split up."

She looked up at the barbarian to get her opinion. Lyan nodded as she leaned down to pick up her gauntlets, complete with the metal rabbit heads.

"I should go after the ogres. I want some payback for my jaw." The Bunny Barbarian growled under her breath, the sharp tips of her newly buckled gauntlet's saber teeth lightly brushing over her cheek. "You would want to see Harby anyway. Wouldn't you?"

The other woman chewed on her lower lip, Lyan was right but there were certain realities to consider. "You're faster and you would still be lucky to reach Dianmeyer by nightfall as it is. The ogres are twice as far as Dianmeyer if you run around the lake."

"Meaning?" Lyan asked.

"If I take a boat straight across the lake, I have less distance to cover and can do it faster." Ophelia arched an eyebrow up at the barbarian. "You want to sail on a boat?"

Lyan frowned. The mercenary knew well the barbarian's aversion to aquatic vessels of any type. Over the years, she often took sedating, sleeper holds or other forms of trickery to even get her onto a boat when it was necessary and she surely wouldn't be willing to do it on her own. She finally nodded, bitterly snatching one of her long boots from the silk cloth.

"So what are you going to do while I get Harby to ready himself for battle?" Lyan asked as she pulled on her other pastel boot.

Ophelia picked up a small leather pouch and opened it. Slipping a hand in, then her arm, the woman reached farther into the thing than it had physical space. After a few seconds, her hand returned to the open air, this time holding Lyan's spear by the base of the stylized rabbit spearhead.

The long shaft finally liberated itself and the mercenary offered it to the barbarian in her right hand while her left made a beckoning gesture. Lyan slapped the still sheathed Havarti into Ophelia's waiting hand as she took her spear back. Then she slipped her shield onto her scarred arm and then her helmet and, for the first time in two days, Lyan felt complete.

"I still look like a svartalfar, right?" Ophelia couldn't stifle a chuckle at how pleased Lyan looked with herself back in her own armor. "Maybe I can cause some confusion, or find some other way to slow them down before they attack the Light Bringers."

"Too bad you cannot warn the Light Bringers directly." Lyan started rolling her shoulders and jogging in place, trying to loosen up after being cinched in that heavy armor.

"I'd have to get through the ogres to get to them and then we don't know where they're positioned specifically." Ophelia agreed. "We'll have to see how things go after I deal with the big, furry stupid people."

"Hey!" Lyan's brown eyes narrowed at the other woman.

Ophelia let a quick laugh slip past her lips. "Relax. You Yo Bunpy are many things, stupid's not one of them."

The disguised mercenary straightened up, slipping her long coat on over her dress before placing Havarti in his proper place on her back. Ophelia gave Lyan a kind smile, not a look they shared often, and sighed.

"Good luck, Lyan. I hope you get to Harby before the svartalfar."

"Good luck, Ophelia." Lyan smiled back. "I hope you kill many ogres before we meet again and I kill the rest."

With that, the Bunny Barbarian sprinted to the south, out of sight in seconds thanks to the hill strewn terrain. Ophelia gathered up the red silk, wrapping it around her armored hand before turning west and starting toward the lake and the army of ogres waiting there.

CHAPTER

TEN

THE SUN SLOWLY sank behind the tops of the evergreen trees and Ophelia was sitting at the back of a small rowboat. The fisherman who agreed to take her across Loch Aeris scowled back at her with every stroke of his oars.

He didn't want to take her across the lake at first. None of the other fishermen she talked to did either. After all, Ophelia came to them looking like a svartalfar and they weren't known for their friendly demeanor (a stereotype that would only get reinforced if Lyan and Ophelia failed to stop the Inquisitor's plan).

This man though, named Hachi, was the only one who let her talk long enough to mention Harbenigyr. One of the Order of Kuan Yin had delivered Hachi's daughter after a complicated pregnancy, saving both the lives of the mother and baby girl. That was the only reason he agreed to help her.

But that didn't mean that he trusted the woman that looked like a svartalfar. He kept his green eyes locked on her, mindful to dump her in the water if she did anything that even appeared threatening. And if Ophelia had been a true svartalfar, that would have been an effective threat. After all, how many swimming holes were there deep underground?

Color started to fade from the world as the sun dropped out of sight and the gloaming spread across the landscape. No stars shined in the sky yet but the moon was already making its presence felt well above the trees opposite where the sun just disappeared.

The boat slid into the shoreline and Hachi jumped out to pull it the rest of the way onto the fine silt of the shore so that Ophelia could disembark. Before she was three steps away, Hachi was already back into the water and heading back the way he came.

He never promised to stay and Ophelia had never asked it of him. The woman only watched him shrink into the distance for a few moments before turning for the trees a short distance beyond.

The ogres Perett controlled were gathered somewhere on the west coast of the lake. Considering they were each over twelve feet tall, they weren't going to be hard to find. The problem was, what was Ophelia going to do once she did?

The woman weaved her way between the trees. Her ears picked up a series of heavy thumps, and though she couldn't see where they came from, Ophelia had a feeling she was on the right track.

As she moved, the thumps became crashes and then the sounds of pine wood being torn and crushed. The gigantic silhouettes of the beasts came into view between the trees as they stomped around a massive bonfire. That surprised Ophelia more than anything else, really. She didn't realize that ogres actually knew how to make fire.

The hairy creatures grunted and growled in what Ophelia supposed was some kind of language to them as she watched and tried to get a rough head count of what the she was up against. Ophelia recognized the ogress that had helped capture Lyan and herself sitting beside the flames and she couldn't help but be pleased to see that the creature had a big patch of burlap wrapped around her head to cover one eye. Lyan's spear had been more effective that either human had thought.

Despite that, Ophelia didn't feel too encouraged when she counted roughly twenty ogres at this camp and could hear more stomping in the woods all around her. She didn't know what she was expecting, but the mercenary didn't know how she'd be able to delay this one group of ogres, let alone multiple camps.

She looked over her shoulder at Havarti's hilt. "I'm thinking, I'm thinking." He whispered in her mind.

Ophelia cursed to herself when a group of skeleton soldiers stepped out of the trees and into the clearing. On their shoulders, they carried a throne carved out of polished wood and sitting atop it was... Caleb.

The man that unsuccessfully tried to kill Ophelia but had successfully guided her into a trap. Ophelia felt her jaw clench and her fingernails sink into the bark of the tree she stood behind.

Caleb was back in his armor, although apparently he didn't want a helmet to muss up his silky blonde hair at the moment. The armor seemed to have a fresh coat of polish, so the fire reflecting off the metal was almost painfully bright.

"Hail to the odoriferous ones!" Caleb called out as the skeletons knelt and rested the chair on the dirt.

The ogress smiled as she rose to her feet. She must have thought "odoriferous" was a compliment. She stomped over to the human with two other ogres flanking her. Then the ogress copied the skeletons and knelt in front of Caleb, bringing her head down level with his.

"Is your whole clan here?" Caleb took the tone of an adult talking to a toddler.

The ogress nodded, as did the two other ogres at her side. Caleb rested a hand on her head and started grunting and groaning. Ophelia scowled, he was speaking whatever language ogres spoke and she couldn't understand a word. But judging by the reaction of the ogress, she was a sucker for a pretty face.

After he finished whatever ogreish sweet nothings he was muttering, Caleb continued. "We attack at dawn. Your clan will charge in first. The red capes won't know what hit them."

"Red capes" must be their pet name for the Light Bringers. Why though? It wasn't like their normal name was too complicated for even the slow witted ogres to understand.

The ogress grunted and pointed up at the sky that was quickly darkening from cobalt blue to black, the first stars of the night just starting to flicker their light. Caleb looked annoyed, for just a split second, before a smile that would have appeared condescending to anyone a little sharper in the brain department stretched across his face.

"Don't worry. Virgil's griffins will protect you from the red capes' nasty arrows." He patted the ogress' head again before speaking loud enough for the entire camp to hear. "These are the words of Perett. This is what will be."

A plan started to form in Ophelia's mind. It wasn't much of one and could fail spectacularly but at least it was a plan. First, she had to get rid of anything recognizable as hers. Pulling the crimson silk out of the pocket she had tucked it into during the boat trip, Ophelia draped it over the ground as quietly as possible.

In spite the growing cold, the woman pulled her long coat off and then Havarti out of the red leather, as well. She quickly rolled the coat up and tossed it in the middle of the silk. Pulling out the pouch that previously held Lyan's spear, Ophelia loosened the ties and positioned the end of Havarti's scabbard at the opening.

"I don't like where this idea of yours is going, my dear." Havarti said telepathically.

"I know but I don't have anything else that doesn't involve me dying in less than two seconds." Ophelia whispered back. "You?"

"And this will let you live for, what, one minute longer?" He sounded like he wanted his comment to be biting but it betrayed his worry more.

She stuffed Havarti into the pouch up to the pummel guard which was too wide to fit past the mouth of the small bag. With a quick twist of his handle, Havarti's hidden dagger stayed in Ophelia's hand while the magically packed sword found itself beside her coat.

Ophelia tied the bundle shut with a tight knot. Lifting the skirt portion of her dress, the woman tucked the dagger away, stabbing it into the fabric of her pants just inside her thigh, and then picked up the crimson bundle.

Looking up, Ophelia aimed for the densest foliage of the evergreen beside her and threw the silk up into the branches. Branches cracked loudly and needles and dust fell from the tall tree but the bundle didn't.

The noise caught Caleb's, as well as the ogres', attention. Two creatures stomped in Ophelia's direction. She was committed now. Taking a deep breath, she gave her long silver tresses a quick flip and stepped out into the clearing.

One of the ogres closing in roared and lifted a tree trunk it had made into a basic club to drop on the woman. When Caleb saw her, though, he rushed between the massive creature and the black skinned svartalfar.

"No, she isn't the enemy!" His face bordered on panicked as he skidded to a stop in front of Ophelia.

Caleb's armor wrapped arms rose, ready to block the blow as best he could and his eyes shut tight in preparation for the immense force he knew would impact but it never came. He opened his eyes to see the ogress gripping the club tightly a couple of feet above the man and Ophelia.

The disguised woman shuddered at just how close she had come to dying, whether from the club crushing her or Ophelia blinking and having them realize she wasn't actually a svartalfar and then crushing her with another club. As Caleb turned to face her, though, Ophelia put on her best bored looking face and rested her hands on her round hips.

"Not a very promising first impression." She did a passable impression of the Inquisitor, which was a mix of her haughty noblewoman voice and sounding like she was complaining about a bad smell.

"Forgive us." Caleb bowed his head. "We were not expecting word from your forces for another day or two."

Ophelia let the silence linger between the two of them. First, it seemed to make Caleb uneasy, which meant that he wasn't thinking completely straight and, second, she had to figure out just what to say.

Finally, she nodded. "As you know, war is a fluid situation. I have to see Perett immediately."

Caleb looked puzzled. "Why didn't you portal to him directly?"

The black skinned woman gripped her hips tighter. "That is part of the reason he and I need to speak." Ophelia added more of a hiss to make herself sound more annoyed. "Now."

"O—of course." Caleb nodded again.

Before he could do anything else, Ophelia stepped around the man and marched for the group of skeletons. "Then we'd best be going, don't you think?"

If she was going to be a svartalfar, Ophelia had to sell it. She stuck her nose in the air as if the entire world and everything lying on top of it was beneath her notice. Her round hips swayed from side to side in a way that drew the eye and knew that it did so as she walked.

The skinless corpses didn't make a move of any kind, try to stop the woman or attack her, nothing. Ophelia sat herself on the wood throne and crossed her legs. Leaning back into the seat, she rested her chin on her fingertips and stared back at Caleb. "I did mean now, upworlder."

Caleb muttered some last instructions to the ogress before hustling over to Ophelia and the group of skeletons that stood inanimately still around her. The ogres glanced back and forth among each other, a mix of confusion and uneasiness in each of their faces.

"*Maltz juoyi tou!*" The man uttered the short incantation and the skeletons suddenly shifted back into unlife.

The dead soldiers lifted Ophelia into the air on the polished throne and, in perfect unison, turned around while keeping the woman in place. Ophelia stifled the yelp of surprise at the motion and tried to keep looking bored. The skeletons again stopped, awaiting direction.

And Caleb gave it to them. "Return to Perett's camp." He said simply, walking several paces behind the undead bones as they started marching.

Ophelia felt Havarti's presence pulling away from her but, thankfully, not fully thanks to the dagger she carried. The plan started off relatively well, now she had to figure out a story that would get this Perett character to delay his attack long enough to, at least, warn the Light Bringers and give them a fighting chance against the brigand forces.

The stomping and wood crunching of the ogre camps were left behind and the group was enveloped by darkness. Closing her eyes, Ophelia could almost imagine that she was on a ship in the middle of the sea with the cool air washing over her. But the reality was that skeletons carrying a heavy wooden chair didn't exactly bob up and down like a ship on the ocean and a jarring step on the uneven terrain of the wooded trail brought her back to reality.

Caleb tried to make conversation a couple of times during the walk. The first time, she simply ignored him. The second, Ophelia gave him a dismissive wave of her hand. He had to believe that she was svartalfar of the Lytyl Tribe and to most of the women of the Lytyl, men were not equals that were conversed with idly.

The trees started to thin and a wide white tent came into view in a clearing a short distance ahead. The center of the tent came up to just below the tops of the pine trees, dropping down in three tiers of height before the eight corners were lashed down by gold cordage much like Ophelia used to tie up the crimson bundle underground. There were half a dozen campfires outside the pale canvas structure but there were no people surrounding them for warmth.

The only signs of life were from the interior of the tent itself. It had its own light sources burning inside, almost giving the tent, and by extension the clearing around it, an ethereal glow. As Ophelia and the skeletons neared, Caleb rushed up and around them toward the gold embroidered flaps that served as the main entrance of the tent.

As the man stepped inside, the skeletons immediately came to a halt and lowered Ophelia in her seat back to the ground. After that, they resumed their statue like stillness.

"I've arrived with an emissary from the svartalfar." Ophelia heard Caleb say through the thin material of the tent. "She needs to speak with Perett."

"Really?" Another man said, sounding familiar to the disguised woman. "Then she must be attended to right away."

Ophelia stayed seated in the wooden throne, trying to look as disinterested and bored and possible as Caleb exited the tent. Moments later another man emerged, wearing an immaculately pressed white shirt and black pants that flared at the bottom to make his thin legs look bigger.

His dark hair waved in the cool night breeze as his equally dark eyes turned and focused on Ophelia. The mercenary recognized him as the man who led the force that had captured her and Lyan on the mountain pass. Apparently, she had already met Perett.

The thin man stepped over to Ophelia, giving her a deep bow. "You are welcome here, of course." Perett said as he straightened back up. "But why didn't you come to me through the portal mechanism we established to your people?"

Ophelia spent the entire trip to see him thinking up a story that could work. She could only hope she could tell it convincingly.

The disguised woman rose to her feet and stepped toward Perett, who was just an inch or so taller than her. "That is why I must see you. The situation within my tribe has become... complicated."

"Oh?" Perett's thoughtful face was interrupted by a polite smile. "I do apologize. Where are my manners? To whom do I have the pleasure of speaking on behalf of the Lytyl Tribe?"

Of all the thinking she'd done on her story, Ophelia didn't even consider an alias. So she used the first svartalfar name that came to mind.

"Stohbease." She said, trying to look proud despite the disgust that suddenly washed through her body. "I am an apprentice Inquisitor with the Lytyl Tribe. Inquisitor Aylosha sent me on this errand."

"Very well." Perett nodded. "I can't help but think that the rest of this conversation should be held inside, don't you?"

The brigand leader turned back toward the tent with Caleb at his side. While it was customary in svartalfar lands for women to go ahead of men, it wasn't in the upworld and Ophelia wouldn't look overly dignified trying to rush in front of Perett and Caleb just to enter the tent first. Besides, who knew what kind of magical wards or defenses could have been just inside waiting for some idiot to stumble into them?

So she followed them in, Caleb holding the flap open for her. This was only one part of the interior of the tent. It wasn't anywhere near as big as it looked outside. The white canvas that served as walls for this "room" had flaps here and there that would allow a person to access other sections.

Inside this portion was sparse but what was here was of the highest quality. Especially the finely polished round oak table, which Perett took a seat at in an overstuffed chair, with three others just like it surrounding the table.

He motioned for Ophelia to sit and she did so. Then he waved Caleb away. The armored man stepped through a set of flaps into another part of the tent behind the svartalfar emissary.

"Stohbease, why is our normal means of communication cut off?" He folded his arms across his narrow chest.

Caleb returned through the same flap he had used to leave, this time carrying two glasses of red wine. The liquid almost didn't allow any light through it, which would make it so mysterious and inviting to a connoisseur of fine alcohol. Ophelia knew that much.

The armored man placed a glass down in front of her first, then Perett. He nodded and Caleb again left that portion of the tent.

Ophelia ignored the glass for the moment, which wasn't easy for her. "The Vizier has grown suspicious of the Inquisitor and is watching her movements." Using some truthful elements should make the lie more convincing. "So she sent me to inform you that she will need to take care of the Vizier before she can commit any svartalfar support to your plan."

She picked up the glass of wine but, as much as she wanted to, she didn't take a drink. Ophelia swirled the liquid around and smelled the teasing aroma that filled the glass with the motion.

"I see." Perett took a long, deep drink from his own glass. "How long will it take for the Inquisitor to 'deal' with this suspicious Vizier?"

Ophelia forced herself to place the glass back on the table. "She must do it within a day. Before the Vizier has an audience with the Matriarch to share her suspicions."

Perett took another deep sip of wine, finishing off his glass. Then he was still for a long moment.

"That seems a reasonable amount of time." He said, his dark eyes darting back and forth as if he was reading some kind of invisible document. "Of course, that would give the Bunny Barbarian enough time to warn the Light Bringers we are coming and allow them to reposition to face us on even terms. But that was the plan, was it not?"

Ophelia's stomach tightened. "The Bunny Barbarian? She is still down in the dungeons with—"

"Ophelia." Perett rested both his elbows on the polished oak. "I know it is you. But I do have to applaud you. My dear, you played the part of a svartalfar perfectly."

He gave her a mockingly quiet clap while his elbows stayed on the table. Ophelia felt her anger start to boil up, her pale blue eyes looking around the tent for anything to use as a weapon.

"Then how did you know?" She figured trying to buy a few seconds now, instead of the day she wanted a moment ago was worth a try.

"Two things really. I will start with the more specific first." He looked so pleased with himself as he spoke. "You may not realize it, my dear, but the runes on your back glow brighter when your emotions are running, shall we say, intense? And Caleb saw them when he delivered our wine."

Ophelia thanked her luck that Perett enjoyed talking. She couldn't see anything outside of the table and chairs that could be potentially lethal but she still had the dagger. Now if she could just figure out how to get to it...

"Second, I knew you were a spy the moment you spoke to me." He gave her such a wide smile Ophelia was sure that his face was about to split. "Any emissary sent to us by Inquisitor Aylosha would have known that I'm not Perett."

CHAPTER

ELEVEN

LOOKING OUT THE window of the bar in which they had taken refuge, Bothan saw the sun dip behind the massive castle that served as home to the Order of Kuan Yin. The svartalfar rose to his feet, reached into his pocket and tossed a couple of coins onto the table. He'd been there for hours now, pretending to drink while listening to the locals gossip without hearing a word about the Light Bringers or coming war.

"You have yourself a good night and walk safe!" The exceptionally friendly elf behind the bar waved to Bothan as he made his way toward the door.

The svartalfar waved back, smiling politely so he didn't appear suspicious. Not that he looked like a soldier ready for war, of course. That would have been beside the point of his mission here. No, Bothan looked like a simple traveler in a plain brown leather tunic with a gray shirt underneath. His pants were worn, much patched cloth and his boots well scuffed. Even the rapier he carried on his hip looked old and worn. Bothan wore his role as a traveler well.

Once Bothan was outside he saw Garak, who gave him a slight nod and motioned to a nearby alleyway. Garak was dressed much like Bothan, although he was pale by svartalfar standards, his skin an ashen gray that practically blended with his shirt compared to Bothan's own onyx skin. Where Bothan had silver hair pulled back into a loose ponytail, Garak's was short and dyed black. He practically plastered it flat against his head just so at least one of his features would stand out against his bland skin. But standing out is the last thing either svartalfar wanted to do.

Still, neither had garnered anything that resembled even a wary glance by the many passers-by. Not one human, elf, dwarf or even halfling gave either a second look. Even as both ducked down into the alley behind the blacksmith's shop.

"Report." The final member of the svartalfar scouting party, their leader ordered.

The Lady Wizard, Kurayakin, leaned against the building that was the a blacksmith's shop, her arms folded across her chest. The far side of the alley had been made a dead end by a pile of wooden crates there that stood over a foot above all three svartalfar. Other than that, there were just the brick walls of the blacksmith's and a wooden building that was probably someone's house. It had a drainage gutter that was as bone dry as the weather had been for weeks.

Where Bothan and Garak were dressed to blend in, Kurayakin was dressed to do anything but that. She wore a sequined violet dress that shimmered even in the fading light of the day, as well as jewelry just about anywhere she could, in her earlobes, around her neck, around her wrists, every finger and even around her ankles, although they only peeked into view when she walked.

"I've heard no mention of the Light Bringers, the svartalfar or the escaped prisoners, my Lady." Bothan gave her a deep bow as he spoke. "I don't think these people are aware of what the Order is planning."

Garak gave her an equally deep bow. "My Lady, I have scouted the grounds immediately around the castle and even listened in on several conversations by those of high rank in the Order." He paused to take a breath, though Kurayakin looked impatient. "No one made any mention of the Light Bringers or preparations for war."

The long silver hair of the svartalfar woman cascaded behind her as she lifted herself away from the wall. She looked at the two men assigned to her sternly as she digested their reports.

"So, after leaving you here for a full day," Kurayakin started. "I have to belittle myself enough to *sneak* into an upworlder stronghold just to be told that you have nothing?"

She hissed at them and the two men almost fell to their knees to beg forgiveness. Only the instinct of trying to avoid suspicious behavior seen by a someone passing stopped them.

"I suppose I should take this as good news. An enemy caught unawares is one easily conquered." Kurayakin mused.

That was when a figure as tall as the wooden crates suddenly shuffled over them with stunning speed. "That is very true." The silhouette only got taller as it seemed to suddenly grow a pair of long ears from the top of its head. "However, an opponent's overconfidence has led to their downfall more than once."

The figure revealed herself to be a woman wearing pastel blue from head to toe. Lyan Yo Bunpy! The escaped prisoner! The Bunny Barbarian brandished her long spear, although she did not yet move to attack.

Her brown eyes shifted from one svartalfar to the next. "I don't suppose I could convince you to come along quietly?" She smirked.

Kurayakin's hands started to crackle with energy before Lyan had even finished her sentence but the flat side of the Bunny Barbarian's spear blade slapped into her chest, interrupting the spell and throwing her back into the brick wall.

Then Garak flew to the ground after Lyan's spear spun around and slammed into his chin. He didn't even get a chance to draw his sword.

The same couldn't be said for Bothan. He charged at Lyan Yo Bunpy, who simply spun around and let him pass. The svartalfar man stopped himself before he hit the crates and turned to face the Bunny Barbarian. When he did, Bothan grinned to himself. Now the svartalfar's enemy was sandwiched between the two that remained.

Lyan's spear swept at the male svartalfar again, this time with the blade swinging to cut. He couldn't step back so he had no choice but to parry with his rapier to keep from being stabbed. His blade was much thinner than even the staff of the spear and the extra mass knocked Bothan's weapon from his hand.

Glancing behind the barbarian, Bothan figured he wouldn't have to worry much longer. Using the time the male svartalfar bought her, Kurayakin had charged up a massive spell to unleash on the Bunny Barbarian.

Her obsidian hands stretched out and a whole storm's worth of lightning leaped from her fingertips into Lyan. The Bunny Barbarian stiffened up as the bolts struck her body, the smell of ozone filling the alleyway as little mini claps of thunder echoed in the space between the walls.

Once the energy ceased spilling from the svartalfar wizard, Kurayakin gasped for breath after expending such an effort. She waited for the much taller, muscular woman to collapse to the ground but, instead, she only saw the Bunny Barbarian's broad shoulders shake.

Then, after a few seconds, the laughter began. Lyan's mouth was wide open, tears of mirth rolling down her face as she grabbed Bothan's collar and tossed him at the wizard as if he barely weighed anything.

Both svartalfar fell to the ground in a heap and Lyan Yo Bunpy couldn't stop her laughing. It just kept coming so insistently that the woman had to brace herself against the wall.

By the time she recovered enough to open her eyes and stand on her own, Lyan noticed that a crowd had formed at the other end of the alley. Wiping the water away from her eyes, Lyan stepped over the svartalfar spies and over to one of the onlookers, a young dwarf that was dressed in white robes.

"You are a cleric in the Order of Kuan Yin?" She only asked the question as a formality.

The dwarf, barely old enough to have started his patchy looking brown beard, nodded as he stepped forward, away from the group. The rest of them started to mutter, already starting to spread the story of what happened around the township.

"Could you go tell Harbenigyr that Lyan Yo Bunpy of the Yo Bunpy Tribe seeks an audience and has dire news that requires his attention." The Bunny Barbarian glanced back over her shoulder at the svartalfar laying in the alley. "As well as proof."

It was only a matter of minutes after that Lyan and the three svartalfar found themselves in the meeting hall of Dianmeyer's castle. It was formerly known as the throne room but after the former owner was ousted by Harbenigyr and his friends (Lyan included, of course) all the gold trim, thrones and anything else that was mounted simply to boast that it was expensive had been removed years before. It was all replaced with fine wooden carvings of their goddess or other decorations that had been created by the clerics themselves.

The two svartalfar men had their hands bound together, the Bunny Barbarian carrying their belts and sheathed swords on her shoulder, while the wizard had her hands encased in specially designed silver manacles that kept her from being able to perform any magicks.

All four were escorted by Gimli, second only to Harbenigyr in the Order's hierarchy and, just by coincidence the father of the dwarf that announced Lyan's presence to the castle. Eight clerics, looking out of place by holding maces that rested on their shoulders, lined the walls of the meeting room on guard duty that, until tonight, had been mostly ceremonial.

They all waited for the Grand Cleric of the Order of Kuan Yin on this continent in silence. Finally, a cleric pushed open the double doors at the side of the meeting room. This cleric was differently dressed than the rest. He was easily as tall and perhaps more heavily muscled than Lyan. He was a human with black hair pulled back into a short ponytail, with a small patch of hair under his lower lip.

His robes didn't even have sleeves, unlike every other cleric in the room, which only served to show his thick arms off to anyone looking. He also wore a jade green sash around his waist. As far as the prisoners could tell, that was the color that symbolically represented the Order of Kuan Yin and the more green a cleric wore, the higher ranked they were. And he was easily wearing more than any other cleric they had seen yet.

All three of the svartalfar looked between each other uneasily. Kurayakin even started to struggle with her bonds before Lyan tapped her shoulder to remind the svartalfar to be still.

The massive cleric straightened up proudly to his full height. "The Grand Cleric of the Order of Kuan Yin, our leader, Harbenigyr!" He heralded.

Seconds later a thin elf who barely came up to the herald's shoulder hopped into the room on one foot, still pulling a jade colored sandal on the other. His hair was black like the herald's but was worn loose, draping down to his shoulders. His pointed ears poked out past his flat hair at an angle that would have been considered wide even for an elf and his black eyes darted back and forth between all the people in the room, looking sheepish as he found his way to one of the two largest chairs in the room.

As different as the herald's robes were from the rest of the rank and file in the room, Harbenigyr's were even more so. While they were still white, they also had silver epaulettes resting on his shoulders, a jade tabard was draped over his chest and a green sash that had a depiction of the goddess Kuan Yin displayed on the flat cloth that ran down in front of his legs.

This depiction of Kuan Yin always amused the Bunny Barbarian. She looked like a sweetly smiling woman carrying a pail of water in a simple robe with one long leg emerging from the folds of the cloth. Harby was often mockingly told, mostly by those that counted among his friends, that his deity had "nice legs".

Lyan chuckled to herself as the svartalfar glanced about in confusion. The Grand Cleric sat across from the prisoners, well out of their reach of course, but his chair wasn't on any raised surface so that he could look down at them. Any sense of intimidation they had before the herald entered the room was replaced with confusion as to what would happen next.

That was the entrance of Harbenigyr's wife, Josie. "There's no need for that, Samson."

She stopped the herald from announcing her as she passed, her scarlet hair draping down to her waist and the way she walked giving her a more regal air than her husband. She wore pants similar to the type Ophelia did with the hips cut out, although hers fit around her legs loosely unlike on the mercenary.

Josie was a half-elf and married to the Grand Cleric but she wasn't actually a member of the Order. That meant that she didn't have to wear white or jade. In fact, her pants were the color of green olives while she wore a sheer black top that was tucked in. On top of that, she was barefoot. Apparently, she had only slipped on her pants over her nightgown after being called to this meeting from bed.

She made her way to the chair that rested beside Harbenigyr. Sitting down, she leaned her elbow on one arm of her chair, leaning away from Harbenigyr as she crossed her legs. Her other hand reached out and interlaced with Harby's fingers while the room remained silent.

The Grand Cleric finally spoke. "Lyan, what is going on?"

The barbarian didn't expect a formal welcome, in fact, she liked that Harbenigyr went straight to business. Even if his tone was more of confusion and curiosity rather than the worry and suspicion she felt the situation warranted. Although, how would he know that yet?

"Ophelia and I have had a... run in with the Lytyl Tribe of svartalfar and learned that they are mounting an army to attack Dianmeyer." Lyan said simply.

"Are these the ones you had your 'run in' with?" Harbenigyr motioned to the svartalfar prisoners. "Where is Ophelia, by the way?"

The Bunny Barbarian glanced over at the prisoners out of the corner of her eye. "I'd rather not say where she is in front of them. But no, they aren't the ones we dealt with earlier. I found them when I spotted the wizard and followed her into town around sunset. Where she met them." She shrugged the shoulder that held the belts and swords of the two svartalfar men beside Kurayakin.

"And they're spies for the Lytyl Tribe?" Josie asked. "Why would they want to attack us?"

The barbarian turned to look at Kurayakin. "You want to take that one?" She grinned at the svartalfar.

If the wizard's eyes had been blades, they would have buried themselves in Lyan's face. "We have nothing to say to the likes of you."

The Bunny Barbarian's eyes stayed locked on Kurayakin's even as she spoke to Harbenigyr. "They think you have formed a partnership with the Light Bringers and are planning to invade their caves."

"Us? Invade?" Both Harby and Josie looked equal parts surprised, confused and repulsed at the idea.

"But we haven't even seen Collen in months." Harbenigyr said. "What would make them think we have any kind of dealings with the Light Bringers?"

"Triton." Lyan answered.

She went on to explain about the wingless griffin being used as a patsy for Perett's attacks. That led to her explaining Perett, Caleb, the silencing heads of wheat, the Inquisitor and, finally, the subject turned to Nyphistra. Again, Lyan was reluctant to get into details with the prisoners standing just beside her.

"So Nyphistra became the Lytyl Tribe's Vizier after we left." Harbenigyr looked thoughtful.

His black eyes, which had more of the effect of a peaceful night sky rather than the dark burning malevolence of the one who captured Lyan and Ophelia, glanced from Lyan to Josie and then finally over to the svartalfar.

When Harbenigyr, Ophelia and the rest of his party met Nyphistra before, she told the cleric of her goal toward restoring peaceful relations between the surface elves. The now Grand Cleric knew better than to push further on the subject in front of those who would likely think such an objective treacherous. So his teeth tapped together inside his closed mouth as he considered everything he'd been told.

"Do you believe everything you've heard here?" He asked Kurayakin.

The svartalfar woman's silver eyebrows pressed together, her pale blue eyes looking from Harbenigyr to Lyan and back. She hadn't heard of this silencing magical item before but that did explain some of the unusual stories she'd heard about the Inquisitor of late. But to admit that any of the barbarian's story made sense would be to betray the plans of her people to the enemy.

So she said nothing.

"You?" The Grand Cleric looked over at Bothan and Garak.

The two svartalfar men looked at each other doubtfully. Then they turned to Kurayakin, who shook her head, although she didn't seem as steadfast as before.

After more silence, Harbenigyr finally lifted himself to his feet. "Then there's just one thing I can do." He started.

Just then a little streak of red rushed into the room, followed by the sound of a crying child. "Mommy! Mommy! Mommy!"

The little red thing ended up being a little seven year old elf girl that latched onto Josie's leg, wiping her tiny nose on her mother's pants.

Josie reached down and pulled the little girl into her arms. "What's wrong, Apple?"

"Apple" was short for Appelonia, Harbenigyr and Josie's daughter. She had flaming red hair like her mother's, although the child was dressed in pajamas that were white like cleric robes. The little girl looked around the room for a second, not seeming to notice or care that the grown-ups were in the middle of anything before she pointed back at the doorway she had run through.

"Ashe is treating me like a baby!" She whined, burying her face in her mother's chest.

As if on cue, Asheram Despana stepped into the meeting hall. The young man had just barely entered manhood by elf and svartalfar standards, standing just barely above Harbenigyr in height. His

pasty skin only made his grass green hair that much brighter looking while the hair itself stuck out in so many different directions it
almost buried his pointed ears.

He was dressed from neck to toe in black, a standard school
uniform for where he studied, that served only to make him look
paler. His hands were deep in his pants pockets as he entered, his
face vacillating between saddened and annoyed.

"I simply told her that she was up beyond her bed time." He
volunteered the information before anyone asked. "I was attempting to examine the soul orbs in the vault when she started scamper-
ing underfoot!"

Towards the end of his sentence his annoyance took control
and Asheram's voice almost squeaked. Catching himself, the young
man, cleared his throat.

"I was not underfoot!" Appelonia glared at him in a way that
Lyan could have only described as 'precious'. "I was helping!"

"You were n—!" Ashe stopped himself, clearing his throat
again. "I appreciate the enthusiasm, Appelonia, but I would also
appreciate if you waited for me to ask for help before giving it."

The little girl looked up at her mother. She had eyes like her
father's, and they looked confused.

"He said thank you, but you should have waited until morning
to help him." Josie grinned and kissed her daughter's forehead. "It is
way past your bed time."

Appelonia started to nod when the Bunny Barbarian's pastel
blue caught her eye. "Lyan!"

The little girl hopped from her mother's lap and rushed to the
barbarian. She wrapped her arms around Lyan's leg so tightly that,
even with all her muscles, the woman couldn't pull the child off.
Appelonia grinned wide up at the barbarian.

"It is good to see you, Apple." Lyan smiled back.

After it was apparent that the little girl wasn't going to let go,
Lyan shuffled over to Josie. The half-elf woman had to resort to tick-
ing to free the barbarian from the child's grip. Everyone around

them looked amused except for the svartalfar prisoners. They stood silently, stunned by how informal everything was in this place.

Harbenigyr whispered something to Josie. She picked up Appelonia and took her out of the room, taking Asheram with her on the way. The Grand Cleric grinned at everyone that remained sheepishly.

"Sorry about that." Harbenigyr said." As I was saying, there's only one thing I can do."

Kurayakin straightened up, a defiant look in her face. Bothan and Garak followed suit readying themselves for whatever these people did to punish spies.

"None of us want war." Harbenigyr took a deep breath. "I don't think your people do, either." He motioned to the svartalfar.

Lyan folded her arms across her chest, honestly not sure what the Grand Cleric was going to say. Her gaze fell on the svartalfar as she waited, the long teeth of her helmet pressing against either side of her nose.

"So, I would ask you to return to your people." All three svartalfar and Lyan looked at Harbenigyr in shock. "I would ask you to take a message to let your Matriarch know that we don't want a fight."

"Harbenigyr," Lyan stepped between the Grand Cleric and the prisoners. "If you send them back, all they will say is that you are unwilling to defend yourself." Her voice was barely above a whisper but the svartalfar could still hear her.

"I didn't say that." Harbenigyr answered, then turning to Kuryakin. "I will send a message with you that will also say that we are willing to defend the innocents who live with us here. Will you deliver it?"

The svartalfar wizard looked back and forth between the elf and the barbarian. Kurayakin stayed silent as she glanced over at the two men under her command. They looked equally conflicted. Scowling, she finally nodded at the Grand Cleric.

"Yes. I will deliver your message." She said.

Harbenigyr sent for parchment and a pen. While they waited, Lyan pulled him far enough away that the svartalfar couldn't hear this time.

"Why don't we just send a cleric with them to deliver your message?" The barbarian asked.

"The svartalfar are notoriously secretive about the entrances into their tunnels, Lyan." He answered.

"All the more reason to—" The Bunny Barbarian started.

"And will you guarantee my cleric's safety?" Harbenigyr interrupted.

There Lyan stalled. She had to get back to Ophelia to aid her against the ogres and whatever additional forces Perett had assembled.

"Fine." The barbarian growled.

Harbenigyr wrote his message, folding and sealing it with wax in a way similar to how Nyphistra sealed the map Ophelia and Lyan used earlier. Then he stepped up to the svartalfar wizard. He looked at her and she looked at him in silence.

Muttering a quiet prayer, Harbenigyr reached down and removed the woman's restraints. The silver manacles fell to the floor.

Lyan readied herself to rush Kurayakin if she tried to cast a spell. The wizard never did.

Harbenigyr gave the woman the folded parchment. "So that you can reach your lands faster, we will provide you with steeds."

Again, both the svartalfar and Lyan were surprised but they were all taken to the stable almost immediately. As they reached the doors leading outside, Josie rejoined the group, taking position beside the herald, Samson, who was serving as one of the three guards accompanying Harbenigyr, Lyan and the svartalfar spies.

They entered the building, the floors lined with fresh straw. A familiar beak peeked out from its stable. As Harbenigyr neared, the massive eagle head of Triton emerged after it. The Grand Cleric gently petted the griffin's head.

"Are you feeling better today, boy?" A look of genuine concern crossed the elf's face.

"What is wrong with him?" Kurayakin asked.

"He's reached a nice old age." Harbenigyr smiled sorrowfully. "I'm afraid his days of hauling me to and from the Land of the Long Toothed Rabbit are over."

All three svartalfar looked into the griffin's stable. Most of the beast's fur was gray and while its feathers were well tended, there were bald spots on Triton's crown and the base where his wings would have been.

"He has no wings." The svartalfar wizard observed.

Harbenigyr nodded, still petting the griffin's feathered neck. "I found him that way."

Kurayakin frowned but then continued on. Samson, Josie and Harbenigyr guided each svartalfar to a horse while the other guards gathered food and water.

The Grand Cleric gave the svartalfar a blessing as they started off. Again both the svartalfar and Lyan were surprised, although the barbarian less so by now.

Once Kurayakin and the svartalfar men in her charge shrank into the distance, Lyan stepped up to Harbenigyr. "So what now?"

"I have to get as many people evacuated and fortify the castle as best I can." The elf answered, turning to face his wife. "We need to get you both back to Loch Aeris to help Ophelia."

"Wait a minute. I'm staying to help—" Lyan started to protest at the same time as Josie. "I can't leave Apple—"

"Both of you, please." Harbenigyr turned to face the Bunny Barbarian. "Josie, Samson and Organa are going to go with you, Lyan. If what you're saying was accurate, you'll need help out there."

Lyan frowned but nodded in agreement. Josie looked far less convinced as she stomped up to her husband. Her green eyes made her look ready to beat him to a pulp.

"You want to send me away from my daughter in the face of a svartalfar invasion?" Josie, who was several inches shorter than her husband was standing nose to nose with him. "Are you insane?!"

Lyan was about to agree with the half-elf archer when Harbenigyr spoke up. The barbarian hadn't expected that. He usually submitted to Josie's opinion when it came to fighting strategy.

"I can't send an army with Lyan, Josie." His voice was barely above a whisper and Josie felt her anger melt as he continued. "You're the best archer I know. You need to go so that Lyan and Ophelia can make it back. I will watch over Appelonia and, if I have to, I'll get her out to safety."

Josie wanted to argue but she couldn't find the words without insulting her husband. He didn't enjoy fighting, that was true, but she knew he was capable. Probably just as good as she was in his own way.

"What's the fastest way to get there?" Lyan asked.

Lyan and Josie both saw something that neither had seen too often before: Harbenigyr with a mischievous grin.

"If Ashe thought our family was underfoot before." The Grand Cleric said. "Then he's really going to be tripped up after he and I have a little talk..."

TWELVE

OPHELIA STOOD BESIDE the table where she and the man who wasn't Perett drank together. She held her hands out as the thin man patted down her sides. With Caleb standing just behind her with his sword drawn. All Ophelia could do to express her displeasure was an annoyed sigh.

One of the woman's thick eyebrows arched up when the thin man knelt down in front of her. When he pulled up the hem of her skirt, Ophelia reflexively stepped back, only to feel the tip of Caleb's sword press between her shoulder blades.

She felt the thin man's fingers slip into the tops of her boots just below her knees. Not finding any weapons, he lifted himself back up to his feet, a wide grin on his face as his dark eyes stared down at Ophelia.

"She's unarmed. Such a shame, I did so admire that sword of hers." He announced to Caleb, who didn't react at all. "I am impressed with your commitment to looking the part of a svartalfar from head to toe, Ophelia."

His voice had a mocking tone as the thin man reached up to the woman's chest and pulled the blue fabric away from one side.

He let himself take a good, long look before letting the sapphire top slip back in place.

"You painted every inch of your skin, and I do mean every, to match theirs." He believed the leather like material of Ophelia's pants was actually her skin painted like the rest of her upper body.

The thin man's hand rose up to her head and gripped the silver wig Ophelia wore. With a hard tug, the pale tresses pulled away from the mercenary's hair, the pins that had been used to secure it scraping against her scalp as her brunette hair was revealed. Ophelia's hair went off in every direction, the braids that had tied it down before tried in vain to keep performing that duty even though most every lock had been pulled out from under them.

With the wig wrapped around his fingers in one hand, the thin man's other hand rose to her ear. "A wig. Makes sense, you couldn't dye your dark hair to match a svartalfar's silver. It is such a distinct color. As for the ears..." For the first time, the thin man had a look on disgust on this bony face. "These are real svartalfar body parts?"

The thin man tossed the scalp to the dirt, wiping his hands against his black pants as if to wipe filth off of them. Then his hand balled up into a fist as he again focused on the woman.

"Wait, Virgil!" Caleb spoke up from behind Ophelia. "If you attack her, she could teleport anywhere around us."

Ophelia smirked, remembering how she did just that to the armored man, knocking him out with just one punch. She looked back over her shoulder at him, to remind him of just that.

The thin man's name was Virgil, eh? If Ophelia's memory served, Caleb, who was somehow controlling the ogres, mentioned that Virgil was doing something similar with the griffins. If he was here, the number of winged beasts he had dominion over had to be much higher than the few that aided in her and Lyan's capture.

Each man seemed to control a different "division" of Perett's forces. They also seemed to have some means of sharing that control. Virgil was able to command griffins, ogres and skeletons the other night on the mountain.

Virgil's hand dropped back down to his side. "Ah, I had forgotten. That does beg a question, though. Just how will we get her to tell us what her rabbit friend is up to?"

The thin man's face hovered only inches from Ophelia's, his pupils starting to flicker like embers growing into a fire. A list of possibilities were going through his head and, judging from his grin, each one was more pleasing, and likely more painful to the woman, than the last.

Then the already cool air in the tent suddenly went cold. If Ophelia wasn't mistaken, the fire light seemed to somehow dim, as well. The flaps to an adjacent section of the tent pulled apart by some unseen force and a massive figure stepped into the room.

It easily dwarfed Virgil, who was taller than Ophelia. In fact, its head almost brushed against the canvas roof as it made its way to the small group.

"Perhaps I could be of assistance here." The figure's voice had a deep rumble to it that reminded Ophelia of the Judicator.

Both men suddenly bowed low, Caleb's sword forgetting to point at the woman at that moment. Ophelia, though, had a feeling that this was not going to be her opportunity for escape with this massive... thing closing the distance.

"Lord Perett." Virgil greeted the figure before straightening back up.

As Perett got closer, Ophelia saw that he wasn't much more than a skeleton himself, albeit a massive one. Dried flesh stretched across what little of his bones the woman could see under his fur robes and unnaturally red hair stretched over the top of the skull, tied back in a short ponytail.

A sensation that Ophelia almost exclusively reserved for the Xaviour Tribe washed over her. Dread was the closest word that could describe it but it seemed so inadequate when she realized what Perett was.

He was a lich, a wizard so obsessed with power that death wouldn't even stop him from working to get more. Liches were more powerful than just about any living wizard because their bodies could handle energies that would burn any living thing to dust. In fact, that was precisely why a rare soul twisted enough would choose such a fate and join the ranks of the undead.

It was safe to assume that he was the one who primarily controlled the skeletons that she and Lyan encountered before. In fact, the unnaturally red hair reminded Ophelia of the old man she and Lyan came across at the base of Etigran Pass.

Ophelia noticed that around Perett's beef jerky looking neck was a gold chain and on it hung two trinkets. One talisman looked like a tuft of hair the same color as the ogress', tied up with some kind of twine Ophelia couldn't identify. The other looked like a small griffin feather with some of the beast's fur coat still sticking to the base of the shaft.

Perhaps those were what made him able to control creatures that were primarily under the control of the other men. It was a safe bet that Caleb and Virgil carried similar talisman.

Perett stepped over to the table, his bony hand reached for Ophelia's still full glass of wine with quiet taps filling the air as each bony finger wrapped around the stem. He pulled a vial of liquid that was a putrescent green color and dumped the entire contents into the glass, making the liquid reach the brim.

He stuck a bony finger into the wine and circled it around in the glass, although the red and green liquids never really mixed as much as swirled around each other. "It is rude of a guest not to drink something offered them. Would you open her mouth, please?" He pulled his finger out of the glass and flicked the excess wine from it as he stepped over to Ophelia.

Caleb stepped up behind Ophelia and wrapped one arm around her shoulders while his other hand wrapped around her jaw. The mercenary wanted to spew some kind of witty repartee at the men but her desire to not have whatever the lich mixed into the wine not in her mouth overrode that instinct.

When Virgil saw that Caleb wasn't having much luck prying Ophelia's clenched jaw open, he reached up and pinched the sword woman's nose shut. Ophelia felt as if she was back on the schoolyard about to be force fed mud by one of the local bullies. She had seen that happen to a schoolgirl once, anyway. Ophelia couldn't remember if it ever actually happened to her as a child.

She could hold her breath for a while, but not indefinitely, and just as her vision started to blur and fade, Ophelia's body usurped authority from her brain and opened her mouth to take in a lungful of air.

She immediately tried to close it but Perett's thick bony thumb wedged itself between her teeth. Ophelia bit down as hard as she could but the undead wizard didn't seem to notice and the hard digit didn't budge at all.

Her foot flew up between the lich's legs, connecting with his pelvic bone under his robes but otherwise having no effect. In fact, Perett looked amused at the effort as he raised the glass to the woman's lips.

The next thing Ophelia felt was like acid filling her mouth. She tried to spit it out but Perett pressed his hand against her lips with every mouthful, leaving the liquid nowhere else to go but up into her sinuses and down her throat.

She couldn't decide which was worse, the burning in her nose or in her throat as the undead wizard continued to force feed her the wine. Finally, once the glass was empty, Perett backed away from her, placing the glass on the table.

Ophelia coughed, red and green spittle flying from her mouth as some of the wine, and whatever it was mixed with, spilled from her nostrils and dripped down her chin. She tried to force herself to retch, only seeming to amuse the men around her more.

"Please, let our guest go, Caleb." Perett said. "She and I are about to have a most pleasant conversation."

"*Like hell we are.*" Came to Ophelia's mind but what came out of her mouth was, "What do you want to know?"

Perett nodded, looking pleased with himself as he leaned against the square table. "Where is your barbarian friend?"

"By now she's reached Dianmeyer to warn Harbenigyr about the svartalfar attack." She instantly rattled the sentence off, her face betraying the surprise and anger at how quickly it came out. "What did you make me drink?"

Ophelia was actually shocked that her question came out and was not blocked somehow. Perett nodded and grinned. Well, grinned as much as taut dried skin around his mouth could move to simulate the motion.

"See, gentlemen? Now this is what a conversation needs, engagement from both parties!" The lich commented to the other two men before turning back to Ophelia. "A potion of my own design that speeds up every system in your body. Since lying takes more time to develop than the truth, the truth always comes out first."

Ophelia suddenly felt as if she'd run miles in only a few seconds. But then her body felt a surge of adrenaline rush through it so intensely, she stumbled and had to grab the back of one of the overstuffed chairs to keep from falling.

"My turn." Perett condescendingly patted Ophelia's shoulder. "How long will the Order of Kuan Yin be able to stand against a force like the svartalfar?"

"Without the Light Bringers, two days at most and it's not likely they would be able to get any other reinforcements in that time." Ophelia slapped her hands over her mouth but too late.

Her blue eyes dug into the undead man beside her. She wanted to reach up and strangle him but he was already dead so it would be useless.

"What is this potion going to do to me after we're done here?" She asked instead, realizing that he was staying silent until she took 'her turn'.

"You will eventually immolate as the potion overheats your entire body but worry not, we will have all the information we need from you by then." He shrugged then took his turn for a question. "Who would be the most likely sources of said reinforcements to the clerics?"

"Lyan's people would take a week to get organized and down to Dianmeyer." Even through her fingers, Ophelia spouted off the words so quickly and loudly that every one of them could be understood. "The only other option is the Romefeller Guild. Harbenigyr and I traveled with their second in command for years but it's still not a given that he would help."

Ophelia bit down on her tongue but her mouth kept moving. Now she tasted her own blood in addition to betraying her friends.

She growled to herself as Perett kept quiet, waiting for her question. "Will you give me an antidote to this if I promise to cooperate from here on in?"

The lich shook his head. "You wouldn't cooperate with us, though. Would you?" He acted as if he already knew the answer.

"No." Ophelia quickly confessed. "I was just trying to waste some time to figure out which of you would likely fight back and make me blink."

She pulled herself away from the table and pulled the front of her dress up to where Havarti's dagger rested inside the uppermost part of her thigh. She pulled the dagger free and charged at Caleb, who still had his sword drawn. In the back of her mind, Ophelia realized that even if she didn't blink and avoid the attack, she would more than likely be dead anyway. Either way, she wouldn't betray any more information about Harby or Lyan.

Caleb's survival instinct took over and he stabbed the woman rushing at him with the dagger. His eyes opened wide as Ophelia suddenly disappeared and he realized what a mistake he had just made.

Before he could move again, Caleb felt a hand wrap around his blonde hair and wrench him backwards. The cold steel of the dagger pressed against his throat and he felt Ophelia's warm breath on his cheek.

Perett's barely mobile face betrayed his surprise but his hands were immediately glowing with maleficent red energy. Virgil took a couple more seconds to let his shock pass, then he drew a pair of daggers from the small of his back that crackled with electric energy.

"What did that accomplish, girl?" Perett started lifting his hand.

Ophelia pressed herself tighter against Caleb's back to make herself a smaller target to the lich. "There's a side effect to blinking that's always annoyed me until now. Whenever I got drunk at a bar, if a fight broke out and someone made me blink, it instantly made me sober. As if I never drank a drop."

The pressure on Caleb's scalp from Ophelia pulling his hair stopped. But he started feeling her fingernails scratch and dig into the back of his neck as she pulled him backwards.

Virgil started slinking to the side, trying to get a better angle on Ophelia. In response, the mercenary pressed the dagger against Caleb's throat hard enough to get a trickle of blood as she shuffled toward the tent's entrance.

"And you were counting on that to negate the effects of my potion as well." Perett said. "And yet you are still spouting information that would be better kept secret."

"That's where you're wrong, lich." Ophelia slid another foot toward the tent's entrance. "I was just buying time again."

With that, Ophelia's dagger sank into Caleb's throat and she pushed his gurgling, dying body into Perett before diving out of the tent. The lich shoved the armored man, dead after only seconds, aside and charged out after the woman. Virgil joined him in the cold night but Perett just stood beside the nearest fire.

"Where is she?" The thin man asked.

"Gone." The lich answered simply.

INTERMISSION

BACK IN SVARTALFAR lands Kurayakin, Bothan and Garak were being marched straight into the chambers of the Matriarch. They hadn't expected this, even if they were carrying correspondence from the leader of the Order of Kuan Yin. Not even Kurayakin, the highest ranking of the three, had ever even seen the Matriarch outside of official functions. Even then it was from a distance in the audience.

Wizards surrounded them on every side as they were instructed to avoid stepping on specific stones in the floor and even in certain spaces. Finally, though, the group found themselves in front of a pair of stone doors that had gold and diamonds adorned onto them in the shape of the insignia of the Lytyl Tribe.

The two wizards on either side of the entryway slapped their hands together and both women started chanting simultaneously. Kurayakin could only understand a random word here and there. The rest was in a language that was even older than that of her people.

The doors slowly pulled open, coming to rest in the hands of either wizard, and the sapphire blue carpet that led to the throne of the Matriarch came into view. The rest of the wizards motioned for the trio to continue on without them and the doors slammed shut the moment Garak was past the threshold.

The throne room was bigger and more magnificent than any of them had imagined. It took Bothan nudging Kurayakin's shoulder to keep her feet moving instead of staring at the golden columns and jeweled frames containing portraits of her ancestors.

The pillars drew the eye up to the ceiling and the arches supporting it. Hanging from an arch at the far end of the room was an immense chandelier with great metal arms that held translucent crystals that were easily the size of a person aloft and gave a shimmer to the lighting. Much like the columns leading the eye up to the chandelier, the crystals guided the eye down to the Lytyl Tribe's seat of power.

Once the Matriarch sitting in her throne came into view, the wizard let out an audible gasp of awe. The aging woman hadn't lost any of her beauty. Her skin was the color of scorched earth and her hair had natural streaks of gold. Kuryakin had seen the Inquisitor trying to ape the effect with gold chains.

The black dress the Matriarch wore sparkled like the night sky of the upworld in the torchlight, the golden spider web of her cloak's filigree swept from her shoulders to blend so perfectly into the intricate gold designs in the massive throne that it was impossible to tell where one began and the other ended.

The three svartalfar spies stopped at the base of the thirteen steps leading up to where their sovereign sat and knelt obediently. The Matriarch's violet eyes locked on them and her ruby red lips spread into a kind looking smile.

"Arise, my children." The Matriarch ordered.

They each did so. Remembering their place, both Bothan and Garak stood a full pace behind Kurayakin who still appeared spellbound at the sight of her leader.

"What word do you bring to me?" The Matriarch's voice echoed in the grandness of the throne room.

"My Matriarch, we bring a message from the Grand Cleric of the Order of Kuan Yin, Harbenigyr." Kurayakin pulled the sealed parchment from a secret pocket in her dress. "He wishes to avoid war with our people."

The Matriarch looked thoughtful, a fingertip idly running back and forth across her chin. "And what of his alliance with the Light Bringers?"

"Mistress, he denies any alliance and none of us could find any evidence of such a thing. Dianmeyer has no hint of a military presence within or outside of the keep." Kurayakin started up the steps to deliver the parchment only when the Matriarch motioned for her to do so.

The older svartalfar woman took the paper and opened it, her violet eyes scanning the document. "And what about the evidence that this Harbenigyr led an assault on several squads of our people?"

"I personally saw this griffin, Triton, that serves as the cleric's steed, Mistress." Kurayakin fought with all her might to keep from bouncing giddily as she spoke to her sovereign. "He is old and wingless and could not have attacked our troops."

For the first time, the Matriarch's eyes looked up without any sense of kindness. "My child, you are not calling our Inquisitor a liar, are you?"

Kurayakin's eyes opened wide. "No, Mistress, not at all! But after seeing Dianmeyer up close, I believe that she is somehow being misled by another in order to force us into war for their own profit."

The Matriarch's eyes narrowed. "Those are very serious accusations, my child."

The younger svartalfar felt her mouth go dry. "Yes, Mistress. But I cannot think of any other reason someone would try to have our people slaughter an opponent so obviously weaker than us."

The older woman lifted herself to her feet. At the top of the pedestal her throne sat upon, even with the sweeping gold filigree behind her shoulders, there was still plenty of room for both women.

"I see." The Matriarch said. "Have you told the Vizier your suspicions?"

"No, Mistress." Kurayakin answered. "The moment I said I had a message from the clerics we were brought to you."

"As it should have been." The other woman nodded. "All of the svartalfar know how personally I take treason."

"Yes, Mistress." Kurayakin bowed her head in agreement. "If it is your wish, I will go and inform the Vizier immediately so that the perpetrator can be found and brought to face your justice."

The Matriarch smiled sweetly, resting a hand on the younger woman's shoulder. "You misunderstand me, my child. It is your treachery that I have taken personally."

The confusion on the young woman's face was replaced with pain as flash of indigo lightning shot from the Matriarch's hand, launching her down the stairs and into a heap at the feet of Bothan and Garak. The two men knelt down over the woman to see if she was still alive.

"Lytyl do not get captured and then turned into pages for our enemies!" The older svartalfar wizard bellowed as she unleashed another barrage of lightning down onto all three underlings.

They fell to the ground, writhing in pain as the Matriarch continued. "You should have had the sense to stay in the upworld and die! Or at the very least, keep your seditious thoughts to yourselves!"

The lightning changed to green flame and enveloped the still twitching bodies of the svartalfar messengers. The rage in the Matriarch's eyes gleamed for a long moment before she dropped her hand back to her side, taking a moment to catch her breath.

The three scorched bodies of Kurayakin, Bothan, and Garak were little more than steaming skeletons with black flesh still sliding off their bones. The carpet under their corpses wasn't even singed, enchanted to withstand the heat of violent magicks. If only the same could be said of the stains the victims left behind.

"Nyphistra will be dealt with soon enough." She spoke as if the bodies could still hear.

Moments later, the Inquisitor entered the throne room, stepping over the charred remains before bowing at the base of the throne's steps. "You sent for me, Mistress?"

The Matriarch nodded. "Aylosha, it is time to end this charade with Nyphistra."

The Inquisitor smiled. "Yes, Mistress."

"She taught me her most powerful spells." The older woman slipped back into her throne. "With our combined strength, we shall destroy Nyphistra's plan to turn us into subservient race for the upworlders rather than their masters. Mastery was our founder's vision for our people. We'll use that imbecile Perett's grudge against the Light Bringers to keep them distracted while we establish a foothold in the upworld at Dianmeyer."

The younger woman smiled as she nodded. "Assuming those idiotic humans don't kill each other, it will leave the supposed victor easy prey for your armies."

The Matriarch nodded in agreement. "I never thought that the fates would place the pieces for our triumph together so quickly."

BACK AT PERETT'S TENT...

"Bring him back. You can do that, can't you?" The anguish in Virgil's face was on full display in the light radiated by the still burning campfires.

The thin man carried the recently killed Caleb, still wearing his now bloodstained armor, in his arms as he approached Perett. The undead wizard gave no indication that he heard the other man speak. His dark eyes stayed directed at the dark sky for a long moment before he turned his chin down to rest in his taut fingers.

"Perett, bring him back!" The shriek in the thin man's voice actually pulled the lich's attention back to Virgil and the armored body in his arms.

The wizard stepped up to him and Caleb, who still rested in his arms. "The enchantment I placed upon the two of you requires a natural life force to wield it. Bringing him back now would make no difference. Ophelia has taken his ability to control the ogres away from him."

"That is what you're worried about?" The veins in Virgil's neck bulged with rage. "He's your brother, Perett. Not to mention the last of our noble line!"

The undead man arched the stretched flesh that used to be where his eyebrows rested. "He and I are share bloodlines, Virgil. You think I am not aware that it now ends with me?" His dried fingers ran across the cooling skin of the blonde man's forehead.

The thin man was surprised at the tenderness in the lich's gesture. It knocked away the vitriolic words he had ready out of his mouth.

"It is the very reason you and he helped me become... this." Perett motioned down his black robed body with his other bony hand. "To avenge the Grissom Clan on the swords of the very men who allowed us to be wiped from the earth: The Light Bringers."

Virgil hesitantly nodded. "You're right, Perett. I apologize. With the power you now wield, I forgot that you have also sacrificed so much to bring us here."

"And as such, we must finish what we have started and sacrificed, including young Adrian and Paul to that barbarian woman." The lich slipped his arms under the corpse of his brother and lifted him away from Virgil. "Ophelia is surely heading straight for the Light Bringers and they will be marching for us come daybreak. You must ready your griffins to take up the role we had set for the ogres."

The thin man wasn't sure what to do with his hands once Caleb was taken from him. "Do you really think we can stand against them now?"

His question was genuine. Their forces had been reduced by half and now doubt was coming to the surface.

Perett nodded. "I gave you and Caleb these powers before I tapped into the ley line under the Lytyl Tribe's control. You still control an entire swarm of beasts. Now that this artery of the planet's energy flows through me, it makes my reach stretch that much further and our enemies defeat a surety. But we will need your griffins to lay the groundwork, so to speak."

"I'll go prepare them." Virgil said but he didn't make any motion to leave. "But what are you going to do with him? Not make him one of your necrotic pages?"

"Necrotic pages?" Perett cradled Caleb's body to his chest like a mother with an infant. "Were you not asking me to do so to my own brother only moments ago? You forget yourself, Virgil."

The undead wizard turned away from the thin man, his brother's lifeless head resting on his bony shoulder. Perett's sunken eyes swept over the open space of the clearing, the stars in the sky just starting to fade to make way for the morning soon to come.

"Caleb is a noble and my kin." The lich turned back to the other man. "I will see that he is put to rest in the proper fashion. Once we've cleared our path of these Light Bringers, we will take the Valen Court itself and turn the ley line they have used to assert their dominion against them. The very earth they stand upon will loathe their presence."

"Can't you do that now?" The thin General asked. "You control the Lytyl's ley line. Didn't you say they were all connected?"

The lich nodded. "As the river is to the ocean. Yet you will never find a kraken in a trickling brook."

Virgil stared back at Perett blankly.

"Once I become the circuit that connects two of the earth's arteries, I will be able to reach every other ley line in creation, make my own ocean of power, and direct the energy to and away from wherever I desire. Meaning I can deny the red capes their power source while imbuing the lands of the Grissom Clan and returning them to glory." The wizard explained.

Awe filled the living human's face as Perett finished speaking. "Does that mean you can bring our people back to life?" He asked, his voice breathless.

"Once I have control of the second ley line." The undead man answered. "Only then will I be able to do whatever I wish. To fulfill any one of our desires, including a proper resurrection for Caleb. But it will only come to fruition if you ready your charges. Now."

A look of appreciation crossed Virgil's face and he gave the wizard a short bow.

"Thank you for insisting on a proper burial for Caleb." He said. "He deserves a peaceful rest until you can bring him back to us. To a world free of the Light Bringers' tyranny."

Virgil again bowed and then marched into the forest toward the nest of the nearest pride of griffins. Once the mortal was well out of sight the wizard's arms dropped to his sides and Caleb fell to the ground in a heap.

"Churl!" The lich called into the chilled air.

The sound of soil rending loose from the ground was the first sign of any response. Shortly after, a man with pallid skin and earth stained robes stepped out of the treeline and toward his undead master.

There was a hitch to his stride as the man now called Churl walked. One of his hips had been injured in the battle that had cost him his life and would never heal. His eyes, once the same blue as the waters of Loch Aeris, now more resembled curdled milk. He had no hair on his head in life and now even the skin on Churl's bare head was showing signs of wearing thin.

The rosary he used to pray to his god in life still hung off his wrist. On it was a silver amulet with a blooming tree carved into it that was tarnished to the point that it looked to be made stone rather than precious metal. The same tree design was embroidered into the front of his robes, though it was barely visible through the caked on mud and dust.

When he was alive, Churl was a cleric as well as a member of the very same clan as Virgil, Caleb and Perett. Churl was the first to taste unlife at the lich's hand, a test to learn the limits of Perett's newly acquired power.

"Prepare Caleb for battle." The undead cleric's master ordered.

Churl knelt down, placing his hand with the rosary on the chest of the armored corpse. Scarlet light, in the shape of a hand like the one tattooed onto Caleb's torso, erupted from the armor and grasped the cleric's wrist as if to stop him from whatever task he was attempting.

Perett, who had already started back to the tent, heard Churl struggling and turned back. "Ah, the life seal. I had forgotten."

When the undead wizard had discovered the enchantment to make the ogres and beasts bend to the will of a human master, it was after he had already taken this new supernatural form. The spell required living, mortal blood.

When Caleb and Virgil agreed to take the power upon themselves, one of the steps required what Perett described as a "life seal". It sealed off the mortal's soul to be used as fuel to run the enchantment. Once the "master's" life force was spent, they would drop dead on the spot, unable to be even reanimated as Churl was.

But Caleb had not fallen as a result of the enchantment. He still had his life force, as it took days for it to drain away naturally after death, and the wizard still had a use for him.

The lich sank to one knee next to the undead cleric. "I am sorry, old friend, but it takes a massive offering to counter a glyph warding against tapping into a life force."

Perett's massive hand wrapped behind the back of Churl's head. The other undead man had just enough sense to wonder what was happening before the lich shoved Churl's face into the light bulging from Caleb's chest.

For the first time since his reanimation, the cleric felt a sensation almost forgotten to him: pain. The glowing hand that had been holding Churl's wrist eagerly changed its grip to the cleric's face when it came within reach. The first scream of genuine emotion to escape the bald man's mouth in years was cut short by the hand crushing his jawbone. It continued crumpling the rest of Churl's skull like a piece of discarded parchment.

Pulverized undead flesh disappeared down some invisible gullet as the hand continued to rend more and more of Churl's now still body. Finally, the seal stopped, peeling away from Caleb's body to blow away on the wind like so many fading embers. All that remained of the cleric was his arm with the rosary still wrapped around its wrist.

Perett lifted the now unclaimed limb from the ground and then himself to his feet. "Caleb, arise."

The metal of the human's armor scraped against the soil as Caleb's lifeless limbs started to move again. The motion was awkward at first, like when a child first learned that it had the ability to stand. The newborn undead learned this lesson quickly and pushed itself back onto its blood soaked, boot covered feet.

"Very good." Perett smirked at the unliving mockery that had been his brother. "You will proceed to the battlefield. Align yourself with the rest of my forces waiting there. Do you understand?"

Many of the sinews in the man's neck had been severed by Ophelia's blade, so Caleb's head more flopped back and forth rather than nodded that it comprehended the instructions given. The armored corpse turned and started across the clearing.

"Oh, Caleb?" The lich called the body of his brother back to him.

Perett held the disembodied arm out to the blonde undead man. Dropping the limb into Caleb's waiting hands, the lich then crossed his arms over his narrow chest and stood thoughtfully for a moment.

"I'm sure that, on some level, you miss the glyph that rested on your chest." The wizard spoke with a hint of amusement to his voice. "See if you can find a way to make that into a reasonable substitute on your way."

Perett laughed as he started back to the tent again. As a living wizard, he long ago learned that words had power. To wield it, one had to speak them. He also learned to take care as to who was within distance to hear said words. With Virgil working his way farther and farther, it was time for him to make his declaration:

"Caleb has thrown off the chains of his irksome, independent living flesh and maintained his usefulness beyond tomorrow. Virgil's use, as well as all living flesh, will no longer be necessary for my needs after the Light Bringers fall. Let this battle herald the rebuilding of the world in my image which, by definition, is the glory of the Grissom Clan!"

With his supposed allies focused solely on destroying Dian-meyer, it was already too late for them to realize he had stolen their connection to the true source of their power, the ley line. The power starvation he will cause alone was enough to destroy the Lytyl Tribe.

But first, he had to let them annihilate the Order of Kuan Yin. Over the years they had become the largest sect of clerics on the continent. The power clerics wielded was nature's counter-balance to the energies a lich like Perrett wielded and was the only true threat to him.

The sun started to tease its presence between the clumps of trees and Perrett realized it was time for him to report to Inquisitor Aylosha that the battle was to commence shortly and make sure she was keeping up her end of their supposed bargain. The lich made his way to the furthest back section of the tent.

As he walked, his skin loosened, taking the pink appearance that it had in life. His face turned from that of a mummified corpse to that of an old man, save for the hair he had dyed bright red during his life.

Thanks to this wrinkled face, the svartalfar thought of him as little to no threat. As did Ophelia and Lyan at the base of Etigran Pass. He couldn't keep this appearance up for long, but if it kept the Lytyl Tribe compliant it was so, so worth it.

CHAPTER

THIRTEEN

LYAN'S EYES WERE shut tight as she tried to ignore the bobbing motion of the boat. She gripped the railing so tight that splinters started digging into her palms.

"Oh come on! You teleport into my room in the middle of the night to bum a ride and I don't even get to touch them?" The captain of the ship whined.

"No, you're not going to touch them because of what I saw when I teleported into your room, Plant Boy." The voice of young Ashe floated across Lyan's ears. "Besides, don't you have a tulip waiting for you at home?"

"Plant Boy", or Isaac as his mother named him, was the same age as Asheram, an experiment to create a person that was a mix of human and plant since his mother was unable to have children of her own. The fact that his mother just happened to be the apprentice of Asheram's wizard father meant that, like it or not, the two boys grew up as practically family. And the familiar banter was causing Lyan to grind her teeth into nubs.

Isaac's father also happened to be the head of a group of pirates, "businessmen" being the title they preferred, that ran out of Craigh Na Troon, a port city a short distance south on the shores of Mare Morte. This was the second, or perhaps third, ship that Plant Boy had been given command of in his short career as an actual "businessman".

"Ha ha, very funny. But you know I have a girl in every port." Isaac sounded as if he was prancing to make his way closer to the Bunny Barbarian. "And you know it doesn't count when you're on the open sea!"

Ashe sighed. "No, Plant Boy, you have a shrub in every port and we aren't even on the open sea!"

"It is water deep enough to drown in, right?" Isaac snapped back.

Lyan could just imagine the young man's blue hands making their way to grab her cotton tail as he spoke. He was always like this, lavishing copious amounts of attention on the closest female. Incidentally, Lyan couldn't think of a time, even when he was a little boy, that it didn't revolve around him touching some part of a woman or trying to get her attention with varying degrees of appreciation from the chosen female that ranged from little to none. And the mention of drowning drove the barbarian's stomach into a lurch.

"But you can drown in a teaspoon deep puddle." Ashe replied. "I don't think that's a fair measurement of the 'open sea'."

"Well, do you see any of my other ladies around?" Isaac sounded close enough to backhand now.

"No, none of the businesswomen want to sail with you, Plant Boy." Asheram's smirk was almost audible.

"Then what's wrong with getting a handful or two, really?" Isaac laughed. "It's like my Dad says, 'Grab what you can today, for tomorrow you may be at the bottom of'—"

"Enough!" Lyan suddenly spun around, her face a mask of rage. "No one is touching anything and if anyone even says the word drowning again they will meet my god a piece at a time!"

Ashe and Isaac looked up at the muscular woman, dumbfounded. Both young men sat on either side of a sealed barrel, a small pile of pastries resting on a piece of cloth on the flat surface. Plant

Boy had one of the frosted pastries hanging from his lips and two more in each hand. His green hair, that the Bunny Barbarian thought was actual grass, was the only part of him that moved.

After some silence, Ashe finally spoke. "Lyan, you really should keep your voice down. We are sailing into unknown, possibly enemy controlled territory."

Isaac quickly chewed and swallowed the pastry in his mouth as he nodded in agreement. "Yeah, and could you please tell goth boy here, " Plant Boy pointed at Asheram, "that the chicks still dig me and I'm not getting fat from too many sweets?"

"Sweets" took Lyan's stomach one lurch too far and the barbarian turned around and vomited over the ship's railing. Both young men were unsure how to proceed beyond the look of concern on their faces.

Thankfully, the door that led below decks, just out of reach of smacking Isaac, opened and two clerics stepped out into the cool predawn air. First came Samson, the muscular herald, who had to slouch to fit through the doorway. After him came Organa.

She was the same height as Isaac, that is to say, about a head shorter than Asheram. She wore the same white robes as all clerics of the Order of Kuan Yin, as well as a jade talisman hanging from her neck that was carved after the likeness of the goddess as she appeared on Harbenigyr's sash. Her auburn hair was braided up on either side of her head and wound up into circles that covered her ears. Something she was especially thankful for when it was cold as it was at the moment.

Samson's eyes locked on Ashe and Isaac as he passed on his way up to the bow. They both shrugged back at him, feeling as if they were being accused of something without a word being spoken.

"Perhaps you should go below and try to get some sleep." Organa stepped up beside Lyan as the barbarian finished her business over the railing. "Everyone else has had a chance and we won't be on the water much longer."

Lyan shook her head. "A Yo Bunpy warrior can go days without sleep if necessary." She breathed a silent sigh of relief when she heard that they wouldn't be on the boat much longer.

"But is it necessary?" Organa rested a gentle hand on the other woman's shoulder. "We will need you sharp if there's going to be a battle."

Lyan shrugged the cleric's hand off. "I will be. As soon as I am off this accursed flotsam." And with that, she stomped back toward the aft of the ship.

Organa turned to join Samson on the bow, giving Ashe and Isaac a kind wave as she walked past. "I told you she digs me." Isaac snickered at Ashe, elbowing him in the ribs. The woman couldn't help but giggle as she stopped beside the tall, thickly muscled cleric at the front of the ship.

"I've never seen her like this." Organa leaned forward against the railing as she spoke.

Samson grunted. "It's the first time I've heard of her getting on a ship willingly, too." He held out a small vial of yellow liquid that rested on a thick piece of cloth. "Harbenigyr said I would have to use this to get her aboard."

"Do you think it's going to be as bad as she says?" Organa turned and rested the small of her back against the railing. "That the Light Bringers and our Order are going to be wiped out if we fail?"

With a softness that was surprising from a man his size, Samson cradled Organa's shoulders. "Remember that monk that helped us realize we should be together?"

She looked at him quizzically. "Jin Vega? What about him?"

"He told us that he had failed in his mission to save his master." Samson's deep voice had a soothing effect on Organa despite his words. "But then he said he wouldn't have found the peace he did in Dianmeyer, or met us if he hadn't left his people after his master's death."

"What's your point?" Her hands glided up and down Samson's arm.

The large cleric smiled, the little tuft of hair on his lip, listing to the side. "No matter what happens, good will find its way out of it."

"It will still be better if we succeed." Lyan chimed in as she stepped up to the bow.

She came up from the side opposite where Ashe and Isaac sat, so the Bunny Barbarian must have taken to pacing around the ship. Both clerics nodded back at her in a combination of greeting and agreement as Lyan continued around the ship.

The barbarian woman made several laps around the deck and up to the bow before she heard the man from the crow's nest, only about twelve feet off the deck but it still counted, call out that he spotted land. Ashe and Isaac rushed up beside Lyan, Plant Boy's collapsible telescope already extended and up to the young man's eye.

"There are rocks along the northwest shore." The ship captain said as he scanned the shoreline of Loch Aeris. "We'll have to land you just south of those."

"You have sharp eyes, Isaac." Josie said as she stepped up behind him. "Too bad you didn't take up archery."

Plant Boy jumped in surprise at her voice, letting out a noise that he was thankful the rest of his crew didn't get a chance to hear. The red haired half-elf rubbed the last of the sleep from her eyes, chuckling at his reaction.

"So there are ogres in there somewhere." Josie scanned the treeline with her emerald green eyes, not bothering with a telescope.

Lyan nodded. "Along with griffins and skeletons."

Samson frowned as Isaac started ordering his men to ready a small rowboat for the landing party. "And how are five people meant to stop such a force?" The herald asked.

"One problem at a time. First, we find Ophelia." Lyan started for the rowboat being lowered over the side.

Josie, Ashe, Samson, and Organa followed suit. Even though she reached it first, Lyan helped everyone else onto the smaller boat without boarding herself.

"I'll provide you with what cover we can before you get too far into the trees. Then we'll wait for you to come back." Isaac gave the barbarian woman a gentlemanly bow, taking her hand and helping her into the boat without any hint of duplicity. "Just don't come back being chased by anything violent. Dad's still plenty steamed at me for sinking my last ship."

The rowboat was lowered into the water before Lyan could have any second thoughts. Samson took up the oars and the group was on their way to the shore.

The sky was just starting to show signs of dawn readying to make its appearance with dark purple hues and Lyan knew that the ship was the fastest way they could aid Ophelia. Even now, she knew the rowboat was faster than swimming to the bank herself but, at least then, her fate would be in her own hands and not left to a piece of wood between her and the water. Still, she stayed in the boat and Samson had them on land sooner than even the Bunny Barbarian had hoped possible.

Lyan was the first off, almost tipping the boat over in her haste. Samson plunged an arm into the water up to his shoulder to keep everyone else dry and stop the small craft from capsizing. Having solid ground, if not completely dry, under her furry boot seemed to bring some sense back to the Bunny Barbarian and she aided everyone else off the boat, giving the herald a quickly muttered apology as they both pulled the boat out of the water enough to keep it from washing away.

Everyone pulled their weapons out of the supplies. Lyan gave her spear a couple of practice swings and thrusts to loosen up her broad shoulders. Josie held a loosely strung arrow in her bow. Ashe slipped a finger into his spell book on a page holding a couple of his preferred enchantments.

Organa's mace had a jade head that seemed more ceremonial than functional but Samson didn't seem to have a weapon at all. He simply pulled out a pair of leather gloves and slipped them onto his meaty hands.

Adjusting her shield against her scarred arm, Lyan looked over her party of warriors. Not exactly Yo Bunpy elite, although she could attest to Josie's prowess in battle. The rest, though, the Bunny Barbarian wasn't sure would last to the end of the day.

"Let's go find Ophelia so I can get back to my little girl." Josie finally said, breaking Lyan out of her pre-battle reflection.

Only a few steps into the trees, the party heard an inhuman bellow echo through the woods. Then what sounded like a stampede grew louder and louder with each second. Each of the party members took up defensive positions, waiting to see the source of the noise, when four ogres smashed down a clump of trees and charged straight for them.

Lyan smashed the base of her spear into the dirt. Bracing it with her foot, she angled the sharp head at one of the charging beasts. The rabbit shaped blade buried itself deep into his chest, the ogre's momentum carried the creature over the barbarian's head like some ghastly pole vault. Dead, the ogre rolled and knocked down the few trees that were between the party and the beach, exposing the combatants to the view of the floating ship.

Ashe muttered something that no one could understand, not even opening his book, and several green arrows appeared out of thin air and launched at another ogre, striking it in the chest, throat and cheek to join the two already in its eyes from Josie's bow. Although, after Josie's arrows struck, they didn't erupt into molten metal like those from the young wizard to separate what was left of the thing's head from its furry body.

Much to the barbarian's surprise, the gloved fist of the herald smashed between his ogre opponent's legs, forcing it to a dead stop as he stood between it and Organa, whose eyes were closed as she chanted. Then a loud pop came from the water.

"Incoming!" Josie yelled as she dove to the ground.

Samson wrapped both arms around the woman cleric and pulled her into the dirt, his body lying on top of hers, just as a cannonball streaked through the air and cratered the ground between the two remaining ogres and sent them flying.

The last ogre struggled to lift itself back to its feet, wrapping two ham fists around the trunk of a splintered tree that was barely standing itself. Lyan stepped up in front of the beast, her spear dripping from the blood of the other it just slayed.

"If you value your life, you should stay down." The barbarian offered advice to the defeated creature.

The ogre's eyes narrowed and, with a heavy grunt, it wrenched the tree from what was left of its stump and threw it at Lyan. The woman ducked under it easily and brought her spear up under the beast's chin, thrusting the tip deep into the creature's head. Pulling the weapon free, Lyan flicked the blood away from the spear's rabbit shaped blade as the ogre's head landed back in the dirt with a heavy thud.

The sound of splashing could be heard as the tree the ogre threw landed in the water. Then the faint, echoing of Isaac's voice drifted from the water. "Plug that leak! Man the bilge pump!"

"Plant Boy's Dad isn't going to be happy about this." Ashe said before they continued into the trees.

CHAPTER

FOURTEEN

LYAN, JOSIE, ASHE, Organa and Samson followed the trail of felled trees that were left behind by the ogres that attacked them. Leaving such a trail of destruction was unusual even for such graceless creatures.

Lyan wondered about that. Being on the warpath was one thing. Those ogres, though, didn't even seem to notice her party even when they were practically on top of them. And then they left a trail even a blind and deaf halfling could follow all the way back to their camp? Something wasn't right about this.

"Lyan? Lyan, is that you?" A muffled voice came faintly on the wind.

Standing on top of a pile of three toppled trees, the Bunny Barbarian looked around. Most of the forest was still standing, fog clinging to the evergreens helping give plenty of cover to possible enemies. Lyan couldn't see anyone but her party in the quickly growing light of dawn, and she knew the voice wasn't any of theirs, but she decided to risk replying.

"Who's there?" Lyan called, although not as loudly as she could have.

"It's Havarti, my dear." The faint voice echoed. "You needn't worry. Most of the ogres have left this area but I, myself, am a bit stuck."

"Havarti?" The Bunny Barbarian walked in the direction of the bastard sword's voice. "Is Ophelia with you?"

"Unfortunately not." The weapon answered, although Lyan wasn't quite sure from where. "She left several hours ago with that Caleb rascal, masquerading as a svartalfar messenger."

"Svartalfar messenger?" Josie asked, her gaze moving up a thickly canopied tree. "How could she pull that off?"

"Nyphistra painted her black and fused svartalfar ears onto hers." Lyan quickly said before calling out to Havarti. "Why did she leave you behind?"

"For her plan to succeed Ophelia needed to rid herself of anything that could be recognizable as hers. And I'm not easily concealable, even in my current condition."

"And what is your current condition?" Lyan asked as Josie pulled her bow from her shoulder, motioning up toward the top of a nearby tree.

"I am currently packed into that leather pou-aaAHH!" As Havarti spoke, Josie loosed an arrow that snapped the branch the crimson bundle of silk had been resting on.

The bastard sword screamed all the way down into the dirt and needles lining the ground. When the bundle landed, though, Lyan frowned. There was no way the sword could have fit into it the way the silk was tied.

Havarti made a sound that would have been clearing his throat if he had one. "As I was saying, I'm currently packed into that leather pouch we used to conceal your spear upon our escape from the Lytyl tunnels."

Lyan nodded as she untied the bundle, revealing Ophelia's rolled up leather coat and Havarti's hilt tucked into the leather pouch he described. The barbarian picked up the bastard sword by the handle, which was half the length as normal, and pulled the gilded scabbard effortlessly from the enchanted leather.

"May I?" Ashe spoke up for the first time, pointing to the pouch.

Lyan tossed the little bag to the wizard as she straightened up. "Do you know which way Ophelia went?" She asked the sword.

"West by southwest." Havarti answered. "But I don't suppose that you could put on the coat and carry me that way? I fear I would otherwise be a hindrance since you no longer have the weapon belt from the guard armor."

The Bunny Barbarian's ears waved back and forth as she shook her head. "I couldn't fit my shoulders in it."

Lyan looked over at Josie, who shook her head. The long coat's armored sleeve would weigh down her shooting arm. Samson had the same issue Lyan did. Ashe refused as well, the weight would be a hindrance to casting spells.

Finally, her gaze fell on Organa. She was smaller than Ophelia but she didn't have to shoot a bow or cast spells using talismans, ingredients or gestures so Lyan held the coat up to the cleric. The woman looked from the barbarian to Josie then Samson uneasily.

"You won't expect me to use you, will you?" Organa focused on the sword, not sure what part she would look at.

"Oh, goodness no, dear." Havarti responded. "It would feel as if both of us were doing something improper. Ophelia is the only one who shall use me unless absolutely necessary."

The cleric let out a soft sigh. "Okay then." Organa caught the coat when Lyan tossed it to her and slipped it on.

She was quite a bit shorter than Ophelia. The red leather reached down to around her ankles and the coat hung on her so loosely it looked as if she was about to be swallowed by it. Lyan stepped behind the shorter woman, slipping the bastard sword into the little slot just below the collar of the garment.

As for Havarti, he started to let out a contented sigh but stopped himself. "Hmm... it just isn't quite the same." Both he and Organa both seemed to shift uncomfortably against each other.

Lyan looked around the surrounding trees. "So which way did she go?"

"That way." Organa's right arm suddenly shot out to point to the southwest as Havarti spoke.

The cleric's face clearly showed her horror when her body suddenly moved independently of her will. Organa looked over at Samson, who glared at the sword menacingly but otherwise didn't say anything.

"Maybe you should not move Organa's limbs without her permission next time." Lyan smirked back at the hilt of the sword.

"Oh, yes, of course. My apologizes, dear." Havarti mumbled as the group started moving again.

The destruction caused by the ogres that attacked Lyan and the others stopped almost immediately after the tree where they recovered Havarti. Other trails of crushed trees, though, lead off to the north and south.

"What happened here?" Lyan asked the sword.

"I can't say with any certainty." Havarti spoke from over Organa's shoulder. "All I do know is that a short time ago, the ogres started fighting amongst themselves and then scattered to the winds. Some of them with more enthusiasm than others."

Lyan grunted, continuing down the faint trail that the bastard sword indicated. Aside from the massive ogre foot prints, the barbarian could make out what looked like skeleton feet but they moved oddly, as if they were carrying something heavy and struggling with the weight.

"Havarti, did Caleb believe Ophelia's story?" The signs of skeleton prints troubled the barbarian.

The weapon responded so suddenly it made Organa flinch. "He certainly seemed to. Caleb even stopped an ogre from attacking her before she mounted his throne and left the camp."

Lyan's brow furrowed. "Mounted his throne?"

"Caleb arrived on a wooden throne that was carried by a group of skeleton shoulders much like the ones that * harumph * escorted us to the Lytyl Tribe tunnels." Havarti explained. "She took his seat to sell the idea that she was an arrogant svartalfar more thoroughly."

"Yeah, that's a stretch." Josie let out a sarcastic chuckle.

Harumph.

The edge of the barbarian's worry ceased but it didn't disappear completely. The ogres were no longer a threat for some reason. That meant that Ophelia probably had some amount of success with her plan. But it also left Lyan without a chance for payback against the massive beasts.

That left an unknown amount of griffins, undead and their generals to contend against. Still plenty of threats to face ahead.

They kept walking, the light steadily growing but everything stayed gray, as if the sun was unwilling to give anything color yet. A large white structure came into view as they neared a clearing. Again, the party readied their weapons.

Lyan motioned for Organa to come up beside her, at the same time motioning Samson to stay back. "Havarti, is that where Ophelia went?" The woman cleric frowned when the barbarian addressed the sword and not her, to which Lyan only responded with a pat on the woman's shoulder.

"I would presume so. I'm afraid I lost any meaningful contact with her about halfway from the ogre camp to here."

Lyan grunted, then let out a whistle that sounded like a spring canary's song toward Josie. All she had to do was point at her own eyes and the half-elf archer was immediately climbing up a tree.

A whistle came back down to the barbarian that sounded like the cry of a baby swallow. Lyan looked up and saw Josie balancing on a branch that looked far too thin and brittle to handle her weight. With a shake of her head, the archer indicated that there was no visible enemy.

"Okay, everyone head for the tent." Lyan ordered, reversing her grip on her spear so it could be thrown with ease.

Josie stayed up in the tree, an arrow in her bow ready to loose at the slightest sign of an attack. Lyan and Organa stepped into the clearing first and were well over halfway across the open terrain before the two men followed, the young wizard's hand looking as if it was encased in metal thanks to some kind of defensive enchantment. It reminded the archer of the claw Ashe's father wore.

Once all four had crossed the clearing without incident, Josie was quickly back down the tree and beside them in short order. They entered the tent only after the wizard checked for any kind of enchantments meant to snare unaware intruders. There were none.

The room they entered was much smaller than the rest of the tent. All there was inside was a small square table and four heavily cushioned chairs. It smelled of spilled wine and blood to Lyan.

Looking at the floor, she could make out what looked like four sets of footprints. One pair had definitely been Ophelia's, the barbarian recognized her boot pattern. Two others looked like men's boots, one a lighter, thinner man while the other was heavier, more than likely wearing armor. Lyan had an idea who those two were and growled. The third set dwarfed the others and the woman couldn't make them belong to anything. They were far too large for a human and their weight dispersal seemed... impossible.

"It looks like they force fed Ophelia wine." Josie said quietly, doing the same thing as Lyan. "She was off balance then attacked the heavier of the two men."

"Caleb." Lyan said. "I don't know the lighter man's name but he was the one that captured us on Etigran Pass. I don't know what this third set of tracks could be from."

Josie stepped up beside Lyan, looking just as confused. "He was the last one in. Whatever he was, he came in from a different part of the tent than Caleb came back and forth from." The archer pointed at the lone set of tracks, the only ones that weren't trampled over in the entire room. "Ophelia blinked, that would explain the gap in her tracks. She backed up toward the entrance... then I think she killed Caleb."

Ashe's green eyebrows pressed together. "Where did she get a weapon? She had to leave Havarti behind."

"Most of me, yes." The bastard sword replied. "She did take the dagger I usually have hidden in my handle as her only means of defense."

Organa walked beside the massive tracks that no one could identify back to the flaps from which they emerged. "You better have a look at this." She waved everyone over after she peeked her head into the next room.

At the back of the room was a short hill that was concealed by the immensity of the tent. At the back of the room, immediately in front of the incline of dirt, was a massive mirror. The glass of the mirror was a square large enough to reflect Lyan Yo Bunpy's entire body on the surface, including her helmet's ears, but it didn't show the Bunny Barbarian as she stepped around Organa and into that portion of the tent. Instead, the glass showed a room that Lyan didn't recognize specifically, however, the architecture was familiar.

"It's some kind of portal generator, I think." Asheram said as the young wizard stepped into the room behind the barbarian. "When it isn't actively transporting people, it defaults into some kind of screen that can be used for communication. Do you recognize the place?"

Lyan grunted as she stepped up to the mirror. The frame, some pewter colored metal that the barbarian couldn't recognize, had a shape that mounted flush with the surrounding the glass but also contoured against the hillside behind it. Lyan hadn't noticed it from a distance but the mirror was slightly inclined, as well. It was like the mirror was custom made to sit on this spot.

The barbarian's brown eyes narrowed as she tried to find something familiar in the room beyond the frame. "It is inside the fortress where the Lytyl held us."

"You're sure?" The wizard's brow furrowed as he stepped up to the mirror, his fingertip lightly brushing along the pewter frame.

Lyan frowned when she did finally see one familiar thing in the room. "Yes. That carpet with the runes must have been moved here after the Inquisitor questioned Ophelia. That blood on the rune, the one that looks like an eyeball with legs, is Ophelia's from the Judicator's torture."

Ashe looked confused. "Inquisitor? Judicator? I'm not familiar with those terms."

Lyan had forgotten until that moment that, despite the young man's albino pale skin, he was actually part svartalfar himself.

From a different tribe and he hadn't lived underground a day in his life, but still, he knew much about the culture even if he didn't live it himself.

"Nyphistra created it for the Lytyl Tribe." Lyan stepped up and hammered the side of her fist into the mirror's glass.

Her movement was so quick and unexpected that Asheram couldn't stop her. The surface of the mirror rippled like water around her hand, creating a sound that was more shrill than the screeching of a colony of bats. The noise made both Lyan and Ashe step away from the mirror, covering their ears.

"Why did you do that?!" The wizard asked, the pointed tips of his ears peeking out between his pasty fingers.

"Why does everything have to have a reason?" Lyan growled, her gauntlet wrapped hands doing little to block out the noise. "Why didn't the glass break?"

"Because it's not glass!" The noise ended just as the wizard yelled that, then he continued at his normal volume. "It's a quantum locked dimensional rift represented by a fold in the fabric of space contained in the frame to link here with the room on the other side."

Just listening to that sentence made Lyan's head hurt. Apparently, the look on her face told the young wizard as much.

Ashe busied himself by pressing down the folds that had formed in his black school uniform. "A portal. An inactive one, which is why you weren't flung through back to the very people that captured you in the first place!" For the first time, he appeared annoyed with the Bunny Barbarian.

Suddenly, movement in the room on the other side of the mirror caught Lyan's eye. It was just at the edge of the visible area of the room but Lyan and Ashe both instinctively rushed to either side of the mirror frame to avoid being seen. The barbarian pressed her face just to the inside edge of the frame, avoiding the not-glass, to see if she could see the source.

A door opened in the other room, revealing a female figure but it was too dim in the room for Lyan to see who it was for certain. "Ashe, can this portal be opened from either side?" She whispered, not sure if the woman on the other side could hear but the Bunny Barbarian didn't want to take the chance.

Ashe's silent nod told Lyan that the figure would indeed be able to hear them as he pressed himself against the frame on the opposite side of the mirror to avoid detection. Lyan waved for Organa and the others, who had barely stepped into the room, to get out. This section of the tent looked empty as the svartalfar on the other side lit a lantern before turning to face whatever mirror was on her side.

"Perett, what do you need?" The Inquisitor's voice was distorted but recognizable as it came through the mirror. "Our forces have amassed outside Dianmeyer and we're on schedule attack at sunse..."

The svartalfar's voice trailed off as she realized that the lich wasn't standing on the other side of the inactive portal. Her eyes narrowed as she scanned the white canvas room.

"Ophelia, is that you?" The Inquisitor's voice took a mocking tone. "Perett told me everything you said to him last night. The poor clerics being left to rot by their so called friends in the Romefeller Guild and even by the battle hungry Yo Bunpy. I guess even they can smell a lost cause."

The svartalfar couldn't see the barbarian or the wizard on either side of the mirror. Unfortunately, Lyan couldn't see her either without risking being spotted at the edge of the frame.

"Perett did say that the potion would have killed you by now but, like most men, I think he underestimated your cleverness. Still, your hundred some cleric friends will be killed by our over a thousand svartalfar strong war machine before you can even hope to make it back to help." The Inquisitor continued, laughing as she spoke. "If by help you mean dying beside them in a futile gesture, that is."

Ashe's forehead looked ready to crumple as he looked over at Lyan, trying to figure out what she was doing. The barbarian woman, pressing her body tightly against the frame, reached up and wrapped both hands around the top of the pewter metal.

"How does it feel to be completely alone again, Ophelia?" Small screeches came from the mirror again as the Inquisitor pressed her hands against the glass on her side of the portal. "Your old friend Nyphistra shall share your pain, at least for a minute when the Matriarch and I turn her ribcage inside out for her treacherous ways!"

Ashe's eyes opened wide when Lyan suddenly wrenched back on the mirror. He shuffled out of its way as the massive mirror teetered over and finally met the flat ground. The young wizard coughed, waving away the cloud of dust left in the mirror's wake.

The Inquisitor's muffled laughing could still be heard through the mirror on the ground. "And don't worry about Lyan Yo Bunpy. I'll find her corpse in Dianmeyer, peel her skin from her body and make it into a new corset. She is rather large, perhaps I'll make a matching garter belt!"

After a few seconds, the dust settled and Asheram was finally able to see around himself. Lyan stood on the back of the mirror, her muscular back to the young elf wizard. Before her was the mouth of a cave that just happened to be the exact same size as the frame that had formerly been mounted in front of it.

"What is this?" Lyan asked.

"Almost surely the cave Perett used for his initial contact with the Lytyl Tribe." Ashe stepped up beside her, avoiding the jagged edges of the mirror's frame. "It's easier to create permanently linked portals with open air between them rather than tons of stone and dirt."

"And the cave makes it so there is open space between here and the Lytyl keep." The barbarian figured.

The wizard nodded. "Why did you knock over the mirror? The link is still active under there, you know."

"But the Inquisitor won't be able to come through." Lyan answered and then motioned to the cave. "The frame's too heavy for her so if she wanted to come here, she'd have to take the long way."

"Why would she come here?" Asheram turned for the flaps where the rest of the party waited. "All her plans revolve around Dianmeyer and killing the Vizier."

"She really doesn't like Ophelia." Lyan stepped off the mirror and back onto the packed dirt.

"So the Inquisitor would jeopardize her whole plan just to kill her?" Ashe held the flap open for the Bunny Barbarian as she stepped through into the room with the table.

"The Inquisitor just might have, if she had the portal as a shortcut." Lyan said. "Ophelia has a way of motivating people in that regard."

The barbarian strode out of the tent and started looking up at the rapidly brightening sky, which had finally obtained a shade of blue. The others followed her out to stand beside one of the many extinguished fires lining up beside the tent.

"It is just past dawn." Lyan muttered, shielding her eyes from the growing light. "Perett is surely attacking the Light Bringers by now so we have to figure where the battle has been joined."

"You figuring that Ophelia will be where the action is?" Josie slung her bow over her shoulder.

Lyan nodded. "She killed Caleb and got out of the tent. If she didn't die in the woods from whatever poison Perett gave her, she will be out there looking for some payback."

As she spoke, the Bunny Barbarian noticed some griffins swooping through the air. They dove, the trees obscuring their target or destination, some distance due west of where the party currently stood.

"With the ogres no longer on his side for some reason," Lyan pointed in the direction of the flying beasts. "Perett is likely to up the griffins' role in the attack. So we go where they are."

CHAPTER

FIFTEEN

THE SOUNDS OF battle started to fill the forest as the party made their way west. All had their weapons ready and Organa was already starting to quietly chant prayers of aid and protection as they walked.

The trees became sparser as they neared another clearing. On the south side, men in armor wielding shields and swords, the insignias on their chests showing them to be the Light Bringers, deflected beaks and claws as griffins stalked and lunged at them from the north end.

What was harder on the men, though, were the griffins that dove into them from above. More than one Light Bringer was snatched from the ground, hoisted into the air and then dropped to fall in a dead heap into the grass.

Arrows whistled into the air around the beasts that swooped and dodged until they saw an opening to sink their talons into another armored soldier. Still, half-eagle half-lion bodies were strewn across the clearing in much the same numbers as the men that fought against them.

Then something none of the party expected happened. A group of ogres knocked down trees at the far side of the clearing from Lyan and her party and charged into the fray. Even more surprising was when an ogre snatched up one of the heavy trunks and swatted a dive bombing griffin out of the air!

It wasn't a fluke. More than one of the furry giants tackled and beat on the winged beasts. Even before Josie loosed her first arrow and Lyan and the others closed the distance, the tide of the battle had turned in the Light Bringers' favor.

Lyan was the first of the party to meet body to body with an enemy griffin, her spear skewering the beast's throat. Samson grabbed two handfuls of beak that lunged for him, snapping it in half before it could bite down on him.

As the Bunny Barbarian and the cleric herald sank deeper and deeper into the fray, Ashe slung arcs of lightning, plumes of flame and other spells into the violent mass of figures. Josie kept launching arrow after arrow into the beasts, quickly eating through the supply in her quiver, though she didn't even touch three black arrows that were tucked into a thin pocket on the side. Organa kept chanting prayers as she stood beside the archer, not using her mace as a weapon against the griffins, much to the chagrin of Havarti, who shook to and fro on the woman's back.

The tide of the Light Bringers, not attacking anything with less than four legs, finally overtook the party and the griffins were driven away from Lyan and the others. The front of the battle moving away from them, the Yo Bumpy and those from Dianmeyer started getting confused looks from the Light Bringer archers, magicians and officers that made their way to their location. The Bunny Barbarian grinned a wide grin when she saw a familiar face approach astride a magnificent looking horse.

"Ho there!" The Light Bringer officer held up a metal stump where his right hand used to be in greeting.

"Ho there, Collen!" Lyan reached up and took the man's other hand in response.

The dirty blonde hair of the Light Bringer bobbed as he nodded and smiled at Josie, who returned the greeting. The man was in the same armor as always, with the symbol of a sword with streams of light radiating from it on his chest. It even had a tiny spot of corrosion, not big enough to affect the overall strength of the armor, that he'd never bothered to get fixed for some reason on the left side of his chest. But Lyan just couldn't shake the thought that something didn't look quite right about what he was wearing.

Then Collen noticed the two in white robes. "Are they from the Order of Kuan Yin?" He asked Lyan.

She looked back at Samson and Organa. "They are."

A look of relief crossed over the mounted man's face as he called to the clerics. "We could really use your help! Many of our own healers were wounded themselves and the rest are over tasked with the injuries the griffins are causing."

Collen called up a Light Bringer to guide them. Both clerics marched after him for where the healers were stationed, which wasn't far. Lyan could still make out Organa's strangely braided hair as she bent down over her first patient.

"What are you now?" Lyan rested a hand on the neck of the Light Bringer's stallion. "A General?"

Collen bit down on his lower lip. "I'm just a Colonel, actually. But I'm in command of the forces repelling Perett's attack." He confessed as he slid from his saddle.

Despite his meekness, Collen wasn't that much smaller than the Bunny Barbarian in height or muscle. As his soft leather boots met the ground, the Light Bringer turned and pulled his shield from the mounting on his horse's rump. It had a clever, custom made mechanism that attached it to the stump of his right wrist and forearm.

"How did you find out about the attack?" Lyan asked as Josie and Ashe stepped up just behind her.

"We were initially warned by Nyphistra. She and I have been corresponding secretly for a long time now." The Colonel said. "That got us at least facing the right direction. But it wasn't until two hours ago that we got the specific intelligence telling us about this Perett character and the ogres. Ophelia told us that the ogres were no longer a threat so we could concentrate our numbers here."

"Where is she, anyway?" Josie asked, her emerald eyes scanning the battlefield.

A ruckus rose off to the barbarian's right, causing her and Collen to reflexively raise their shields. A woman riding the back of a charging griffin barreled through the Light Bringer lines.

The beast had one wing hacked away, so it couldn't fly, and it struggled to twist its head back far enough to snap its beak at its unwanted mount. The woman's black boot kicked against the griffin's head, the dagger in her left hand chipping yet another piece away from the yellow bone of the beast's beak, even as the sword in her right finally plunged into the griffin's ribcage, just under the base of the amputated wing.

As the now dead creature skidded to a halt. A couple of Light Bringers rushed up and helped the woman back up to her feet. Flipping her brunette hair out of her face, Ophelia's baby blue eyes came into view. She still had pointed ears, although most of the black make up from her forehead to her jawline had long since rubbed off. The same thing could be said for her chest, it was mostly back to her normal skin tone except for immediately around the low cut material of the dress itself. As Ophelia made her way over to Collen, Lyan and the others, the barbarian heard the young wizard gulp.

"Is it wrong that I think she kind of looks enticing in those ears?" Ashe muttered, rubbing the back of his neck in embarrassment. "This is going to cause me so many issues..."

Despite the obviously strenuous physical activity the woman had been undergoing, the svartalfar made dress was in remarkably good shape with little more than grass stains where Ophelia's knees had met the ground to betray the wear it had been under.

"I thought I saw some sparkling blue over here." Ophelia grinned wide, reaching around Lyan's broad shoulders to give the Bunny Barbarian a tight embrace.

With a spear in one hand and a shield mounted on the other, Lyan simply stood, smiling awkwardly in response to the other woman's greeting. When she saw the rest of the party over Lyan's shoulder, Ophelia didn't bother to try and hide her surprise.

"Josie? Ashe? What are you two doing here?" She stepped around Lyan to face the other two members of the party."

"We came with Lyan from Dianmeyer." Josie answered as she gave Ophelia her own quick embrace. "The Grand Cleric thought you and the Light Bringers could use the help."

Ophelia knew what that meant. Whenever the red-haired woman referred to him by his title it was common knowledge that his wife was upset with him. But an angry Josie was also a focused Josie, which meant that she would be that much better of a fighter in this battle.

The mercenary turned her attention to Asheram and gave him a little wolf whistle. "And why haven't you been where I've been drinking, Ashe?"

The young wizard's cheeks, which were already flushed to begin with, just got darker and most anyone could practically see steam rising from them. Ophelia laughed and gave him a quick peck on his cheek before she turned to the Light Bringer.

"You were right, Collen." She said to the Colonel. "Most of the ogres didn't understand why they were going to attack you in the first place. Once Caleb was dead, the ones that didn't leave decided to help us against Perett."

"Having us take off our capes was a brilliant suggestion, Ophelia." The Colonel replied. "That way we didn't even have the 'red cape' moniker to be used against us."

Now Lyan realized what was bugging her about Collen and the other Light Bringers' armor. The red capes they usually wore were nowhere to be seen. Odd that an entire army's strategy could be changed by simply not wearing one article of clothing, although there had been battles decided on less.

"Wait a second." Josie made her presence known to Collen and Ophelia again. "Once Caleb was dead? What does one man have to do with an army of ogres fighting or not?"

"Caleb was one of Perett's generals. He was controlling the ogres and making them fight at his command. Perett's other General, named Virgil," Ophelia raised her hand above her head to represent someone taller than her and Lyan understood just who the other woman meant, "Is controlling the griffins. Although I haven't seen him out on the field yet."

A Light Bringer messenger ran up to Collen, his armor dented from battle but otherwise unscathed. "Sir, the griffins are retreating into the tree line to the north. Did you want us to pursue?"

Collen shook his head at the other Light Bringer. "No, have the men rally back here and regroup."

Once the messenger was on his way, Ophelia pulled out a string with a griffin feather and what looked like a small bone attached to it. "Each of Perett's Generals control a type of creature that's a portion of his forces. Perrett and Virgil use talismans like these to give the others at least partial control over the other creatures, too. This was Caleb's. I think the feather gives the wearer the ability to command the griffins—"

"Why didn't you just command them to go away with that one, then?" Ashe chimed in, folding his arms across his chest.

"And why didn't Perett and Virgil use their ogre controlling totems to keep them on their side?" Josie chimed in.

"It only works on a few that are immediately around you." Ophelia explained. "And, you know, not doing stabby things to them at the time. I figured that out when one grabbed me just outside of Perett's tent when I escaped."

"What about the bone?" Lyan asked, mirroring Asheram's pose.

"That gives you control over undead like the skeletons that attacked me and Lyan." The mercenary answered.

"We haven't faced any undead yet." Collen straightened up, trying to see over all of his troops to scan what little of the battlefield they weren't occupying. "Do they have to wait until nightfall to come out?"

Ophelia suddenly let out a curse.

"What?" Lyan, Collen, Josie and Ashe all said.

"We're spread out all over." The mercenary said. "Collen sent out word to regroup but it'll take an at least an hour to get everyone back here and organized. This is what Perett wants: Us all over the place and unable to communicate."

"Have I mentioned how much I despise intelligent women?" The lich suddenly appeared, his furred robes billowing as the very air around him exploded, sending armored soldiers flying in every direction. "They spoil surprises and take the drama out of a good entrance."

Collen ducked as a limp Light Bringer flew over him but his horse was toppled by another lower ranked soldier caught in the blast. Lyan crouched into a defensive stance, her spear already pointed at the newly revealed lich. Another soldier flew into Ophelia, who blinked somewhere out of the barbarian's view, while a glowing red tower shield appeared in front of Ashe to shield him and Josie from the debris and other flying soldiers.

"If you dislike women, perhaps allying with the svartalfar was not the best idea!" Lyan started to slowly circle around Perrett, her spear resting in the natural notch that was created where the edge of her shield and her arm met.

Ophelia didn't mention that Perett was undead himself and also a magician by the looks of it. Lyan couldn't help but wonder if the element he preferred to use as a weapon was lightning. Josie's fingertips brushed over the feathers of her black arrows but, living or dead, Perett didn't appear to be svartalfar so she instead pulled one of her remaining standard arrows and readied to shoot.

Collen followed suit with Lyan, circling around Perett's other side to force him to face two separate targets. The Light Bringers that weren't blown away by Perett's arrival started to organize into small groups around him as well.

"The svartalfar are a means to an end, girl." The lich didn't seem concerned that he found himself surrounded. "Virgil sent his beasts to face you just so I could press the advantage the under-dwellers have given me against all of you."

"What advantage is that?" Collen said, his sword between himself and Perett. "You're outnumbered, surrounded and your griffins have been forced to flee!"

The lich arched a hairless brow at the Light Bringer Colonel. "You were the one who figured the undead could only come out at night, yes?"

Collen didn't say anything back. The only response he did make was slowly shifting his shield squarely in front of his body.

"That is a myth, of course." Perett turned his attention up to the sky. "The dead can come forth at any time. Just ask your friends."

With a series of inhuman wails, the Light Bringers that had been slain by the griffins clamored to their feet and attacked the living soldiers that had their attention fixed on the lich. The ones whose arms were broken simply swung their damaged, armor wrapped limbs like clubs. The ones who had their spines or legs shattered, crawled after their living brothers in arms.

A look of horror crossed over Collen's face when he heard his horse and the man who fell into it shuffle to their feet behind him. The Light Bringer heard the undead soldier's feet shift in the dirt as he charged at the Colonel. With an instinct sharpened in battle, Collen turned and lopped off the attacker's head before he was within reach of the undead man's arms.

"Blake." The Light Bringer recognized the man as his head and body fell to the ground separately. "I'm sorry."

The horse wasn't the only beast to rise to its feet. The griffins, too, rose to unlife letting out gurgling shrieks of rage at those mocking them by having blood still pumping within their bodies.

"You do have one point though, Light Bringer." Perett spoke in very even calm tones even as chaos erupted around him. "The sun... it does hurt our eyes."

Out of nowhere, just where the lich seemed to be looking in the sky, black clouds suddenly formed. In moments the sun was blocked from the clearing, stealing all the color from everything around them and leaving it all gray.

"That's much better." Perett grinned as he turned his attention back to Collen and Lyan.

CHAPTER

SIXTEEN

WHEN THE SOLDIER was thrown into Ophelia by the explosion of Perett's arrival, she blinked to the opposite side of the horse only to be thrown to the ground again by a loose Light Bringer gauntlet flung through the air and hitting her across the face.

Shaking her head, the woman looked around to get her bearings and saw... herself. No, wait, it was someone wearing her coat! With Havarti! The woman was standing beside a table that came up above her waist where a Light Bringer was laying on his back.

Jumping to her feet, Ophelia picked up the dagger and sword she was carrying and rushed over to the other woman. Ophelia pushed the dagger half of the bastard sword's handle back into place and used that to pull the woman around to face her.

"Organa?" It wasn't a face she expected to see. "Did you come with Lyan and Josie?"

The shorter woman nodded, still holding a vial of some kind of medicine in her hand. "And Samson, too."

The taller, heavily muscled man was too busy closing the eyes of the Light Bringer that just died on the table in front of him to notice Ophelia and Organa. He shook his head and started whispering a prayer just under his breath.

The man on the table just behind Organa groaned in pain. Even though the gash across his leg looked bad, Organa had already stopped the bleeding so he wasn't in any danger of dying.

"I feel whole again." Havarti let out a contented sigh. "Thank you, my dear."

Ophelia smirked at the hilt of her sword. "Can I get my coat ba—?"

Before the question was even completely out of her mouth, Organa had the long leather off her shoulders and was holding it out to Ophelia. The taller woman reached out with her free hand when she suddenly heard an alarmed gasp come from the bastard sword.

"Ophelia, how could you use a weapon besides me?!" Havarti wailed.

"Oh, uh..." Ophelia quickly tossed the sword over her shoulder and slipped the coat around her body. "It didn't mean anything, Havarti. Honest! I just needed something to keep my head from getting cut off."

"Harumph."

"Don't be that way. You know you're the only sword for—"

A gurgling shriek came from Samson's table. The man who was dead moments before suddenly lunged for the herald's throat with his bare hands. Both men tumbled to the ground as Samson struggled with the corpse's unnatural strength.

"No!" Organa lunged for her jade headed mace leaning against the table.

Ophelia noticed six other men who were just laying down beside the medical station in shredded armor lift themselves to their feet and start straight for her and the cleric. "Hit that thing across the head so we can get Samson and get out of here!"

The mercenary slashed the first undead Light Bringer to come within reach, splitting its head from its neck and then kicking the still standing body into the next one trailing behind it. Decapitation seemed to keep them down for good, as it did for most things. Turning back to see if the woman cleric had done as she ordered, Ophelia saw Samson about to have his jugular bitten into by his former patient.

"Organa, what are you doing?!" Ophelia's rage flared as she turned to the other woman, only to be grabbed by another undead knight and lifted off her feet.

"Oh, ye clingers to unlife..." The cleric woman chanted, pressing her forehead to the smooth stone head of her mace. "I pray for thee this dawn. Oh, ye mockeries of true life, thou undead begone!"

A flash of pale green light, the spiritual energy of the goddess Kuan Yin that her clerics commanded, erupted from the mace and the creatures fell back into natural death. The one atop the herald was quickly rolled off of him and onto the ground. Ophelia fell butt first onto the one that grabbed her, a sickening squelch welcoming her landing on the breastplate of the newly dead again Light Bringer.

The green light continued to glow around the aid station, protecting the wounded closest to Organa and Samson. Ophelia jerked up straight in surprise when the light hit Collen's horse and it collapsed back to the ground, revealing the Light Bringer severing the head of one of his comrades and exposing the Colonel's back to the lich.

The sky almost instantly turned black as thick, pendulous clouds came out of nowhere to block out the sun. No doubt it was Perett's work.

And, as if to confirm it, the lich's eerily red ponytail bobbed as he spoke. "That's much better." He said.

Ophelia jumped to her feet, rushing toward Collen, who was still looking down at the Light Bringer he just chopped down. Perett raised his hand and pointed it at the Light Bringer. Between the lich's fingers was an opal that glinted in a way that wasn't possible in the suddenly limited daylight.

A fireball as big as a man leaped loose from the jewel for the Colonel's back. Ophelia lowered her armored shoulder and shoved with all her strength against Collen's side to knock him out of the path of the flame projectile... and her right into it.

Ophelia felt sunburned when she realized that she'd blinked out of the way, a good second choice since dodging it wasn't possible. The fireball enveloped a dying Light Bringer and the Colonel's steed, the smell of charred horse meat making the woman cringe.

"What was that, Perett?" Ophelia asked as she kicked a crawling undead Light Bringer away from her, his head easily separating from his body thanks to the wound across his throat that killed him. "No declaration of your attack? That's considered a cowardly move in some circles."

Ophelia smirked over at Lyan who changed her grip on her spear to ready herself to throw. The lich chortled back, his hands slipping into the baggy sleeves of his robes.

"Were the man eating zombies and the blotted out sun not enough of a hint?" Perett freed one of his bony hands and it held a diamond that held something moving in the middle of the jewel.

Ophelia sneered. "I see where Caleb got his pansy fighting technique."

The lich grunted. "How is this for a declaration of attack?"

Just as Lyan was going to throw her spear, an eviscerated griffin dropped to the ground in front of her. It shrieked, spraying globs of blood all over Lyan's shield before the spear crushed through the brain cavity of the creature's skull.

Before Lyan even had a chance to pull her spear free, an ice dragon's head grew from the diamond in Perett's hand and breathed the equivalent of a blizzard at the barbarian. Snow, making her skin cold and sensitive to the damage, and razor sharp chunks of ice pelted and sliced into her arms, legs and torso. The only part of her spared from the onslaught was her face and chest behind her wooden shield.

When the dragon's head disappeared, Lyan fell to her knees. Thin cuts lined her arms and legs, an icicle impaled her left shoulder, to add to her collection on of scars on that arm, and two through her muscular right thigh. The Bunny Barbarian was still conscious but her breaths came heavy with enraged growls.

"Or perhaps this?" Perett opened his mouth wide, wider than a skull coated in skin should be able.

One of his molars glinted with gold as his face turned toward Ashe and Josie. A buzzing sound grew louder and louder from the lich's mouth until, finally, his head reared back as if it was a cannon that had just fired a shot.

A sound like a swarm of enraged hornets screamed across the clearing and struck the young wizard's tower shield. The mystical defense cracked and Ashe stumbled back off balance but stayed on his feet.

Perett's head reared back again and Ashe's shield was again struck. This time, noticeable chunks flew away from the magical construct and the wizard fell to the ground.

Josie loosed an arrow through one of the newly made gaps in the energy shield as Perett screamed out another shot. The arrow and the invisible force of sound met, and the shaft of the arrow shook and bent in the turbulence but continued to its target, striking the lich in his eye.

The sound, though, also continued on its way. Josie tried to pull the wizard out of the spell's path but Ashe pushed her away just as his shield shattered and he took the full strength of the invisible force, laying him out flat on his back. Ophelia couldn't tell if he was alive or dead from her location.

Josie saw the young man who was family in every meaningful way lying limp in the grass. Suddenly a scream of fury only a mother could have roared from her mouth and arrow after arrow flew into the lich. The archer marched closer and closer to the undead villain, each shot hitting Perett and with more force after each step.

The lich doubled over after his other eye, his jerky like throat and his narrow chest were hit twice but Josie kept shooting. An arrow buried itself in the crown of Perett's head and he buckled down to his knees.

Josie would have kept shooting but she ran out of arrows about three steps away from the lich. Her hand went for one of the black ones she'd held in reserve when a marionette made of green...

something tumbled from Perett's robes to the ground between him and Josie. The marionette suddenly hopped to its feet long enough to perform a curtsey before it exploded into a cloud of green gas that enveloped both the lich and the archer.

As loud as Josie's screams of rage were, her cries of pain were even louder. As the gas started to eat away at her skin, her scarlet hair fell from her head as the poison started eroding her skull. Perett straightened up and started pulling the arrows from his body as if they were little more than splinters. Then Josie stopped screaming completely and lay motionless on the ground as the gas dissipated away.

"My, that was unpleasant." Perett snickered as he dusted off the sleeves of his robes.

Collen rushed to where Josie lay, he shook his head to Ophelia before rising back to his feet and facing the lich. "You killed her. But one of us *will* stop you!"

He was about to charge at Perett when the lich raised his hand. "But, my dear Light Bringer. I haven't even unleashed the advantage the svartalfar gave me yet. So far this has just been trinkets and the power you've given me yourselves with your dead. Don't you want to know what could have been so important to me that I'd have dealings with underground elves?"

"I don't care!" Ophelia muttered and she and Havarti charged.

Collen resumed running at the undead wizard as Lyan pulled herself back to her feet. With a battle cry that would make her ancestors proud, she rushed to bury her spear into Perett. Three warriors from three different directions closed the distance to the evil lich.

Perett let out a sigh. "No one appreciates a well laid plan anymore."

Skeletal hands, what little flesh remaining on them being black as a moonless night sky, burst from the ground, wrapping around Collen's legs and tripping him flat onto his face where his arms and body were enveloped by more obsidian hands with protruding bones.

A fully armored corpse still wearing its pale skin, rose up behind Lyan and tackled the Bunny Barbarian to the dusty ground. Rolling onto her back, the barbarian's vision was immediately filled with the zombie's face. Only inches from the woman, Lyan recognized it as Caleb! Perett's former ogre controlling General!

Caleb screeched inhumanly as he wrestled the barbarian for her spear with two hands. With the sound crunching sinew and tearing flesh, a secreted third, skeletal hand pushed out from behind the dirt smeared armor and inside the former General's ribcage to wrap around her throat. A tarnished silver medallion hung off the wrist of the revealed appendage, the cold metal only slightly warmer than the emaciated flesh around the barbarian's neck.

Ophelia expected to trip any moment but was shocked when she was able to keep going. She didn't feel anything grabbing at her legs and she didn't blink, the mercenary would have felt that. She forced herself to run faster before whatever luck made it so changed its mind.

"I have an army positioned in all the tunnels immediately underneath this clearing! They are used by the svartalfar as burial tombs and, as you can see, I control the dead. All of them." Perett turned to Collen and Lyan to gloat. "There was no way any of you were going to leave here without becoming my slave."

Havarti plunged into the lich's back, between the shoulder blades right where his shriveled heart would be. The lich let out a grunt of surprise before his head spun around completely to face Ophelia. The woman quickly pulled Havarti free and readied for another attack.

"Why didn't my skeletons take you?" His eye sockets narrowed, thin trails of black what used to be blood trailing down from them. "Virgil?!"

Havarti swiped for the lich's neck to remove Perett's head from his shoulders. He ducked just in time, his head swinging around to face its normal direction.

"Virgil!" The lich screamed again, just as Ophelia's bastard sword slashed down his chest, completely severing his ribs from one side his solar plexus.

All the bluster the wizard had only moments before was gone. Full skeletal soldiers, along with long deceased Lytyl tribe members, crawled out of the ground all around the undead man and mercenary but none approached either. Perett's hand dug into his sleeve again and Havarti chopped it off at the elbow, the bony tips of the lich's fingers still clutching the opal that launched the fireball earlier.

"Virgil!"

Ophelia raised Havarti over her head, ready to sever the lich's skull into two perfect halves when two griffins swooped into the only skeleton free area outside of Organa's defensive dome. The first pinned Ophelia to the ground, the weight of the beast holding her down. The bird of prey's head reared up and plunged down for her throat.

It got a beak full of the woman's armored sleeve. But it wouldn't last long, Ophelia could already feel the metal starting to bend against the pressure of the beast's jaws.

The other griffin landed beside Perett with the tall thin man, Virgil, slipping from its back. He helped the lich to his feet, concern etched all over his face. Apparently Ophelia and Josie's attacks were more effective than he had let on. Ophelia would have been pleased about that if she hadn't seen what became of the archer.

The griffin let Ophelia's arm go to rear up for another strike when a sword impaled itself through the side of the creature's feathered throat. Collen had freed himself just long enough to kill the griffin before the black skinned zombies grabbed him again. The ground under him started to crater from the force of the undead sinking back into the dirt, pulling the Light Bringer down against the hard surface.

"Virgil!" Perett was noticeably startled. "Kill her! For me!"

The thin man pulled one of those electrically charged daggers from his belt and threw it at Ophelia's head. She quickly rolled the griffin's body in the blade's path and shuffled away as an electric charge arced through the beast. Ophelia rose up to her feet, Havarti in both hands as she made her way around the dead animal.

Ophelia noticed the arm that she severed from Perett's body, laying on the far side of the griffin the lich was struggling to sit upon, it twitched, the hand shifting as if to get a better grip on the opal between its fingers.

"I think he should go now, don't you?" She said, motioning to the griffin Perett was still awkwardly trying to mount.

With a majestic screech the part falcon creature reared back, dumping Perett back to the dusty ground, and launched into the air. With only two or three wing beats, the creature was already past the treeline of the clearing.

"Don't worry, I'll call another one." Virgil said as he helped Perett back to his feet.

"I don't think so. Not as long as I have this." Ophelia pulled out the feather and bone talismans from her coat pocket. "That's why the skeletons didn't touch me. I didn't figure that out until I heard the griffin yelling that it wanted to get away from here. Thanks to the talisman, I was able to understand it and give it permission to leave. And since it wanted to, I was able to override your control. Wasn't I, Virgil?"

The thin man frowned. Ophelia knew she was right. She just wished she'd been smart enough to realize it earlier. Before having the motivation of a griffin trying to eat her head.

"Right next to each other, it doesn't matter whose control is strong enough to control an army." Ophelia reared up Havarti to bat away Virgil's dagger if it came. "It comes down to the slave picking which order they want to follow when they get here."

"Throw it!" Perett muttered at the thin man.

Virgil took a step away from the lich, his arm with the charged blade rising. "She'll beat it." He whispered back.

"Just do it!" Perett growled.

The sound of metal hitting metal filled the air as Ophelia struck the dagger so hard it flew into the trees. The lich's disembodied hand lifted the flame opal from the ground and it started to glitter with unnatural light again.

Lyan Yo Bunpy watched her spear sail through the air as she stood over the thoroughly crushed remains of Caleb, panting for breath. Her eyes stayed glued until it skewered Perett's chest. The rabbit shaped blade dug into the ground, hitting the lich's disembodied hand and spinning it away from Ophelia as flames launched from the opal.

The fireball careened toward the treeline until some unknown force called it back toward the clearing. Virgil raised his hands in front of his face as the ball of flame as big him enveloped and ignited his entire body.

There was something satisfying to Ophelia, hearing him scream after what happened to Josie. But the cries didn't last long and he started to smolder as he fell into the grip of Perett's remaining arm.

"What? How?" He managed to groan through his scorched flesh.

"It was tuned to seek out the nearest human to burn." The lich said.

He sounded more like a marksman who was frustrated by missing the bull's eye rather than one regretful that he accidentally killed an ally. Virgil's skin cracked and peeled as he turned his head to look towards Lyan, who had dropped back down to one knee.

"So it was her fault." Virgil rasped.

The burned man's eyes opened wide as he saw who the barbarian was kneeling beside. "Caleb! You said that he'd been given a proper burial! One worthy of our nobles!"

"And he will be." Perett growled back, shaking the dying man with his bony arm. "I required his services for the plan!"

The lich was staked to where he stood. He didn't have the strength to pull the spear out, it would seem. So he simply stood there, waiting for his General to die.

"I..." Smoke slipped from Virgil's mouth as he coughed, the last of his life eking away. "I won't let you do that to me, too."

As the thin man groaned his last, a flock of griffins started circling overhead. cling overhead. The last orders that their master gave matched the bird of prey instincts of the griffins, so Ophelia couldn't stop them even if she wanted.

One by one, the beasts dove. Each tearing a part of Perett and Virgil away. Again and again they came, wrenching arm from shoulder and ribs from torso. Finally, there was nothing left but Perett's ripped robe, Virgil's blood, Lyan's spear and scorched earth marking where both men had stood. As the last of Perett's body left, the undead reverted back to their natural slumber.

Collen groaned as he lifted himself up. Hero, his wife, was going to be so upset when he got home. At least until he could explain that the new dents in his armor didn't have matching wounds underneath. Still, too much of his body to cradle any particular part as he turned to see to his men.

The midday sun also returned to the clearing. Ophelia found it hard to believe that so little time had passed. It felt as if the moon should have greeted them with its cold light.

The Bunny Barbarian limped up to her spear beside Ophelia. Lyan pulled the weapon from the ground with a quiet grunt as she slowly scanned the remainder of the battlefield. The enemy was gone, mostly sunken back into the dirt from which they emerged. What was left of the griffins took to the air and, surely, back to their nests. Even the few remaining ally ogres started back for the trees.

"This was a battle worthy of many songs." The barbarian's gaze fell on where Josie rested. "For one of us in particular."

Both women walked over to Josie's prone body which looked... surprisingly whole. Ophelia slipped Havarti back into his scabbard as she knelt down beside the red haired woman. Both jumped when a soft groan escaped from the archer's lips.

"Josie? You're alive?" Ophelia reached out for the archer's shoulder, reluctant to touch as if doing so would somehow undo this turn of events.

Josie's skin was intact, unlike how it looked only minutes before. It was warm, just as if she were living. The half-elf woman rolled onto her back, a slow shuddering breath escaping her undamaged mouth.

"Am I?" Josie lifted her hand into the air her green eyes locked on it. "I could have sworn I was... melting."

"I don't understand what happened." Lyan leaned her shoulder into the tall spear to hold herself upright, her eyes darting back and forth from Ophelia and Josie.

"I believe I can explain." Ashe stepped up to them, his voice as shaky as his knees.

The wizard dropped heavily beside Josie, slipping his hand under the half-elf's neck. After a few seconds, he pulled the green marionette out from under the scarlet haired archer.

"I noticed something about the talismans that lich used. They're based on puns." The young wizard started to explain.

Josie opened her eyes, immediately stiffening when she saw the marionette in Ashe's hand. Noticing her reaction, the young man stuffed the green item into the leather pouch Lyan gave him earlier.

"A marionette is a tool that gives the illusion of life when it's used in its traditional role." Asheram continued. "This did just the opposite. While the pain was very real..."

Josie agreed completely with the young man's statement. Ophelia helped her up into a sitting position in the grass.

Ashe finished. "...that talisman provided the illusion of death."

"To what end?" Lyan asked.

"If you think one of your party is dead, you think they are beyond help and that, if that person were surely already wounded before this was cast, would be free to wither and die. One less person to worry about in battle, isn't it?" Ashe shrugged and held up the opal that had formerly been in the lich's severed hand. "This is a fire opal. Get it?" He didn't look amused by the pun either as he tossed that talisman into the pouch then held up the diamond. "Some people call diamonds 'ice'."

"Ugh." Josie groaned at either the bad puns or the effort to get back onto her feet or both.

"Let's get her back to Organa and Samson." Lyan started to limp in that direction.

"We'll let Organa look at Josie while Samson patches you up. Deal?" Ophelia slipped under Lyan's arm to help the barbarian support her own weight.

"I'm fine, by the way." Ashe said as both he and Josie supported each other for the walk. "Thanks for checking."

"I've been checking you out since you showed up." Ophelia smirked back at the young wizard.

CHAPTER

SEVENTEEN

"SERIOUSLY, DID NO one think to check on me?" Ashe looked astonished at the sea of blank faces in front of him. "I mean, I was flat on by back and possibly dead by a mad lich's violent magicks!"

Organa turned her attention back to Josie, who was lying down on the table as the woman in white robes examined her. To the archer's left, the Bunny Barbarian's tall pastel boot was on the ground while she lay on the next table. Samson had already bandaged the wound on Lyan's shoulder and was busy wrapping a thick strap of cotton around the barbarian's thicker thigh.

"You'll need to get the hole in your boot patched up when you get the chance." The cleric herald's baritone voice carried to everyone's ears even with its gentle tone.

Asheram sighed, slumping dejectedly. Ophelia stepped up beside him, putting a comforting hand on his shoulder.

"You know we all love you, kid." She gave him a kind smile before motioning over to Josie. "But we've known her since before you were even born and you didn't look like you were melted alive."

The young wizard nodded. "I understand. I'm simply relieved that my spell worked out."

Everyone's eyes shot to look at Ashe, who suddenly felt very self conscious. He rubbed at the back of his neck as he started to explain himself.

"I have studied liches on occasion. They are notoriously powerful and most wizards want to know the benefits and costs to that state of being." He couldn't help looking sheepish as everyone's faces when from different shades of horrified to disgusted. "In my studies, I learned that physical attacks alone don't do much and many magicks can be absorbed to make them even stronger."

"And?" Ophelia moved to stand in front of him, cutting Josie out of his field of vision.

The mercenary's pale blue eyes stared into the young wizard's with a hint of distrust in them. The feeling seemed to be shared by most everyone else Ashe could see over her shoulder.

"I'd been working on a spell that displaces the trans-dimensional energy from the physical manifestation of a target as well as severing any potential energy reserves from possible forms of synthesis or osmosis." As Asheram spoke the blank stares returned. "I made it so your strikes drained his magical energy and he couldn't absorb power from any spells that hit him."

"Oh!" Everyone finally understood and Ashe's face twitched in frustration.

"When did you cast that spell?" Ophelia slipped her hands into her long coat's pockets.

Ashe perked up when at least one person wanted to keep speaking to him instead of moving on once he dumbed down what was said before for them. "As Perett's last shot was smashing though my shield. He's not the only one that can cast spells that can't be seen." That last part came out with a hint of pride.

"Great work, ki— Asheram." Ophelia suddenly looked surprised and looked down at her hand as she pulled it out of her pocket. "I totally forgot about this thing."

In her palm was the puce talisman that looked like a head of wheat. Ashe bent down to have a look at it, his nose only inches from Ophelia's palm.

"What does this one do?" He asked.

"Let me show you." The woman flipped the trinket in her palm.

There was no flash of light, no ominous noise or any sign that effect had taken place. Until, of course, Ashe tried to speak. He immediately noticed that no sound came from his mouth. Instead of looking alarmed, though, he jumped up and down with excitement.

His pale fingers pointed from the trinket, to Ophelia and then to himself. Ophelia's thick eyebrows pressed together as a confused look came over her face. Ashe repeated the motion of pointing from her to him.

"It would probably be easier to undo the enchantment so you can actually tell us what you want." Ophelia said.

Just as Ashe started nodding in agreement, Ophelia stepped up to him and pressed her lips to his. Ashe's purple eyes almost burst out of his head as the woman kissed him. When she finally pulled away, the puce trinket was already in his hand.

The young wizard's mouth opened and closed but no sound came out, although this time it had nothing to do with the enchantment. Ophelia folded her arms across her chest and smiled back at the man.

"I deactivated the spell, Ashe." She said. "You can talk now."

"You I— you me, I mean you," The wizard shook his head in an effort to regain his faculties. "You have to kiss the target to undo the spell effect?"

Ophelia laughed as she stepped between the tables where Josie and Lyan rested. "No, you just have to flip the trinket. The rest was just for fun."

Asheram was sure his cheeks were about to erupt in flame. To distract himself, he pulled his newly acquired pouch and added the wheat head to the others he scavenged from the lich's torn robes and slipped it back into his pants pocket.

"I see, if that was designed by the lich, that means they are all probably Will Talismans." His voice was still a little uneven as he tugged strings to close the pouch.

"Okay, I'll bite." Josie had to shoo Organa away just to be able to sit up on the table. "What is a Will Talisman?"

For once it wasn't a sea of blank stares that greeted the wizard's explanation. "There are three basic types of talisman that are used as outward sources of magical power. Invocation, that requires an exact spoken phrase or hand movements to activate, Blood obviously requires a sacrifice of life energy, and Will, which simply need the wielder's desire to be activated."

"And how do you know those are the Will Type?" Ophelia could feel the young wizard's eyes locked on her so she took a few seconds longer than was actually necessary to bend over, pick up Lyan's furry boot, and hand it back to the barbarian. Just to give him a show.

The blush in Ashe's cheeks just wouldn't fade. "Blood is impossible for a lich, who literally has no life force. Also, a common side effect of process to become undead is a tendency for the target's fine motor skills to become limited. But Will, a lich would have that in abundance."

"So you decide who you want to target and the trinket does the rest." Ophelia said and the young man nodded in agreement.

"Thanks for the magic lesson but we'd better get a move on." Lyan started pulling her long boot back onto her leg. "We have to get down into the Lytyl tunnels and figure out a way to force the Matriarch to call off the attack on Dianmeyer."

"I don't understand what they get out of all this." Ophelia said as she handed Josie her quiver, refilled with a new supply of arrows courtesy of the Light Bringers. "Why would the Matriarch back the Inquisitor in a deal with an upworlder? Even worse, a male upworlder."

Lyan shook her head as she hopped onto her feet to test the bandaging and, finding it satisfactory, started for her spear and shield leaning against a barrel of water. "I don't know about that. I do know that killing Nyphistra seems to be the foremost part of their plan."

Ophelia grunted. "As much as I hate to admit it, we need her help. If we have to take out the Matriarch and the Inquisitor, Nyphistra can take the throne and stop the tribe from destroying Dianmeyer."

"We'll come." Organa and Samson volunteered.

Lyan shook her head. "Collen's forces are in much greater need of your help."

"I'll go with you." Ashe stepped up.

This time Ophelia shook her head. "Your father is involved in svartalfar politics up to his slanted eyebrows. If anyone even thinks he sent you to take out another tribe's Matriarch, that would be just the thing to spark another war."

"I'm coming." Josie said as she slid off the table and onto her feet.

"Josie, you really shouldn't—" Both Ophelia and Lyan started to object.

"I have three arrows tipped with poison specifically formulated to kill svartalfar with just a scratch. I'm the best shot with a bow of all of us. It's my home they're going to attack where my daughter is waiting with my husband." The archer's emerald eyes glared holes into the two other women. "So why am I not going again?"

Lyan and Ophelia looked at each other and shrugged. Collen appeared and walked up to the group, his red cape back in place on his shoulders. His blonde hair was wet and pressed tightly against his head and he looked a bit cleaner. He must have taken a minute to dunk his head into one of the barrels of water around the camp and washed up after one of his healers tended to him.

"I have our fastest horses saddled up to take us wherever we need to go." He announced.

"We?" Josie, Ophelia and Lyan turned to face the Colonel.

He nodded. "I've been helping Nyphistra in her efforts to ready the svartalfar to rejoin the surface world so if she's in danger it's my duty to help." Then he motioned to Organa and Samson. "And the Order of Kuan Yin came to our aid when we were in need so I am honor bound to help them."

"Who's going to look after your men while you're gone then?" Josie asked.

"I've already asked Captain Riker to do so." Collen said. "He's my number one man when it comes to logistics and keeping up morale."

Josie, Ophelia and Lyan looked at each other and again shrugged. Ashe stepped up to the end of the table the archer had just vacated and rested his hands on top of it.

"So where are we all going then?" He asked.

Lyan grinned at the young wizard. "Do you think you can get that mirror working?"

EIGHTEEN

AS LYAN AND Josie took the lead to guide the Colonel, Asheram pulled Ophelia back so that they could speak at the rear as the party rode along. He looked confused by something, which wasn't a look the young wizard had very often outside of his studies.

It took Ashe a moment to find the words he felt appropriate to use. "Ophelia, I can understand why Josie wants to go after the Lytyl Tribe Matriarch. Her family is threatened. Collen is protecting a colleague with whom he's had dealings that have put her in danger. And, as a barbarian of the Yo Bunpy tribe, Lyan defines herself from battle.

"What I do not understand, though, is why you are willing to go back down into those tunnels. You escaped captivity already, delivered word of the Matriarch's plot to those it would affect and even delivered the Valen Court from the danger it faced. What could you possibly hope to gain by putting yourself into the fray yet again? Especially for people with whom you have no blood nor organizational connection."

"Blood or organizational connections?" The woman in the red leather scowled slightly at the young albino svartalfar atop her horse after he finished. "I've known Harby and Josie longer than you've been alive. Isn't that enough?"

"I spend much of my time not only with my father in the Emerald City but also in Dianmeyer." Ashe answered. "You do not stay with the Order of Kuan Yin very often."

"That doesn't mean I don't care about them." Ophelia answered back. "Harbenigyr has brought me back to life more than once."

The mercenary had to consciously keep herself from flinching as the image of the chortling face of Mistress Stohbease flashed across her mind's eye. Glancing over at Ashe, she was thankful that he didn't seem to notice.

The wizard arched a green eyebrow in response to what she said, though. "I know resurrection of the dead to true life is impossible, but why do I feel that you do not mean that figuratively?"

Instead of answering, Ophelia reached over to the young man's waist for the rope that peeked from his pocket and pulled the pouch that held the talismans free. "You know, it would be easy for this to fall out having it in that pocket. You should put it in one of the pockets in your jacket for safe keeping."

"I have no pockets in my uniform." Ashe replied.

The look the woman gave the man back showed that she didn't believe him. He sighed and stretched out his hand for the pouch.

"Very well. I do have compartments meant for components for my spells." Ashe confessed. "I will put it in one of them. Good enough?"

Ophelia dropped the leather bag into his hand and watched the wizards hand slip between the buttons that held his uniform jacket closed, slipping the pouch into a hidden pocket on the left side of his chest. The mercenary nodded, giving him a lopsided smile before motioning that they should rejoin the group.

The horses were as good as Collen's word. They carried the Colonel, Josie, Lyan, Ophelia and Ashe back to Perett's white tent only minutes later, although the amount of uprooted trees, courtesy of panicked ogres stomping and making their own paths that morning, did make it easier for them.

Reaching their destination the party dismounted and slipped back into the tent. As they walked by the table, Ashe picked up the long silver wig that was laying under it.

"This is what you wore to look like a svartalfar?" He said, trying to make it look presentable again by brushing away the dust that had coated it. "It looks so real."

"It is." Ophelia answered, her voice monotone.

"Oh." He didn't drop the hair to the floor but he did drape it over his other arm and, when his hand was free, started wiping it against his pants.

The group continued on into the room with the mirror that Lyan toppled earlier. Nothing appeared to have changed since they left earlier that morning.

"Ophelia." Lyan called to the other woman as she slipped her hands under the edge of the mirror's frame.

The mercenary did the same thing on the other side of the mirror, having to hike the skirt portion of her dress up over her knees to get it out of her way. The mirror was even heavier than it looked. It took the two women all their strength just to get it knee high.

Once there, Collen slipped his hand and stump under to add his strength to theirs. Josie and Ashe were just about to step in when they again seemed to stall at their shoulders when the mirror suddenly tipped away from their hands and fell back into place over the mouth of the cave with an echoing thud.

The room Lyan and Ashe had seen earlier was still on the other side. No one was in there and it was almost completely dark except for the hints of torchlight that came in through the edges of the door.

"Alright, magician. It's your turn now." Lyan huffed, still getting her breath back from the effort of lifting the mirror.

Ophelia grabbed Ashe's arm as stepped toward the portal generator. "Wait. Before you do, can you enchant us to look like svartalfar?"

He arched a green eyebrow at her. "A glamour? You know that won't get you past any of the security measures."

Ophelia nodded. "But most of the svartalfar won't look twice at us if we look like them. Otherwise we're fighting and searching for Nyphistra at the same time. And I'm not one for multitasking."

The wizard nodded, obviously having seen this request coming, and pulled the silver wig off his arm. "Put this back on."

Ophelia looked down at the wig then at Asheram. "Why?"

"A strong glamour takes time to concoct." He explained. "Hair is always the hardest part. You wear that, all I have to do is change your skin color to black. Easy." He pointed back at Collen. "Some svartalfar are blonde so I only have to change his skin and make his armor look like a Lytyl." Then he looked at Lyan, his lips pursed tightly in thought. "You escaped dressed as a guard, yes?"

Lyan nodded.

"I thought so. They're the only ones big enough for you to pass as." He muttered. "Lyan's glamour will be the trickiest because if anyone touches her, the enchantment will be seen through instantly since she isn't actually wearing metal armor."

"So keep her between me, Josie and Collen. Got it." Ophelia forced herself to not shudder as she placed the wig back on her head.

As he turned to Josie, the red haired half-elf shook her head. "I won't look like a svartalfar." She said simply.

"You can't go looking like you do now." Ashe said. "You'd be killed on sight!"

"Can you make me invisible?" Josie asked. "I can't take any more 'Evil Josie' jokes. Besides, it's one less complicated glamour for you to create, right?"

"Everyone thinks that invisibility is so much easier!" Asheram protested. "You know that to maintain the illusion you can't speak, or shoot or trip or even bump into anything without breaking the spell, right?"

Josie motioned to Collen and the others. "They'll be able to talk. I'll watch their backs and only break the spell if they're attacked. Deal?" She gave the young wizard a reassuring smile.

Ashe sighed, rubbing at the bridge of his nose. "Very well. But remember, don't talk or touch anything. I may be able to make it so you can strum your bow to let them know where you are but that will only be if everything goes perfectly."

"I understand." The archer nodded.

Ashe stepped up to her first, bringing his hands up on either side of the archer's head. "If you can keep the illusion here while I'm working on everyone else, I'll have faith that you can keep it going down there. Agreed?"

Josie again nodded, her scarlet hair falling over her eyes. Ashe chanted under his breath, his eyes closing as a soft hum filled the air. As he finished, the archer didn't disappear instantly, more like she was enveloped in a cloud of unseen smoke.

Everyone looked around the tent but couldn't see any sign of Josie, not even footprints. Lyan even reached out and waved her hand through the area the half-elf had occupied moments ago.

"She's gone!" The barbarian looked shocked.

"No, she simply moved." Ashe smirked before turning his attention to Ophelia.

"A quick cleaning cantrip here." Ashe pressed his fingers into Ophelia's wig as he helped her position it and then the skullcap properly again. "And here."

He pressed his hand against Ophelia's chest, his palm lingering between her breasts, was much lower than he had to touch to make the spell work, the woman was sure. The black makeup that lingered at the edges of the dress disappeared in a faint hiss of steam and Ophelia was in her own skin again.

"Oh, those are actual svartalfar ears." Ashe couldn't help but stare. "Nyphistra's smart, I'll give her that. She did everything she could to make you pass any security measure they have down there. You may have even been able to get to the Matriarch before if she had given you the passwords."

A second later and Ophelia's skin was black again, thanks to Ashram's magicks. "But not now?" She asked.

"No. Using non magic make up to darken your skin is a trick even real svartalfar with, shall we say, uneven skin tones use to beautify themselves. Even if someone noticed your makeup, they would think that was all you were hiding. But with the glamour it's obviously magicked camouflage."

The young wizard's hand lingered just a moment or two longer before he pulled away and moved on to Collen. The Light Bringer insignia on his armor disappeared and the breastplate turned polished black along with the shield on his arm, although Ashe added an illusory hand holding the defensive piece of metal in place. His skin followed suit and became as dark as char cloth.

"Don't look anyone in the eye." Ashe instructed him. "You may be an officer but women are still considered your superiors, no matter their rank."

Collen's armor now had gold etching that was similar to what was on the clothes of the massive Lytyl officer Ophelia fought while trying to find Lyan. Only just now did the mercenary think it was odd that he didn't have any armor on at all. But that had likely been due to being roused out of bed at that predawn hour rather than it not being part of his uniform.

Ashe stepped over to the Bunny Barbarian and started waving his hands in front of and behind her, but never actually touching the woman. The air around the barbarian shimmered and inky blackness started to engulf her, as if some giant unseen hand were painting over her. After a minute, the Bunny Barbarian again looked like one of the big guards from the fortress. Not only was she wrapped in black metal but her spear looked like their pole ax, as well.

Lyan's free hand lifted up and she looked down at herself. "I don't look any different." She said, jumping in surprise when her voice sounded tinny.

"It's a one way glamour." Ashe said, looking in the direction only he knew Josie was to let her know he was addressing her as well, then he turned to Lyan. "Only people looking at you see it. Just be sure to duck your head when you go through doorways. If the ears of your real armor get pushed back, your glamour will look as if it's decapitating itself."

The barbarian nodded at the wizard as he turned and walked over to the mirror. He started chanting under his breath again, his hands making different odd gestures as he paced from one side to the other and back. After a bright flash of light nothing looked different.

"It's open now." Asheram announced. "You'd better get through fast and get out of that room. Chances are the Inquisitor has some way of knowing when the portal is active."

Lyan pressed a hand where the 'glass' would have been. When her hand went through without resistance, she quickly followed it. Collen gave Ashe a thankful nod, the glamour making his gesture look sufficiently malicious as he passed into the room.

Ophelia stepped up to the mirror beside Asheram. "Oh, I almost forgot. I need to pull a Josie on your coat!"

He wrapped his hands around Ophelia's shoulders, pulling her around to face him. "I'm not my father, you know. I can still come with you." He said.

Ophelia's red jacket started to fade from view, exposing that much more of her chest to the young wizard's eyes. "I know. But there are some svartalfar just looking for an excuse to go after your father, even if it has to be through you. Besides, I think you met your quota of almost getting killed for us today."

She started to turn to go through the portal but Asheram held her still. "Unsheathing Havarti will undo the glamour on your coat but not the one on your skin. However, wizards don't wear anything like that down there so they would know you're an outsider. Don't use your sword unless you absolutely have to."

After he said that, Ashe looked conflicted about something. She'd only seen the young wizard this way when he was trying to figure out what he should do next to improve a spell, his grades or whether or not to take advantage of the latest shenanigans Isaac was up to.

Ophelia gave him a wide smile and a playful pat on his chest. "I already stole a kiss from you. You want it back, you're going to have to take it yourself." And the woman jumped through the portal into the other room.

Once her feet touched the rune covered rug, Ophelia turned back to the mirror. Ashe's cheeks betrayed his embarrassment. "So many issues." The wizard muttered as he gave them all a quick wave before turning and leaving the white tent.

After he was gone, Ophelia let out a little sigh. "I feel guilty."

Both Lyan and Collen looked at her. "Why?" The Bunny Barbarian asked.

Ophelia lifted the leather pouch that had been in Ashe's jacket pocket and bounced it in her hand. "He's sweet and I stole these from him."

"Why would you do that?" Collen asked, looking genuinely shocked by her actions.

"He said not to use Havarti unless absolutely necessary." Ophelia tucked the pouch into one of the invisible pockets of her coat. "So I can use those to fight and still sell ourselves as svartalfar to any others we come across."

As the Light Bringer shook his head, Lyan asked. "How were you even able to take that? You're no pick pocket."

"You don't have to be a master thief when you use your assets." Ophelia folded her arms in front of her, making her soft breasts press tightly together, although she didn't have any hint of amusement on her face.

She couldn't see it, but Ophelia was sure that Lyan rolled her eyes before marching over to the door. Collen muttered something about women not fighting fair but neither the barbarian nor the mercenary caught the full gist of what he was saying.

Then, as the thought just occurred to him, Collen spun around where he stood to scan the entire room. "Josie? Are you here?" He asked the air.

The faint strumming of the archer's bow, like a lute with only one string, was the only response the group received.

The group was out into the hallway seconds later. All three of the visible ones looking this direction and that but there wasn't any sign of the Inquisitor or anyone else coming to check on the status of the portal.

"Let's wait here a minute and see if she shows up." Ophelia motioned for them to duck down the nearest intersection. "Then we'd only have one more to worry about."

As the disguised woman watched the door that led to the portal's hiding place, Collen and Lyan kept eyes on every other direction. They weren't sure what direction anyone would be coming from and they surely didn't want to be caught unawares.

thump

Still, no one came.

"I don't like it." Ophelia finally said. "It's not paranoid enough for a svartalfar to not have a way of knowing something that can be used against them is, in fact, being used."

Lyan grunted in agreement. "Do you suppose she's busy with Nyphistra by now?" Her tinny voice asked.

"I don't know. Maybe." Ophelia frowned.

"We'd best be moving anyway." Collen finally chimed in. "It's only three hours until sunset and we have to hope the svartalfar have a fast way to communicate with over a thousand troops to not attack Dianmeyer or this is all going to be for nothing."

"Josie, keep us in sight. I know you like to scout ahead but it's too easy to lose each other in this place." At the sound of the bow string being plucked, Ophelia started down a hall and stopped at the first intersection to look around. "Tribe Matriarchs are too controlling to not have a way to communicate with their armies directly. We just have to find out what it is."

thump

Collen and Lyan stepped up beside Ophelia as they started in a direction they hoped either woman would recognize something. Eventually. The hallways looked identical to their first visit, decorative armor along the walls, gold edging on the corners. Everything looked exactly the same from hallway to hallway.

After passing a few intersections, Ophelia looked back at Lyan. "See anything familiar?" She asked the barbarian.

Lyan shook her head. "Not so far."

"How can anyone find their way in this place?" Collen whispered, peeking his head around the corner and seeing yet another decorative suit of armor.

It was designed to be like a maze and they were caught in it. Lyan was fairly certain they hadn't gone in a circle but she there was no way for her to be sure. The barbarian found herself wondering if anyone ever came across the skeleton of an assassin who got lost so thoroughly that he died before finding a way out.

thump

"What is that noise?" Ophelia hissed.

Collen and Bunny Barbarian shrugged back at her, not knowing what she was talking about. The thumping must have been too weak for the Light Bringer or Lyan to hear and Ophelia honestly couldn't tell what direction they thumps were coming from but they were getting stronger. Strong enough to annoy the woman disguised as a svartalfar wizard, anyway.

Ophelia cocked her head to the side, the ruby earrings swinging around to tap against her jaw. "It sounds like something heavy hammering and crushing stone, maybe. But... I think I hear voices with it." Her pale blue eyes narrowed. "No, the voices are coming this way!"

Both Collen and Lyan strained to hear the voices Ophelia was talking about but couldn't. Still, they followed the woman when she went down a different hallway. When she stopped again at a T intersection, Ophelia looked to the left, then the right and finally turned back to face the other two.

"Svartalfar are coming from both directions." She said. "Now's the time to see if these disguises are going to work."

"And if they do?" Lyan whispered. "We still have no idea where we are going."

Ophelia didn't answer. Instead she listened, cocking her head from one side to the other. Then she pointed to the right and started down that hallway. Lyan and Collen hurried to keep pace with Ophelia, who started to carry herself differently as she marched down the hall with her nose in the air and looking as if something smelled bad.

Moments later, they came upon another group of three svartalfar. A wizard in a black velvet dress led with two wizarding students flanking just behind her in their plain brown robes. They hadn't been through the Mage Trials yet, so they hadn't earned the privileges of the rank of wizard among the Lytyl but they were still dangerous enough to burn the humans alive if they were found out.

"What are you doing here? You're out of position!" The velvet dressed wizard frowned as her attention turned to Collen disguised as a military officer. "You should be on the south end of the throne hall!"

Collen glanced over at Lyan, who tightened her grip on her spear that looked like an ax, out of the corner of his eye. He opened his mouth to say something, being careful not to look the wizard in her eyes as Ashe instructed when Ophelia suddenly spoke up.

"No, Veracose, you know you're the one not in the correct position." Ophelia pointed back the way she, Collen and Lyan had come. "You are supposed to be three halls back and four to the left that way!"

Both women, one disguised as a wizard and the other a true magic user, stared each other down silently. The velvet dressed wizard's jaw ground but there was also a noise that sounded suspiciously like the string of a bow being pulled back to shoot an arrow. The students behind her looked as uneasy as Collen and Lyan while the two women stood off. Collen's hand slipped over the handle of his sword on his belt, readying to attack at the first violent motion.

Finally, the true wizard's head bobbed down. "You are right. My apologies. We will take up our posts immediately."

The three real svartalfar skirted around Collen and Lyan with their heads bowed while Ophelia kept a stern eye on them until they turned the first corner. Only then did the woman practically fall against the wall and let out a sigh of relief.

For the first time she was thankful for Ashe's enchantment that made her skin black. It made it so she could wipe the sweat from her brow without worrying about whether the color would be rubbed away.

"How did you do that?" Collen whispered excitedly.

"I heard the two students complaining about being lost." Ophelia explained as she pushed herself away from the wall and started walking again. "I sent them where the other group I heard said they were going. With any luck, they'll argue amongst themselves about who's right long enough for us to be long gone from here."

"How did you hear all that?" The Light Bringer asked as Lyan pulled him back a step so he wasn't walking beside Ophelia.

"Enchanted for better hearing." The disguised woman lightly tapped at the rubies hanging from her ears. "It's nice to know that even they get lost in there sometimes, isn't it?"

Ophelia grinned back at her two compatriots before her face turned stern again. Seconds later another group of svartalfar, two armored guards and a male officer, came up the hall and gave Ophelia a solemn bow as they passed.

As the group continued on, the thumping had gotten loud enough that Lyan and Collen could hear it now and was definitely cracking stone. They were on the path to reach wherever the noise was coming from and it was also a good bet that it was Nyphistra and the Inquisitor, with or without the Matriarch, causing such damaging violence.

As long as the noise continued, that meant that the living shadow was still alive and Ophelia, Lyan, Collen and Josie still had a chance of success. They just had to get there to shift the odds to their favor.

"Is it just me or does this hallway look like it has more expensive stuff in it?" Ophelia pointed down the newest corridor, the thumping actually making the ground under their feet vibrate now.

"If I were to hazard a guess, I would say that this is the throne hall that Veracose woman referred to." Collen said.

"Probably leading to the throne room." Lyan interjected. "And where the Inquisitor likely decided to spring her trap on Nyphistra."

The strumming noise got frantic and was quickly getting quieter as Josie started running down the hallway without them. Ophelia reached out to try and grab her but, even if she'd been able to see the archer, Josie would have likely been too quick for her to catch.

"Nyphistra said there would be traps!" Ophelia said loudly, but not wanting to shout and draw unwanted attention but also warn the invisible half-elf.

"And wizards assigned to protect the Matriarch that were supposed to be loyal to Nyphistra." Lyan added.

Again, the only response they got was a strumming bow string but at least it wasn't charging away now. Collen drew his sword and Lyan held her spear at ready. Ophelia reached into her pocket, pulling out the leather pouch filled with magical talismans. There was no sign of the wizards around so that left only one immediate worry.

"Okay, don't run and keep an eye out for traps. If you see one, then run." Ophelia took a step into the hallway.

Nothing happened. Another step and still nothing. As she was taking a closer look at the walls and ceiling in an effort to avoid traps, Ophelia noticed that some of the stones looked loose. Another thump shook the hallway and dust rained down on the four of them, making at least the outline of Josie ahead of them visible for a moment. If there were traps, chances are whatever battle was going on had damaged the triggers and the traps were for all intents and purposes disarmed.

All their strides got faster and they reached the doors leading to the throne room. One of the massive slabs of stone was flat on the floor, the other one looked permanently wedged in place in the doorjamb.

Ophelia peeked her head in and, sure enough, Nyphistra was facing the Inquisitor with her back to the throne while the Matriarch stood atop the steps in front of her gold etched chair. Apparently, the Matriarch chose to side with Inquisitor Aylosha in their particular argument.

The bodies of at least a half dozen svartalfar women were strewn all around the throne room. Whether the wizards died defending the Matriarch or Nyphistra, there was no way to tell.

What surrounded the living shadow, though, gave Ophelia pause. A gigantic spider, constructed from pieces of gold, silver and other random metals to fight with her in this battle. It's eight massive legs, the tips made of those tall slabs of bronze in Nyphistra's office with runes carved into them, shifted to block the Matriarch's attacks, slamming into the stone floor to absorb the force of each arc of lightning the aging svartalfar loosed.

Every time the golem like spider moved its legs it obscured Ophelia and the others' view of the Matriarch. "Josie, find a good spot where you can use those svartalfar slaying arrows on both of them, if you can." Ophelia pointed a black finger into the throne room.

The mercenary dipped into the leather pouch and came out with the diamond. She looked back at Collen and Lyan, blowing long silver strands of hair out of her face.

"I'll run in first and use this thing to draw their attention, you run off to the left and find a good defensive position on their flank. Sound good?" Ophelia said.

Collen's face turned stern, which looked even more accusatory with his currently disguised face. "Who decided you were in charge of battle strategy?" He asked the woman.

"Nobody." Ophelia answered. "I'm just the bitch with the ice."

And with that the woman dashed into the throne room. Ophelia's long silver hair trailed behind her as she ran, the diamond glittering in her hand as she raised it towards the svartalfar at the base of the throne.

"Another of your treacherous wizards, Nyphistra?" The Inquisitor flicked a wrist and launched a barrage of arrows made of fire that suddenly appeared out of the air at the Vizier.

Another of the golem-spider's legs crashed down between the black skinned women deflecting the burning attack. "I think if you look closer, you'll see a woman with a more personal vendetta." The living shadow hissed back.

Ophelia's hand felt as if it had been dunked in a mound of razor sharp snow crystals as the ice dragon's head formed around it. It opened it's cobalt colored maw and a blizzard spilled out, straight for the Inquisitor.

The svartalfar woman whipped both hands around into the space between herself and this new threat. Her fingertips drew a line on the ground and a wall of flame leaped to life, absorbing the freezing attack Ophelia unleashed.

That momentary diversion was enough for Nyphistra to unload a spell at Aylosha. She threw a handful of black sludge at the Inquisitor and it landed on the front of her shoulder and coated her clavicle.

The hissing of her satin dress being eaten away by acid, followed by the stabbing pain of needle-like teeth digging into the svartalfar's shoulder made her buckle to her knees. "What is this?!" She yelled, clawing at the sludge with her opposite hand.

Lyan and Collen dove behind two separate golden columns, waiting for an opening. Ophelia's distraction worked perfectly, the Colonel had to admit. The Inquisitor's back was to the warriors and she was already down on her knees. Perhaps this was going to be easier than they had all hoped.

With a crack of thunder, the Matriarch was suddenly at Aylosha's side. With the sound of crackling frost, the elder svartalfar woman dug her nails into and froze the convulsing sludge, pulling it off the Inquisitor's bloody shoulder.

"A void leech." She identified the otherworldly thing before tossing it away. "How maniacal, Nyphistra, eating away at a woman's magic and then her very lifeblood just so she can feel useless before she dies? I'd almost be proud, if you hadn't taught me how to counter it yourself." She gave the living shadow a mirthless grin that a politician often gives another.

Ophelia ran up the steps to the throne. She had to get around the wall of flame that stopped her talisman's ice attack. The human's fingertips were still shivering as she looked down at the diamond.

It had a crack running through it and whatever had been moving inside was gone, so it was surely useless.

But she could still get to the Matriarch. When she reached the top of the throne, though, the woman was already gone. To Ophelia's surprise the elder svartalfar was standing beside the Inquisitor with Nyphistra and the giant golem-spider between her and them.

The svartalfar disguised woman tossed the broken talisman away and reached for another. The fire opal came up between her fingers. Ophelia took aim at both the Inquisitor and the Matriarch and let the ball of flame throw itself.

Aylosha gasped when she saw the burning orb launch from above the metallic golem-spider, bringing up her good arm in a vain attempt to defend herself... but then the fireball veered away. Both the Matriarch and the Inquisitor looked at each other as the flames passed and shot for the nearby gold columns.

"Incoming!" Collen yelled as he dived from his hiding place and into the middle of the throne room.

The column went from solid gold to a pile of melted metal instantly as the Colonel rolled to a stop on the long carpet that guided visitors to the throne. The ceiling gave a shuddering groan at the sudden loss of support but otherwise didn't budge.

"What's this?" The Matriarch looked as if she'd been given the finest of gifts. "A Light Bringer? His body will make a perfect prop when I tell the tale of your failed attempt to assassinate me, Nyphistra."

Collen looked down at himself and, indeed, the glamour disguising him as a svartalfar officer was gone, likely due to his impact with the floor. The sword symbol on his armor betrayed him for what he was and it suddenly felt like a bull's eye on his chest.

As the Matriarch raised her hand and started making contorted gestures with her fingers, a svartalfar pole ax impaled the ground in front of her and interrupted the building power of her spell. Like wet ink getting rinsed off a piece of parchment, the black suddenly washed away to reveal the spear of Lyan Yo Bunpy.

At the same time, the guard glamour around her collapsed, revealing her standing beside the golden column behind which she'd been waiting. "Collen get back into cover!" She screamed.

"Ah hell." Ophelia could only stare as the fireball flew off course and into the column hiding the Light Bringer.

When the lich said that it targeted the nearest human, Ophelia thought he meant person, and said human because that was just what Virgil happened to be. Apparently not. She shoved the opal back into the pouch.

Havarti cleared his nonexistent throat. "Perhaps we should resort to a method of battle to which we are both more accustomed?" He almost sounded excited.

"Why not?" Ophelia reached back over her shoulder for the handle of her bastard sword.

There was no point to subterfuge now. As Havarti came into view, so did Ophelia's long red coat. Her skin, though, kept its obsidian hue.

The woman pulled the silver wig off her head and tossed it onto the throne. For a split second, Ophelia thought there had to be some irony in that image, then she turned her attention thirteen steps below.

The Matriarch was about to unleash a spell at the running Light Bringer when the living shadow beneath the golem-spider suddenly announced from behind. "Don't forget who your true enemy is." Nyphistra whispered as the metal beast's leg crashed down on the elder svartalfar and the Inquisitor.

Both jumped out of the path of the brass leg with the Inquisitor finding her feet first. "You've been mine ever since you took the Trials!" Raising her hand, a cloud of yellow gas started expanding in front of Aylosha, becoming bigger and bigger as it neared Nyphistra.

"Acidic Haze." The Vizier easily identified the spell. "A truly horrific enchantment if your target has to breathe."

The golem-spider lifted its leg, the bronze end flat as a shield, and started waving it like a fan to dissipate the acid based magic.

When the metallic minion lifted the shield, though, the Matriarch launched a spell of her own at the living shadow.

A beam of green light struck Nyphistra's chest, forcing her and the golem-spider to take several steps back to steady themselves. The Vizier turned to look back at the elder svartalfar woman, glaring before she felt the first effect.

Her shoulder twitched. Then her hand. After seconds, what looked like black tree branches suddenly erupted from the living shadow's body. Seven of them stretched away from her, curving toward the ceiling after two feet when the tips suddenly burst into blue flame.

"Crucible Candelabra." The Matriarch smirked. "Burns your life blood as fuel to light my people's path to glory."

The mercenary leaped atop of the golem-spider with Havarti drawn. Her black skin made her stand out against the gold and silver beast and her pale blue eyes burned as she looked down at the Inquisitor.

The Inquisitor, in turn, couldn't hide her shock when she realized who was staring down at her, even through the dark skinned disguise. "Ophelia?!" It took her a moment but she found her composure. "Have you done something with—"

The woman didn't let Aylosha finish whatever passed as a witticism for her. She jumped from the back of the golem, intent on chopping the svartalfar woman in half vertically.

The svartalfar shuffled just out of the way, drawing her rapier from her hip. The Inquisitor's hand shook as the woman held the weapon out in the air between herself and Ophelia. The human marched straight for her, the much heavier blade of her bastard sword snapping the rapier in two as she closed in.

The Matriarch rolled her eyes when she saw Aylosha in trouble again. "Must I do everything myself?" As she raised her hand, she heard the first thing that was beyond a whisper come from the mouth of Nyphistra.

"I taught you that spell as a jest!" She screamed, her voice sounding as if it came from a demon's throat, and the branches crumbled to dust around her.

The Vizier turned to the Matriarch, her voice returning to its normal hiss. "It is little more than a parlor trick, my mediocre student. Now this..."

Nyphistra pointed at the Matriarch's feet where the golem-spider's leg pulled away as quickly as it struck, leaving an opalescent sphere as big as a fist in its place. It expanded with explosive force and the sound of invisible, wrenching metal. The Matriarch was thrown from her feet, the blast burning away one of her eyebrows and littering her violet sequined dress with rips and tears.

"Ultima." Nyphistra said as the golem-spider growled after her. "A spell an old friend showed me."

The Inquisitor scrambled away from Ophelia, just avoiding the human's blade. She needed some distance, a little time that's all. Aylosha then felt the long carpeting come under her feet and smiled.

"Assassin!" She screeched, and ten foot tall metal bars suddenly shot up from the edge of the carpeted path between the Inquisitor and Ophelia.

The throne room was a deathtrap to potential murderers if the target knew how to activate the mechanisms. Inquisitor Aylosha did and it had just worked in her favor. That particular trap barred an assassin on one side of the room while giving the noble a chance to escape.

Now she had a chance. But when she turned to run, the Inquisitor suddenly had a face full of pastel blue. Spitting stray bits of fur from her mouth, the svartalfar looked up to see the grinning face of Lyan Yo Bunpy.

"I officially declare my attack." The Bunny Barbarian said in a strangely calm voice before her fist smashed into the side of the Inquisitor's face.

Meanwhile, Collen's blade found itself at the base Matriarch's throat. "If you surrender and call your troops back from Dianmeyer, I'll see that you live the rest of your life in exile rather than have you executed."

The Light Bringer stood over the woman who was flat on her back. His armor practically glinted with pride and the Matriarch could see her face reflected in the polished surface of his sword.

The svartalfar looked back up at him, every ounce of rage and maleficence bubbling behind her violet eyes as she spoke. "Your terms seem reasonable, human."

"So you accept?" He wasn't naïve enough to lower his guard and he didn't seem convinced she would, in fact, agree.

The Matriarch pursed her purple lips, as if trying to find the right words. "Yessssss." When the hissing sound escaped her lips, the Light Bringer was met with a stream of steel needles spitting from the woman's maw. Thanks to his distrust, Collen's shield, instead of his face, met the projectiles with a percussive symphony as they bounced harmlessly to the floor and disappeared. With another clap of thunder, the Matriarch was again upon her throne.

Aylosha's cheek was pierced all the way through by the barbarian's ridiculous rabbit head shaped gauntlet. She felt blood streaming into her mouth and down her chin as she struggled just to get to her hands and knees.

She let out a pathetic sounding yelp when she suddenly found herself above the ground, the barbarian holding her so high that her face was level with the much taller woman. Her feet just barely reached past Lyan's knees.

Both women could hear the sound of metal striking against metal as Ophelia chopped at the rods barring her way. As the Inquisitor dangled from the barbarian's hands, she noticed the bandage around the muscular woman's broad shoulder and one sticking out of her thigh high boot as well.

"I can't decide if I'm going to eviscerate you, leave you to your Judicator's punishment or let Ophelia have her way with you." Lyan growled at the svartalfar woman.

Each option sounded more horrific than the last to the Inquisitor. She knew there was no way that she could physically get herself free from the barbarian's grip, the human was far stronger than the Inquisitor. So, she went back to her true strength.

"I see you've been wounded in battle." Aylosha's tone was conversational, even with blood dribbling from the wound in her cheek. "Those injuries must hurt badly." The corner of the svartalfar's mouth flicked up when she noticed the other woman wince. "The pounding of your blood rushing out of your body as your soft flesh is pierced and torn into. Oh, the tragedy of it all..."

Lyan suddenly felt her knees going weak but she didn't let herself buckle. She stayed on her feet.

"The burning as an infection sets in..." Aylosha whispered.

The Bunny Barbarian groaned, sweat starting to drip down her face. The bandages covering her wounds from the battle with the lich started to turn red as blood started to pool against the cotton.

"Oh, no, they may just have to amputat—" The Inquisitor was pulled away from Lyan and thrown against the bars she raised at the edge of the carpet.

Ophelia had scaled the bars and held the svartalfar woman by the neck much like the barbarian did seconds before. "You don't look so good yourself, Aylosha." The human gave the svartalfar a mocking grin.

Having an outsider address her by her name was beyond insulting to the Inquisitor. "You will address me by my prop— erkk!"

The mercenary's armored forearm pressed against the other woman's throat, stopping her in mid-sentence. "You know and I know you are one cold hearted mother." Ophelia pressed her lips to the Inquisitor's pointed ear and rasped. "Fortunately, I have just the thing for that."

Lifting her middle finger, Ophelia revealed the fire opal in her palm, thin wisps of smoke still rising from the talisman. The Inquisitor began to laugh.

"You almost killed your friends with that before!" Tears started to roll down her black face. "I'm starting to think you want us to win!"

"That's because the fireball seeks out the nearest human target." Ophelia roughly turned the Inquisitor around so that her face was pressed against the bars. "See any closer than me?"

The fireball was sailing for the corner of the room when turned back toward the place Aylosha and Ophelia now stood. The Inquisitor struggled to pull herself away from the bars but the other woman held her firm, her larger body pressed tightly against the svartalfar's back.

"I wonder if you'll have grill marks." Ophelia snickered in Aylosha's ear.

"You'll die, too!" Blood spat from the Inquisitor's lips and cheeks as the horrific fate approached.

"I blink away from danger." Ophelia gave her a mocking kiss on her pierced cheek, coating her lips with the other woman's blood. "Remember?"

"Wait, Ophelia! Wait!" The bars shook and vibrated as Aylosha thrashed around to unsuccessfully pull away and save herself. "No, don't—"

The Inquisitor shrieked as the fireball engulfed her. Only for a few seconds before she fell deathly silent, her skin still burning as her corpse slumped against the bars.

Ophelia felt the fabric of the blue carpet under her back as her eyes slowly opened to reveal Lyan standing over her. "Am I missing an eyebrow?" The mercenary said as she lifted herself up to her elbows and found herself literally steaming.

"It would take more than that to burn one of those off." The Bunny Barbarian offered her hand to Ophelia to aid the other woman back to her feet. "I guess you're blinking ability didn't kick in?"

Ophelia shook her head. "What was your first clue?"

"You took my kill." Lyan frowned.

"Sorry." Ophelia said, almost an afterthought as the Matriarch caught her attention.

A dozen ten foot long streams of light whipped around the svartalfar aristocrat as she sat in her throne, keeping Collen and Nyphistra, along with the golem-spider, at a distance. The living shadow materialized a barrage of arrows radiating with mystical energy out of the air and shot them at the leader of the Lytyl Tribe.

The light whips swatted all but one away from their target. The Matriarch had to duck to avoid the last arrow, which snapped in half against the back of the throne.

"You will not survive the night, my Vizier." The elder svartalfar sneered at the living shadow. "Every wizard is on their way to kill you, Nyphistra. There is no way that you can stand up to them all, even with your new toy."

"This is hardly new, Matriarch." Nyphistra hissed. "Every artifact I've created for our tribe found its way into my spider. Including the one that was made to be beyond both of our powers and judges us all."

"What are you talking about?" The other svartalfar snapped.

In response, the metals in the golem-spider groaned. "You, my Matriarch, agreed to a contract that was offered in good faith by the Light Bringer Colonel Collen Quilland."

The metal in the spider shifted around until the massive eyeball of the Judicator appeared, the amber iris shifting in the Matriarch's direction. The pupil dilated as the mechanism for Lytyl justice focused on the leader of the tribe. The Matriarch's eyes opened wide as she saw the Judicator resting on the front of the golem-spider's torso.

The immense eyeball groaned, making the the floor and walls shake. "Do you deny this charge, my Matriarch?" Nyphistra's whisper could still be heard clearly over the throne room shaking at the Junicator's groan.

The elder svartalfar's lips pressed tightly together. Her violet eyes darted back and forth from the spider-Judicator to the living shadow.

"You must answer promptly, my Matriarch." Nyphistra hissed.

The older svartalfar woman's face flushed with rage even as her shoulders slumped. "No, I don't deny it."

The Judicator-golem groaned even louder, making everyone in the room cover their ears, until a single word could be heard. "Gohma!"

Indigo blue lightning shot from the iris of the Judicator. The light whips reached out to stop the beam and shuddered with the effort.

The Matriarch let out a relieved laugh as she caught her breath, watching the oldest and last line of defense enchantment of the Lytyl Tribe leader wrestled with the tribe's new instrument of justice.

"See, Nyphistra? Justice only applies to those who don't have the power to make its will her own!" The svartalfar woman laughed and leaned back in her throne, untouchable.

Her cackling echoed through throne room as the Judicator groaned with the effort of fighting against the Matriarch's light whips. The elder svartalfar woman's voice was suddenly cut short and the light whips disappeared into vapor.

The shimmering energy from the Judicator struck the elder woman but she didn't react. A short time later, the lightning stopped and the giant eyeball sank back into the metal golem.

Ophelia, Collen and Lyan looked at each other, wondering if it was some kind of set up for another trap. Slowly, each stepped up to the throne to see what happened. Nyphistra never moved, staying at the base of the steps under her golem-spider.

As they reached the Matriarch's body, they could see a black arrow sticking out from the svartalfar woman's throat. The shaft was pointed up at an angle so the shot had to come from high above...

A smiling Ophelia slipped Havarti back into his scabbard as she looked toward the ceiling, seeing a chandelier she didn't even know was there mounted into the rock cave face that made up the throne room ceiling. The crystal structure swayed slightly from side to side and, sitting on one of the bars that the crystals hung from was Josie, the string of her bow still vibrating from the shot.

A black arrow. One that had poison that could kill a svartalfar instantly. Ophelia rested her hand on Havarti's hilt, not intending to unsheathe him as much as simply enjoying his company.

Lyan pulled her helmet off as she looked up to the archer herself. "Josie, how did you get up there?"

The scarlet haired half-elf waved back down at them. "Wasn't easy!"

"Want to come down and check out your handiwork?" Ophelia hollered back up.

Josie already started climbing the mounting that led to the roof support beams. "I'll just be a minute!" She called back down.

The archer was as good as her word. Watching her navigate the polished beams, the rock outcroppings and gold edging was truly impressive to see. Especially how quickly she got back down to the ground, without injuring herself to boot.

She strode up the stairs and looked at the limp Matriarch. "I was a little to the left."

Both Lyan and Ophelia chuckled. Collen slipped his sword back into its sheathe and started back down the stairs.

"Are you alright, Nyphistra?" He asked as he reached the ground.

The living shadow under the metal golem-spider nodded, though no one could really tell. "I'm a bit... drained but otherwise fine."

"Do you have a way to contact your armies to stop the attack?" The Light Bringer asked.

Before she could answer, the Matriarch's throne began to crackle with energy and a ghostly form of the Matriarch that looked to be constructed of the very light whips that defended her in life. "My final solution." The white glowing Matriarch form said. "Surely, my assassin needed a weapon of great power to murder me. I hope you are ready to die with it!"

With that the Matriarch form exploded into lengths of white tendrils. One enveloped Havarti and another latched onto the two remaining black arrows in Josie's quiver while the rest arced down toward the golem-spider, enveloping it in blinding light.

The massive metal beast scraped against the stone floor, slicing the carpet to shreds under the bronze tips of its spider like legs. The pastel blue fur armored barbarian started for the stairs.

"We need to leave!" Lyan grabbed Josie's arm and pulled.

The black arrows being held by the dead Matriarch's spell slipped out of the quiver, flipped through the air and onto the lap of the svartalfar woman's corpse. Josie reached back to try and grab them but the barbarian pulled her down the stairs.

The golem-spider stumbled halfway up the stairs as the white lightning pulled it closer. Nyphistra fell to the ground at the sudden movement, sliding along with the metal beast.

Collen bent down to help the svartalfar wizard back up. "Why is this thing dragging you with it?"

Nyphistra pulled a medallion on a chain out of an unseen fold in her dress. "This medallion is connected to the golem." She explained.

"Take it off then!" He tried to wrap his hand around the medallion but the light wrapped around the enchanted metal blasted him away from the woman.

Skidding to a halt some distance away from the arachnid beast construct, Lyan and Josie helped the Colonel back to his feet. The Bunny Barbarian pushed the Light Bringer and the archer toward the exit of the throne room.

"Ophelia!" She hollered up to the brunette woman. "Let the sword go and get out of there!"

"No!" Ophelia grunted, trying to force herself away from the glowing throne that was trying to pull her in along with Havarti.

"Don't be an idiot!" Lyan started to charge back up the stairs.

But the golem-spider lost its grip on the ground again, knocking the barbarian back to the bottom level as it flew. Its first two legs buried themselves in the top step, blocking the entire stairwell from Lyan getting to Ophelia.

Nyphistra was pinned under the shifting gold and silver of the beast, the medallion hovering in the air. The taut chain dug into the unnaturally dark skin of the wizard's neck.

Ophelia pulled herself down to her hands and knees beside the living shadow. "Do you have a way to stop the svartalfar attack?" She had to yell over the sound the metal being wrenched away from the golem's body.

Chalices, daggers and jeweled artifacts already covered every part of the Matriarch's corpse. The increase in enchanted objects on the throne only seemed to increase the spell's magnetic power.

"Yes." Nyphistra hissed. "I was the one who taught the Matriarch the spell. Now that she is dead, I can use it."

"Then do it now!" Ophelia screamed, a gold plate flying from the golem and striking her on the forehead. "Before we die!"

"I can't." Nyphistra tried to pull her arms free from under the golem-spider. "I need ingredients."

Ophelia cursed loudly. "Fine. Give me that damn medallion!"

"You cannot take it." Nyphistra kept struggling. "The enchantment attacked Collen when he tried."

The sword woman ignored the wizard and snatched the medallion out of the air, snapping the chain in half. Nothing shocked or attacked Ophelia when she took the thing.

Ophelia growled at the artifact as if it was mocking her. "Go get the ingredients and send the damn order!"

The human pulled the medallion up over her head and the golem-spider lifted itself back onto its legs, revealing Lyan standing just on the other side. Seemingly without any effort, the Bunny Barbarian hoisted Nyphistra back to her feet as she marched toward Ophelia.

"And get Lyan out of here!" Ophelia screamed as Havarti slipped free of her leather coat. "No!"

Nyphistra again nodded and as the barbarian reached for Ophelia. Ophelia reached for Havarti. The svartalfar wizard rested a hand on Lyan's shoulder and both women suddenly disappeared.

The medallion slipped from Ophelia's grip and hit the throne. The entirety of the metal beast loosed itself from the ground and flew into the mercenary, sandwiching her against the throne. Blindly slapping her hand through the piles of metal, Ophelia finally found the handle of her bastard sword as the air was steadily crushed out of her chest.

"You should have left me behind!" Havarti said as the woman gripped him tightly.

"Now... you... say... that." Ophelia could barely chuckle.

The throne exploded and the shock wave shot through the whole room, ripping the chandelier from the ceiling, portraits from the walls and gold filigree from the heavy stone pillars. The blast finally reached the hallway, toppling the other throne room door to the floor next to the first.

CHAPTER

NINETEEN

"GIVE ME YOUR hand you idiot!" Lyan screamed, suddenly finding herself in Nyphistra's office.

The room was far less cluttered without all the piles of different metals. There were still plenty of vials and containers full of items that were apparently not magically enchanted.

But that didn't mean that they couldn't be used to create a spell. Nyphistra stepped over to a drawer and pulled what looked like a heavy, gaudy ring out of it. It was made of gold, which wasn't shocking. It also had the crest of the Lytyl Tribe etched across its surface.

"What is that for?" Lyan fumed but she tried to sound at least marginally civil.

"I need this to claim my place as Matriarch." Nyphistra explained. "Then I will send the message to cease the attack before it begins in twenty minutes."

The Bunny Barbarian had no idea how the magician knew exactly what time it was. Lyan's knuckles cracked as her hands balled up into fists. She had to keep her anger in check long enough for Nyphistra to keep her word to Ophelia.

The living shadow uttered something that sounded like a dragon's growl and the ring began to glow. She slipped it onto her left hand. Turning to another drawer, she pulled out a heavily jeweled dagger out and held it in her right.

The woman's whispering voice echoed in the small room as if she were yelling in a canyon as she ordered the svartalfar armies to stand down. "Divisions Oleander and Hemlock are to return to Lytyl lands. Division Foxglove will await further orders." That order made Lyan arch an eyebrow.

"What are you having them wait for, magician?" The barbarian eyed her suspiciously.

"I need to speak with Collen." Nyphistra put her hand on Lyan's shoulder and they were standing beside the Light Bringer and Josie before the Bunny Barbarian could protest.

"Why didn't you do that to Ophelia? Or yourself earlier for that matter?" Lyan frowned.

"The medallion's effects prevented me." The wizard answered.

"What happened to Ophelia?" Josie stepped up to the two new arrivals.

Lyan pointed into the ruined throne room. "She was in there."

Collen and Josie both looked into the smoke filled room in disbelief. Quiet filled the hall as the dusty air settled. And a figure in a red jacket, caked in heavy lairs of silt and dirt, slowly walked toward the collapsed doorway.

As she reached the group at the door, Ophelia shook the debris from her hair. Everyone stepped away as dust and grime fell to the ground all around her.

"That..." Ophelia, her skin still obsidian black under all the dust, cleared her throat as she spoke. "...was unpleasant."

Lyan and Josie involuntarily laughed, the archer throwing her hand over her mouth to stop herself. But the barbarian looked puzzled, looking from Ophelia then back in the throne room, as everyone started to ask if everyone else was okay.

"How did you survive?" Lyan simply asked.

"I blinked." Ophelia answered as if it was obvious, then she looked back over her shoulder. "Right, Havarti?"

The bastard sword didn't reply. The woman's thick eyebrows pressed together as she shrugged her shoulder to jostle the sword resting on her back.

"Havarti?"

The sword stayed silent. Ophelia's mouth went slack, her knees buckling under her. Lyan caught the woman as she fell. The mercenary's shoulders shook but no sound escaped from her.

"What happened?" Lyan asked everybody but Ophelia, who only stayed vertical because of the barbarian's arms wrapped around her.

The living shadow answered. "The fail safe destroyed the enchantments of all the artifacts in the blast radius."

"I thought blinking saved him like it did me." Ophelia mumbled.

"The spell was designed to kill." Nyphistra started to explain, her voice even and unemotional as usual. "The enchantment of the weapon that was to have killed the Matriarch would have fueled the spell enough on its own. There would be no need to disenchant someone who would be dead anyway."

Lyan pulled Ophelia up, forcing her back onto her feet. Then she kept an arm around the mercenary's shoulder to make sure she stayed standing.

"I'm sorry, Ophelia." Josie said.

Nyphistra turned to the Light Bringer. "You and I must talk."

The living shadow and Collen suddenly disappeared.

Josie looked around the ruined halls. "Okay... really starting to wish I was invisible again."

Lyan nodded in agreement, looking back the way they had come from initially. She almost jumped when the archer tapped her broad shoulder.

"Here's your spear, by the way." The archer handed the weapon to the barbarian.

"So what are we supposed to do now?" Lyan asked.

Both other women had no answer. They all stood in front of the throne room. Ophelia turned back to look inside.

While it was littered with wrenched gold and silver, the room itself was in decent enough shape. Dust from the ceiling coated everything under it and the gold from columns was bent out of shape from the shock wave. But the throne itself didn't appear to be damaged at all. A good polish and it could be sat on again in no time.

Nyphistra and Collen reappeared. The Light Bringer gave them a sheepish wave at their return.

"I told her that we should all be somewhere safe before we talked in depth." He said.

"I agree. I cannot teleport all of us though." Nyphistra whispered. "If you will follow me."

The wizard's office was surprisingly close but cramped with as many people as now stood inside. After the group's short walk, Josie closed the door behind them and stood uncomfortably close to the backs of Ophelia and Lyan, barely able to see over either woman's shoulders.

"I wish to request that the Lytyl Tribe be allowed to establish a colony on the west shore of Loch Aeris. We wish to take responsibility for rehabilitating the land after Perett's attack." Nyphistra announced.

"Are you crazy?" Lyan's reaction was the first off of anyone's lips.

The living shadow ignored her. "Will you support me when I take this request to the Valen Court, Collen?"

The women all stared at the man. He tapped at his chin thoughtfully for a long, long moment before nodding.

"It will be a hard sell, Nyphistra." The Light Bringer warned.

"Those who have been loyal to me have been very patient." The newly crowned Matriarch whispered. "They wish to return to the surface as allies rather than enemies. This will provide them an opportunity to prove their peaceful intent."

It took the two leaders hours to cover the details. Josie lost interest somewhere around the time they were figuring out how to use svartalfar caves as trade shortcuts. Lyan fell asleep even before that, after they decided that the Foxglove division of the svartalfar army would escort the colonists to the lake.

Eventually, though, Collen and Nyphistra decided that they had a strong case for a colony and it was time for the Light Bringer to deliver the proposal on behalf of the Lytyl Tribe.

"It would probably be best for us to take the portal back to the camp at Loch Aeris and head back to Valen Court from there." Collen said as he finally lifted himself from the only other chair in the room besides the one occupied by Nyphistra.

"I need to get back to Dianmeyer." Josie agreed the portal was the fastest first step.

"I will accompany her and then continue on to my homeland." Lyan added.

"Ophelia?" Josie and Lyan both had to speak to get the other woman's attention.

"Hmm? Oh, yeah, that's fine with me." Ophelia said when she noticed everyone staring at her.

"She'll come back with us." Josie announced.

After removing the svartalfar ears and black skin from Ophelia, Nyphistra gave the mercenary the dress as a gift... that Josie accepted for her. Back in her normal clothing, Ophelia and the rest of the party were ready to go.

They met Ashe back at the camp. With Isaac's ship sunk, Collen provided horses that were fast enough to make the trip back to Dianmeyer were fast enough to make in only two days. In that time, Ophelia only spoke to her now inanimate sword for any length of time.

Lyan hoped that, maybe, it was like when she and Ophelia first met, that the sword was somehow responding to her telepathically. But when she was asked, Ashe told her that there wasn't any sign of the enchantment that was Havarti no matter what spell or technique he used to detect it.

The next afternoon they reached the small town that surrounded the castle and even took on its name, Dianmeyer. Once

Josie noticed a little red and white blur charging for her and the others, she slid off her horse and braced herself.

Appelonia slammed into her mother at full speed. The archer wrapped her arms tightly around the little girl and didn't even think about letting go until Harbenigyr ran up behind her, panting for breath.

"Cleric Took saw you coming in." He quickly said, motioning back to the castle. "He told us and I tried to keep up but she's quick." The Grand Cleric grinned, wiping stray beads of sweat from his brow.

Josie finally loosened her grip on Appelonia, who moved on to wrap herself around Lyan's fur covered leg. The archer straightened up in front of her husband, her face stern and hard as iron. Her emerald eyes dug into the man, neither of them saying a word. The Cleric, though, started to fidget uneasily, his hand lifting up to rub at the back of his neck.

Then Josie rushed at him, planting her lips heavily against his and wrapping her arms around him even tighter than they were around her daughter. Harbenigyr's dark eyes opened wide in surprise for a moment but then he melted around her, his arms finding their way around her slim waist.

After they decided to come up for air, the Grand Cleric, his wife and daughter escorted Lyan, Ashe and Ophelia back to the castle. They ate, Lyan and Ashe told Harbenigyr what happened after they boarded Isaac's ship and about the battle with Perett. Josie was careful to keep the details mild due to Appelonia's presence. Then they described the events down in the svartalfar tunnels, including Nyphistra's plan to establish a colony above ground.

Afternoon turned to night as they talked together, Lyan practically singing songs of glory about the battles they experienced. Ashe tried to talk to Ophelia a couple of times, but she barely acknowledged that he was even there. Finally, while Ashe adjourned to the vault to again study the soul orbs encased there, everyone else was escorted to rooms where they could rest.

Lyan had intended to start back for the Land of the Long Tooth Rabbit the next day. The wise man Rayflintr would surely want to hear the tales, not to mention the leader of the tribe, her father, the Mighty Corthek. But she didn't leave.

Ophelia didn't hole up in the room provided for her, although she did keep an arm wrapped around her torso, the injuries including the broken ribs she'd sustained bothering her more than they had previously. She used her injury to decline invitations to spar and exercise with the clerics, activities in which she would have usually participated. But she always carried Havarti with her.

After three more days of barely as many sentences, Lyan searched for Ophelia the next morning. She expected to find the mercenary in her room, or perhaps in the gardens, but she ended up finding Ophelia in the stables. She was slipping a set of saddlebags onto a horse when the Bunny Barbarian stepped in, crushing loose hay underfoot.

"What are you doing?" Lyan asked.

The other woman shrugged. "I think I'll go south for a while, see what's out that way."

"South? Why would you want to go down there?" Lyan asked. "There are no reports of coming battles, unrest or even brigand activity that way."

Ophelia slipped the dress Nyphistra had given her into the saddlebag and tied it shut before she answered. "That's true. But there's a group of monks that make weapons out there. They are why it's so boring down that way. I was thinking I might go talk to them."

Lyan stepped up closer to her sister in arms, resting a hand on the open gate to the horse's pen. "You intend to try and resurrect Havarti? Want me to come with you then?"

Ophelia shook her head. "Thanks, Lyan, but I'll be fine. Besides, it probably won't yield any real fruit."

"Then perhaps you should let him rest as an honored warrior instead of wandering off to far away lands by yourself." Lyan spoke with a gentleness that was surprising from her. "You shouldn't be alone. Not after everything you've—"

Ophelia knew the Bunny Barbarian wasn't just referring to the last few days but everything bondage into slavery to her subsequent recovery. Her friend meant well, but the mercenary realized that she hadn't even thought about Orison since escaping the tunnels to intercept the ogres and warn Harby. Shaking her head, the mercenary slipped a saddle onto the horse's back.

"Havarti may be gone but he's still my sword." Her voice came out hesitantly. "If I have to get used to him being just a hunk of metal, I'd rather do that on my own before getting back into the fray, Lyan."

The barbarian sniffed at the air... just because. It wasn't because she felt any stinging at the back of her eyes, to be sure. The Bunny Barbarian stood silently for a long moment before she nodded.

She strode up to Ophelia and the women gripped arms in a traditional Yo Bunpy farewell, including the head butt. "When our next battle comes, I will break out the chromatic armor."

"My retinas are already burning." Ophelia smirked and slipped onto her horse.

"Don't stay away for too long." Lyan said.

"Would you go tell Harby and Josie what I'm up to?" Ophelia nodded back. "Oh, and give Appelonia a hug for me."

The mercenary started the horse out of the stable and down the road to the south. She rode for hours, making the easy decision to set up camp when the sun hit the horizon. Ophelia started a fire, not bothering with food. The pattern continued the next day, the next, and the one after that.

After she laid out her bedroll, Ophelia pulled Havarti out of the back of her coat, scabbard and all. She rested it on the edge of the roll just as she did the previous nights.. Pulling her long coat over her like a blanket, Ophelia stared at the flames, feeling sleep starting to tug at the back of her mind.

"Sweet dreams, Havarti." She said to herself.

The campfire crackled as silence filled the campsite. The woman's eyelids got heavy.

"I don't mean to be a bother, my dear, but do you mind if you put me more directly in front of the fire?" A familiar poncy voice said.

"Hmm?" Ophelia's pale blue eyes snapped open.

"I would like to be closer to the fire, please." The sword repeated.

The woman pulled Havarti out from under her coat and laid him on top of the red leather. She stared at the weapon.

"Hello again, Ophelia. And thank you." His voice came to her ears again.

Ophelia's voice caught in her throat several times before she was able to get anything out. "How... how did you get back, Havarti?"

"I don't know how long it has been since I was last... here." The sword answered, his voice unsure and wavering, just a little. "But we've been together for a long time and, perhaps, some of... me... remained safe within you after the throne room. I don't think I would have found my way back into the blade if you hadn't kept that part of me with you after I was gone."

The woman's eyes started to sting. "I started to give up hope, Havarti."

"But you hadn't completely, Ophelia." He answered. "That is what's important."

Her vision blurred and she let out a shuddering sigh. The silence lingered for a long moment before the sword spoke again.

"What destination did you have in mind, my dear?" Havarti asked.

"Destination?"

"I couldn't help but notice we are not in Dianmeyer or in the Yo Bunpy village or any of our usual sanctuaries." The sword responded. "That leads me to believe you were en route to somewhere new."

"Oh." Ophelia said. "I was heading south."

Havarti let out a soft, thoughtful grunt. "South? I do not recall any reports of battle or badyguarding jobs down in that direction."

"There aren't." She answered.

"Hmm..." The bastard sword stayed silent for another pregnant moment. "You know, the Matriarch of the Xaviour Tribe was killed not too long ago, causing quite a bit of political strife in the region. That would provide ample opportunity for profit and, dare I say, action."

"Action?" Ophelia arched an eyebrow at her sheathed sword. "You're sure you want to get back into the thick of things so soon? I mean, you were effectively dead until just now!"

"Oh, pish posh!" Havarti snickered back. "What is death but the heaviest form of sleep? I would say that I have rested up long enough. Wouldn't you?"

The woman felt an uncontested tear roll down her cheek even though she laughed in response. "Well, I haven't. I was just getting ready for bed when you woke back up. I need some beauty sleep."

"Sleep cannot make you any lovelier, my dear. But you are right, of course." Havarti wiggled in his sheath like a camper trying to get comfortable in their sleeping bag. "You will need your rest for what is surely to come."

Ophelia slipped back down onto the bed roll, resting a hand on the gilded scabbard. "I'm so glad you're okay."

The bastard sword cleared his nonexistent throat. "And I always shall be, as long as I'm with you."

SPENCER STONER

A SPECIAL BONUS SHORT

GIRL TALK

AN OPHELIA LEGACY STORY

NEVER BEFORE AVAILABLE IN PRINT

AN OPHELIA LEGACY SHORT STORY

GIRL TALK

"YOU HAVE TO love the male ego." Ophelia chuckled as she counted the gold coins that spilled out of the pouch in one hand and into the palm of the other.

The mercenary named Ophelia sat at a small square table in the middle of the the now, save for herself and the other woman sitting across the table, vacant tavern. Her auburn hair was pulled back, tied into a ponytail with the two long braids that grew from her temples on either side of her face.

The long red coat Ophelia usually wore when working was draped over the chair alongside the table to her right. The rest of her wardrobe, though, wasn't what she would usually wear into battle.

She wore a skirt that was little more than a tan piece of cloth tied together against her hip. It was likely that it was a simple sheet or drape before taking up its new job as attire. The white cotton top she wore was buttoned up to just halfway to make sure to expose as much cleavage as possible. The back of the blouse was also mostly cut away and replaced with a sparse system of laces to expose Ophelia's back.

That was because of the violet runes tattooed there. From between Ophelia's shoulder blades down to the small of her back, they were laid out in a rough diamond shaped pattern. They were sensitive and cloth made them itch.

"Indeed." The other woman sitting at the table, Lyan Yo Bunpy, responded. "Some of them were half my size and they still thought they could defeat me."

At just about six feet tall Ophelia wasn't at all diminutive but Lyan easily outmatched her. The Bunny Barbarian was so muscular, in fact, that she was larger than most men they encountered, let alone other women.

Unlike Ophelia, who wasn't dressed as usual, Lyan looked the same as she always did. Pastel blue fur wrapped around her broad chest to cover her ample bosom with leather straps over her shoulders and a rabbit shaped metal clasp holding two more strips of leather across her chest. Her furry blue shorts had the cotton tail of the massive saber toothed rabbit Lyan slayed to create the armor and the thigh high boots were formerly the front legs and fore paws of the beast.

Her black hair was tied up into two massive braids that draped over her broad, brown skinned shoulders. The left braid blended into the skin of Lyan's muscular left arm that had been permanently scorched black from the shoulder down in the battle that ended with the barbarian taking the beast's skin.

"Chauvinism doesn't let little things like facts get in the way of a guy proving a point." Ophelia smirked at her friend. "But some of them were pretty cute, weren't they?"

Lyan's eyebrows pressed together. "Cute? I beat every one of them."

"That doesn't have anything to do with a guy's looks." Ophelia leaned back in her chair.

"It does for me." Lyan said.

Ophelia scowled back at the barbarian. "Even that bald one that was even bigger than you? You know, he gave me the key to his room to give to you." She pulled the mentioned bauble out of the coat draped over the adjacent chair.

Lyan shook her head. "It doesn't matter."

Ophelia cocked an eyebrow back at the barbarian. "What if I told you that the only reason he lost was because of me?"

The other woman had started taking a long drag of ale from the pewter mug when the question was asked. Her first answer was to gag on the liquid.

Slamming the mug back onto the table, Lyan wiped at the foam that went errant around her mouth. "How could you say that? You were not even involved in the contest!"

Again Ophelia grinned, tucking the pouch now refilled with their winnings into the same pocket of the long coat from which the key emerged. "I wasn't? Remember when I leaned in close to him and whispered in his ear?"

Lyan nodded. "I figured you were telling him to give up. That he couldn't beat me."

The auburn haired woman stifled a laugh. "No. I didn't say anything like that."

After Ophelia didn't elaborate further, the heavily muscled woman rapped on the table with her knuckles. "What did you say then?"

The mercenary was about to take a sip of her own drink but thought better of it and put her mug down before she answered. "I told him that if he let you win you might just let him see your birthmark."

Lyan looked confused. "But I do not have a birthmark."

Ophelia didn't say anything in agreement.

And the barbarian noticed. "Why would that have made him lose, anyway?" She asked.

Now Ophelia looked confused. "Really? I mean, have you seen yourself? You have a firm body and enormous breasts."

Lyan shrugged her broad shoulders, the leather straps making a soft slapping noise against her chest as she did. "I know that. But these have little to do with arm wrestling."

"And not everyone concentrates on just one thing all the time like you. I just... made him split his focus." The other woman answered.

"You still have not explained what my chest has to do with it." Lyan said.

"You can't be this dense." Ophelia rested her palm against her forehead. "You *have* noticed that guys stare at you as you pass, right?"

The Bunny Barbarian nodded. "It is unusual to see a woman of my size walking around. It is natural to stare."

The mercenary noticed Lyan didn't mention anything about wearing pastel blue fur with a rabbit theme drawing attention. But, even then, that wasn't the point that Ophelia was trying to make.

"Men stare at me, too. I'm tall, but not unusually so, but they stare anyway. Why?"

Lyan looked as if she'd been asked some kind of riddle. Her brown eyes locked onto Ophelia as if she was trying to find some clue.

Then the Bunny Barbarian sighed and, sure that the answer she was about to give was wrong, she said, "You are an attractive woman."

Ophelia nodded. "Thanks, the guys whose eyes make it to my face seem to think so, too. What about the ones who don't look at my face?"

"Don't look at your face?" Lyan muttered then came to a realization. "They keep looking at your chest. There is rarely much covering it."

The barbarian pointed just where she mentioned. She looked proud of herself that she had figured out the answer to which the mercenary was trying to guide her.

Ophelia pointed right back at Lyan's chest. "Your top is covering even less and those are even bigger than mine."

The Bunny Barbarian's face slowly turned insulted. Not at Ophelia, at least not directly, but at the memory of all the men who failed to make eye contact with her. She had taken it as a compliment previously, assuming they were simply in awe of a warrior of her reputation (word of the battle prowess of her tribe had spread wide, thanks in no small measure to her efforts over the years). Now, realizing that they only saw her as a piece of meat...

"Don't take it personally, Lyan." Ophelia responded to everything the heavily muscled woman was feeling. "All anyone can see right off is our looks. Let them look. Most of the time it's just like they're looking at a painting. They appreciate the view but they aren't going to touch anything." The mercenary leaned back in her seat as she continued. "Best case, people will treat you better because of your looks. Worst case, they may try to take something like sex or our lives."

Lyan's thick arms folded across her wide chest. "So why accept it if it can lead to harm?"

"You did hear me mention that people treat us better, too, didn't you?" Ophelia scowled back at the barbarian. "That happens way, way more often."

"At the risk of violence if we don't return the favor?" The muscular woman looked genuinely enraged at the idea.

The mercenary chewed on the inside of her cheek for a long moment. "It's the same danger as carrying around that pouch full of coins. But I'm still going to. I'm not going to let something that may happen change what I want to do."

"I do not, either." The other woman straightened up in her seat proudly. "Still, I do not seek out the saber toothed rabbits of my land needlessly. Their ferocity in the face of possible food is an instinct that they seem unable to control."

Ophelia nodded. "What I'm talking about is an even more base instinct. This is how every species keeps going. Favor is shown to those you want to mate with because they appear to have traits favorable to the survival of the species. As people, though, we've gained a measure of control over ourselves and don't jump on others on a whim. With the exception of a small percentage of—" The word used described a certain anatomical part that wasn't meant literally but it got the idea of unfavorable, unpleasant types of people across.

"You sound like the men I just crushed tonight." Lyan rested her elbows on the table.

Ophelia shrugged back. "Hey, I still pick and choose who I'm going to be with. Not everyone makes the cut. Of one of the rejects try to force me into something..." She pantomimed a punch and an imagined target falling to the ground with a quiet whistle.

Both of them were quiet for a long moment. The Bunny Barbarian drained the remaining liquid from her mug and placed it back on the table.

"With me willing and available as back up." Lyan said matter-of-factly. "So what is the point of this conversation again?"

"I was just trying to say that it takes more than muscle to win." Opheia answered.

"And you provided this 'more'?"

The auburn haired woman nodded. "A couple times. Although that bald guy, what was his name, Orison? He was the only one that really worried me."

The barbarian's eyes narrowed. "I don't believe you."

"So you're saying you want proof?"

Lyan nodded, her face as hard as stone. Ophelia felt her lips stretch into a wide smirk before emptying the contents of her own mug.

"Okay. You're sure you can beat me arm wrestling, right?" The mercenary said. "Even though I can swing a bastard sword around like a rapier in one hand?"

"I suspect you get some help from the enchantment within." Lyan's answer showed her somewhat haughty agreement.

Ophelia rested her elbow on the table in position to ready herself for the coming contest. "Tell you what, if I win you take the key and go up to Orison's room. If you win..."

"What do you expect me to do if I go to this Orison's room?" The barbarian interrupted.

The other woman shrugged. "I don't know. Whatever you want, really. Wrestle, ask him trivia questions, talk until dawn, knit him a sweater. It's up to you."

Lyan let out a quiet grunt, looking thoughtful. "And if I win?"

Again, Ophelia shrugged. "What do you want?"

Lyan chewed on her thoughts for a moment before speaking. "Harbenigyr has asked me to scout out a location to the west he called Nauterhaus and I do not wish to go out all that way. If I win, you will go there for me."

"Okay. Shall we go then?" Ophelia smirked, wiggling her fingers playfully.

The barbarian glanced down at the other woman's arm ready on the table. "That is your left hand."

"I'm a lefty, remember?" The mercenary grinned back. "Is that going to be a problem?"

Lyan flexed her scorched arm. It was scarred and black, unlike the brown tone of the rest of her skin, but the muscles were just as large as her dominant right arm. That meant that it was still bigger than Ophelia's dominant arm.

She wrapped her hand around Ophelia's and readied for the contest. The barbarian's chocolate colored eyes stared into the pale blues of the mercenary.

"When should we start?" Ophelia smirked.

"On the count of three?" Lyan's eyes narrowed.

"One... two..." They said together.

Neither got around to saying "three". The arm wrestling match had already begun. Both women pushed to drive the other woman's wrist to the surface of the table for the win.

Lyan was surprised at how much resistance the other woman gave her. Ophelia was stronger than she looked. Still, it wouldn't be enough...

The strain of the match up started to show on the mercenary's face. Her breath started to catch in her throat as the effort of trying to keep her arm up strained her elbow and shoulder.

"What's the matter?" Lyan's words came out of her mouth tersely. "Too much muscle for you?"

Judging from the sound of the barbarian's voice, Ophelia definitely wasn't making it easy for Lyan. That pleased the mercenary... a little. Ophelia's arm was starting to shake but it was holding. That wouldn't last long. The second her arm gave out

Lyan would smash it into the table and, even worse, the barbarian would think she was right.

Ophelia couldn't have that and she felt herself grin when an idea popped into her head. The mercenary lifted herself until she was just barely touching the edge of her seat and leaned across the table. She lost leverage but was just able to keep her wrist from touching the wood of the table.

Her face only an inch from Lyan's, Ophelia pressed her lips to the other woman's. The barbarian stiffened in shock and the mercenary took the opportunity. With a quick wrench of Ophelia's arm, Lyan's furry bracer thumped against the surface of the table and that, officially, marked the barbarian's defeat.

Lyan sat in stunned silence for a long, long moment. Her mouth moved several times before words actually started coming out.

"You cheated." She muttered.

Ophelia shook her head. "My arm never left the table. I never left my chair. The rest, well, it's not written out that it couldn't be done."

There weren't many rules to the game but the other woman was right. Lyan slumped back in her chair when she realized that Ophelia had won. Still, her brown eyes dug into the mercenary.

"Was the tongue really necessary?" Lyan had to ask.

"Got your attention, didn't it?" Ophelia laughed.

The barbarian sighed and nodded in agreement. "It did."

"It takes more than just muscle to win." The mercenary declared, sliding the key across the table until it rested right in front of the heavily muscled woman. "And it's time for you to pay up."

Lyan's eyes went from the key back up to the other woman. "Why is this so important to you, Ophelia?"

The auburn haired woman leaned back in her chair, resting her hands behind her head. "Important is the wrong word. I think that "fun" would be more accurate."

Lyan's head tilted to show her confusion. "I do not understand."

"Orison seemed like a nice guy. I think you'd have fun doing, well, something with him. Though I doubt that he's the type to try and pressure you into anything." Ophelia explained. "Even showing him your birthmark."

"I do not have a birthmark!" The Bunny Barbarian protested.

"Not where you can see." Ophelia smirked. "Maybe you can have him describe it to you."

Lyan let out a quiet growl, though her anger didn't boil too high. She lifted the brass key from the table and lifted herself to her feet.

As she turned and started for the stairs to the upper floor, Ophelia spoke up again. "If you don't mind me asking, do you have any idea what you're going to do when you get up there?"

The Bunny Barbarian looked back over her broad shoulder at the other woman. "I believe he deserves a rematch. If he is as mighty as you think... we will have to see what happens next."

ABOUT THE AUTHOR

Spencer Stoner was born in the state of Nevada, where he still lives today. His day to day life includes weekly meetings with the patrol for whom he serves as an Assistant Scoutmaster. He is also a black belt in American Kenpo Karate who is always willing to teach a willing student.

As for hobbies, he loves comics and hopes to eventually spread his storytelling to that format. He draws portraits of his characters to make sure their descriptions stay consistent through all his stories because of the art form's influence.

To waste time, he plays video games... a lot. In particular, he enjoys role playing and fighting games. Spencer also has almost every older video game system from the original 8-bit NES up to the Wii and PS4.

Even though he's not currently married, Spencer's family (including his mother and three sisters) comes first to him. Did he forget to mention his brother-from-another-mother Jim? After thirty years, you would think his memory would be better.